Praise for Leah Braemel's *Personal Protection*

"...impossible to forget...incite the imagination...I've developed a real fondness for so many of these characters"
~ *Chrissy, Romance Junkies*

"Once again, Ms. Braemel demonstrates her ability to create a vibrantly refreshing story that sizzles with a burning sensuality, all with a depth of emotions that will unlock the reader's hidden desires. Personal Protection weaves a compelling and intriguing tale layered with an edge of incredibly intense conspiracy that is sure to have the reader's interest captured. ...This is a delightful tale of deception and passion that is sure to stand the test of time."
~ *Shannon, Coffee Time Romance*

"...a fun and sultry ride from the author's warning to the very climactic ending. The kinks of the BSDM life are brought to the pages in tantalizing bites while the overlying erotic love of the two are entwined with emotion and humor ... the dialogue and interactions between the two main characters and the staff of Hauberk Protection kept me entertained throughout. This was more than a delectable and arousing romp, and I highly recommend this book."
~ *Beautiful Reads*

Look for these titles by
Leah Braemel

Now Available:

Hauberk Protection Series
Private Property
Personal Protection

Personal Protection

Leah Braemel

A Samhain Publishing, Ltd. publication.

Samhain Publishing, Ltd.
577 Mulberry Street, Suite 1520
Macon, GA 31201
www.samhainpublishing.com

Editing by Angela James
Cover by Natalie Winters

First Samhain Publishing, Ltd. electronic publication: May 2009
First Samhain Publishing, Ltd. print publication: March 2010

Dedication

I had a lot of help from authors who graciously helped me in my research. So thank you to CJ Lyons, Red Garnier, Tempest Knight, Rae Monet and Diana Cosby along with the members of Crime Scene Writers. Thanks also to my critique partners, Sue, Marley, Wylie and Dani for investing their time and energy, and boosting my morale when I needed it most.

And thanks again to my family who have supported me as I chased my dreams. I love you guys.

Chapter One

The hood of his raincoat pulled well over his head, he strolled past the empty security desk. The pungent smell of marijuana drifted through the lobby, telling him his diversion had worked. Even so, as he inserted the security key that would bring the elevator to him, he kept his head lowered and away from the lobby's concealed camera. Not that they could easily identify him past the hood, especially with the wig and fake beard he'd donned.

The hallway to the penthouse suites was empty when the elevator doors slid open, though a dog yapped and growled in a suite at the opposite end to his objective. Assured there'd be no witnesses, he walked to the door of 1201 and withdrew the spare key he'd procured.

Once inside the apartment, he disengaged the alarm and took a deep breath. The multimillion dollar penthouse sprawled in front of him, large leather couches and massive chairs, flat screen TV hanging over a gas fireplace in the living room. He'd been here so often, he didn't even need to use his flashlight to find his way to the master bedroom. He briefly considered trying to find the safe room he knew was concealed in the suite. Knowing Sam Watson's tastes, it had probably been outfitted as a personal dungeon for those days he couldn't get to La Porte Rouge.

Some guys had all the luck.

Not that Sam's involvement in the private club had started with anything remotely to do with luck. Which reminded him just why he was breaking and entering the apartment of the one man he trusted more than life itself. Who after tonight might never—should never—trust him again.

He pulled the photograph from the envelope and carefully positioned it on the pillows at the head of the wrought-iron bed.

After a moment's thought, he headed to the kitchen and grabbed the ketchup bottle. Less than two minutes later, a scarlet threat left on the ivory comforter, he walked to the French doors leading to the terrace. Light glinted off the end of the telescope from a suite in the building opposite Sam's where his compatriots, his co-conspirators, waited and watched.

He started to lift his thumb to signal the job's successful completion, then hesitated. Was he—were they—doing the right thing in forcing Sam like this? For three months they'd waited for him to make his move. Hell, for eight years, they'd bided their time. Yet nothing had changed. And so they'd decided to take action. To set right the wrongs that had been done.

But did the end justify the means? And what happened if their plan backfired?

Chapter Two

The sun hadn't yet risen when Sam waved his passcard at the card reader guarding the entrance of Hauberk Protection Services' D.C. facility. The front door unlocked, granting him access to the reception area.

The bulletproof doors were overkill, because that area only held the Accounting and Human Resources departments that were responsible for not only Hauberk's Protection division but also for the newly acquired Security subsidiary. A half dozen empty desks occupied one corner for the local Close Protective Officers to do background checks or fill out reports. At the back of those sections was the executive office area that his operatives jokingly referred to as the Inner Sanctum. But the heavy steel doors he'd had designed to resemble the wooden gates of an ancient English castle he'd once stayed in impressed the hell out of potential clients.

Most mornings he would have headed into his office. This morning he turned toward the indoor firing range and its armory. He placed his hand over the new-to-America palm vein scanner. Another device he'd been recommending his mid-level security clients start installing instead of the easy-to-fool fingerprint scanners.

Hearing the muffled sound of gunfire beyond, he opened his locker and selected a pair of ear plugs, then signed out a box of ammo and a couple of paper targets.

As it did every time he entered the range, the familiar scent of gunpowder both soothed and irritated him as it reminded him how much he missed the camaraderie out in the field. Now he drove a desk, having to get his thrills through reading others' reports, instead of the adrenaline rush of guarding a principal himself.

Two shooting booths were already occupied, including his favorite one at the far end. Chad—he should have guessed his area manager would be on the range this early, and... Well, well, well, instead of wearing her usual pair of baggy cargo pants, Ms. Rosalinda Ramos wore a pair of hip-hugging blue jeans. Jeans that hung low enough he could tell that she wore a blue thong and had some sort of tattoo on the small of her back. Aw, damn, he didn't need to know that. Now he'd be thinking of taking those jeans off her all day to discover what the rest of the tattoo was and just how far down it went.

She raised her gun and fired. The shot hit directly in the heart of her target. She fired again. The second shot doubled the size of the original hole. She glanced over her shoulder, then muttering something he couldn't hear, put her gun on the counter and bent over to fiddle with her left shoe.

Oh, mama, her jeans pulled taut over the tight round globes of her ass. An ass that begged to be squeezed. To be fucked. With a groan, he adjusted his pants, his dick firming at the thought of being buried in such a tight channel.

Ever since she'd won him in the charity bachelor auction three months before, he'd sensed a carefully hidden sensuality in Ms. Ramos. As if deep within, she guarded a slow burning ember waiting to be ignited. A fire that would set his world ablaze.

He'd been hard pressed not making a move on her the night he'd fulfilled his obligations and taken her to dinner. Though he'd wanted to see if he could add a little oxygen to the fire and kick start the inferno, he'd held back. He'd had to. She was his employee after all. So instead of making a move, inviting her up to his place or pressing his case when he'd escorted her home, he'd been the perfect gentleman. At least that's how she'd described his behavior the next morning, much to his disgust and everyone else's amusement.

But damn, it was getting tougher to maintain his hands-off policy. That element of danger and the heat he was sure would envelop them both was too enticing to resist. If he just had the right reason to breach her defenses...if he could find some way to let her make the first move.

Rosie straightened and took two more shots. Both shots were low and outside, yet the center of the target had a good half-dozen holes from where she'd been firing before he'd arrived. Interesting, had he thrown off her concentration?

Seeing his opening, he strode over to her. His body touching her in all the right places, he wrapped his large hand around hers over the gun barrel, repositioning her fingers. Dayam, it was like holding a sparrow, her hands were so tiny.

He leaned down and nudged her earmuffs so he could murmur in her ear, lowering his voice to a whisper, "It's better this way."

Her pulse jumped, racing beneath his fingers. Oh, yeah, that ember was definitely burning brighter. He should have made a move that evening three months before. He should have invited himself into her apartment at the end of the evening, given her more than a chaste kiss on her cheek. He should have put on some soft jazz—Diana Krall maybe—pulled her against him as they danced so she could feel what she did to him.

"Thanks." Her tongue darting out to moisten her lips. Did she realize she was doing that?

The scent of her shampoo—apricots—filled his senses. She always wore her hair in a rigid bun making him wonder if her hair were long or short, curly or straight. He had the strange compulsion to pluck the pins taming it just to satisfy his curiosity.

Yeah, he'd watch that hair spring free from its confines, push her jeans down—no, she wouldn't be wearing jeans, she'd be wearing that little black strapless number she'd worn to dinner that night. Even better. He'd push the skirt up as he slid his hands up her thighs. Then he'd remove her thong and go down on her. Hell, he wanted to stretch her petite body over the firing counter right now and pound into her from behind.

He nearly groaned when her breasts brushed the side of his forearm. The heat of her body snugged up against his blasted a shot of pure lust to his groin. Dayam! *If she turns around right now and sees the hard-on you've got for her, you're gonna get yourself sued, boy! Or your dick shot off. If not both.*

Going against the natural instinct to grind against her, he

eased his hips away from hers and resettled her earmuffs back in place.

Muttering something about needing to get back to work, he whirled back through the soundproof door and tossed his earplugs into his locker. D.C. didn't need him here—he could work out of the Atlanta office, no problem.

Atlanta. Where there were no spitfires with bitable asses to tempt him. Maybe then he could avoid future cases of blue balls he'd constantly been dealing with lately.

Sam checked the water temperature before stepping into the private shower he'd had specially built to accommodate his height. He palmed his cock as the warm water sluiced over it, wondering what he should do about his little problem. He'd not been so drawn to a woman in a long time. Oh, sure, he had a ton of phone numbers in his PDA, women all willing to jump into the sack with him. Not to mention he could always find relief at the Rouge. But no one in a long time had made him as hard as the one woman he couldn't have.

Was that what made her more of a challenge? That, as his employee, he couldn't have her? Was that why his cock was turning into a compass needle with Rosie his magnetic north?

His workout had gone to shit earlier when he'd spied her doing her standard two hundred pushups, her firm breasts reminding him of ripe peaches gently swaying in a summer breeze. He'd been hard pressed to find an activity that wouldn't draw attention to the return of his hard-on. It hadn't helped his control when she lay down on the stability ball and did crunches.

There'd been two other women operatives in the gym at the same time but neither of them attracted him like Rosie. No one else smelled of apricot shampoo and Ivory soap when they jogged on the treadmill. Well, okay, Vince smelled like Ivory too, but he was a guy, and the clean scent wore off within five minutes on the treadmill. Plus Vince sure as hell couldn't put his leg over his head like Rosie could. Thank the good Lord for that.

So here he was, fleeing to the privacy of his shower for the second time that morning, jerking off in order to stop a potential lawsuit. Could be worse things he'd have to do. But damn, he wished he'd dragged her out of the gym for a little personal exercise session.

He'd start by stripping her of the T-shirt that hid those ample curves. Then he'd peel off her bra and expose her completely. Nothing manufactured about those lovely breasts. They'd be firm but not fake. Cuppable. Squeezable. Fuckable. Her nipples would probably be dark brown but would they be large or small? It didn't matter. He'd lick them and blow on them until they hardened. Then he'd capture them between his thumb and fingers and play with them, squeezing gently at first, then harder.

His fingers squeezed his dick, mimicking what he would do to her nipples.

After a while, he'd exchange his fingers for his mouth, tasting them, catching them between his teeth, suckling while his hands explored every part of her. Those big brown eyes of hers would close as he discovered what made her hot. She'd start panting, making tiny mewling sounds with each touch, each lick, each taste.

He tightened his grip, flicking his thumb over the head of his cock, spreading a drop of leaking come over the sensitive foreskin.

Then he'd pull off her shorts, let them pool around her feet. Ever since he'd seen the thin straps of her thong, he'd wondered if she shaved, leaving what would be a beautiful pussy completely bare? Or did she leave a thin triangle of dark curls? He hoped she left a triangle. He'd love playing with her crisp mat of hair before he went down on her.

He'd kneel between her thighs. Would her clit be hard yet? It didn't matter. Her lower lips would be creamy, and he'd thoroughly kiss them. A soft kiss at first, then he'd trail his tongue between them. Down and then up.

What would she taste like? Sweet? Or musky? Either way, he'd gather her essence on his tongue, lapping until she squirmed beneath him, her hands clutching his shoulders or perhaps his head, her hips thrusting in time to his licks. When she started moaning louder, he'd thrust a finger into her pussy, curl it slightly and slowly drag it along that sensitive spot at the front. Then a second. All the while his tongue would be paying particular attention to her now pulsing clit.

His balls aching, he rested his head against the cool tile and closed his eyes as he continued to palm his throbbing cock.

He'd cup her firm ass in his palms and lift her until she wrapped her legs around his hips, then nudge the head of his cock against her warm moist entrance. Obeying his murmured instruction, she'd open her eyes and watch as he slowly pressed into her, kissing him as he slid home.

His hand slowed, letting the heated water from the shower gather in his palm warming his cock until he could believe he was buried in deep within her. Then it sped up again, mirroring the thrusts of his imagination.

Would she be a moaner or a screamer? A moaner, he hoped. Soft sounds would spill from her lips as she arched her back, her heels digging into his butt, pulling him deeper. He'd touch her sweet little clit and watch her eyes glaze. He'd flick the sensitive bud once more. Twice. Then her body would tighten around him. She'd be unable to draw a breath as she orgasmed, her muscles clenching his cock and milking him.

He barked his own release, his come jettisoning against the shower wall in a pulsing stream.

One hour later, his cock finally wrestled into submission, the door to the outer office opened and his assistant walked into the inner sanctum.

The poster girl for the stereotypical girl next door, Sandy was one of those people who matched their name, sandy-colored hair, blue eyes, even a smattering of freckles across the bridge of her nose. He could picture her growing up with the proverbial white picket fence and tire swing. But behind that façade was an iron-hard backbone. Which was one reason he'd hired her as his assistant. He needed someone who wouldn't take any bullshit from anyone. Including himself.

Sandy placed the mail she'd brought from reception on her desk, then took off her jacket and hung it beside his in the closet. "Morning, Sam. Good to have you back. How was Miami?"

"Mornin', Sandy. Miami's hot as usual."

As Sandy set to work booting up her system, Sam scrolled through the weekly reports the other offices had emailed him. The solution to the problem in Miami he'd proposed seemed to be working, his station head there reported. The New York office had three new clients requiring 'round the clock coverage. They needed him to sign off on their request to hire more manpower. He copied the HR department and gave his approval. The manager in Nashville had a potential problem that may head to court—he'd be receiving a letter by courier soon. Chicago and Atlanta reported no problems. And as expected, the Dallas and Houston offices were running just fine—though Mark had made a note that he had something he wanted to discuss in private. Hmm, wonder what that was about.

He'd made it halfway through his inbox when his nose broadcast his taste buds a caffeine alert. "Hey, Sandy? That coffee ready?"

"Sure is, you want one?"

He answered her question by stalking past her desk to the coffeemaker and filling a mug. Damn it, he needed a big slug of java injected straight into his veins. His concentration was shot. All thanks to not being able to finish his workout that morning.

He chugged down half of the black coffee, ignoring the pain as it scalded his esophagus. No other woman had his balls drawing up and his dick getting hard, preparing to send his little soldiers out on field patrol. What exactly was it about Rosie that had him so horny?

He downed the rest of his coffee. Goddamn it, he was going to have to move back to Atlanta if his dick didn't start behaving itself.

Realizing Sandy was watching him as she handled the letter opener like a surgical instrument, Sam gestured toward the coffeemaker. "You want a coffee? I was just fixin' to pour myself another."

Sandy nodded at her own Hauberk mug. "No, thanks, I've barely touched mine. Do you want to go over today's agenda here or in your office?"

"My office, I guess. But give me about fifteen, will you?"

When the outer door opened and Chad walked in, Sandy's head lowered. She stared up at Chad through her bangs in a Lady Di pose. With anyone else, Sam would have said it was practiced, but with Sandy it was a natural movement.

"Good morning, Chad. Can I get you a coffee?" Her voice had a little breathy hitch to it he'd never noticed before. Now wasn't that interesting?

"No, thanks, Sandy. Sam, you got a minute?"

Anyone not knowing Chad would look at his businessman's haircut with a few prematurely silver strands at his temple, and his double-breasted black suit, and be taken in by the relaxed image he projected. They'd assume he was just another mid-level management type. Or perhaps they'd catch his dark grey eyes and notice his sharp assessment and think him one of the hundreds of lawyers that populated the nation's capital. Only if they managed to spot the shoulder holster he wore beneath his jacket, or the baby Glock strapped on his ankle, might anyone guess he was former FBI agent now in charge of the D.C. office of Hauberk Protection.

But today all trace of his relaxed persona had vanished. He prowled into Sam's office and paced until Sam followed him. Once the door was closed, he folded his arms across his chest. "Why do I have to hear from my receptionist of all people that you had a break-in while you were away?"

"It's no big deal, Chad. There was no damage." Other than the word "*Bang*" written in ketchup on the comforter his mother had given him last Christmas. Sam pulled the envelope containing the photograph and slid it across the desk. "It's basically the same as the others, though this one is a bit better quality."

Chad cursed under his breath. "You touch it?"

Puh-leaze, like he'd make such a rookie mistake. "Nope."

Once they'd both donned latex gloves, Chad peeled open the envelope and shook the contents onto the desk. When he saw a photo of Sam standing in line at Reagan National, half his head missing, brains trailing down his shoulders like snakes, Chad exhaled noisily.

"Jesus! It's worse than the last one." Chad grabbed a pen from his pocket, and turned the photo right side up. "I've seen real crime scenes with less gore."

"Yeah, the addition of the blood and exposed brains is a new touch." Sam pushed himself away from the desk, wanting to pace, but forced himself to stay seated. There had to be a clue here. More than just a threat. Some key to the identity of whoever was stalking him.

"Good thing the bastard didn't have a gun at the airport instead of a camera," Chad muttered. "Ink jet quality photo paper, eight and a half by eleven, same as last time."

"Yup." Sam lifted his coffee cup then swore when he realized it was still empty.

"Which means it was probably printed with a home quality printer as opposed to a professional printer."

"Yeah, can't see Wal-Mart processing that."

Chad carefully slid the photograph back into the envelope. "This has been going on for three months now, Sam. At least let me assign a couple of CPOs to you."

Sam scowled. "Come on, Chad, I don't need close protection. Of all people, you know I'm trained in escape and avoidance techniques. In fact, I'm better than anyone you'd assign." Sam shifted in his chair. "Besides, what's it say to clients if the owner of a protection agency can't protect himself?"

"It says he's smart, that he knows he needs an extra set of eyes. Damn it, Sam, this is no idle threat. You're being followed. Stalked. Someone broke into your apartment, remember? The bastard could have set a bomb to go off when you opened the door."

"Yeah, well..."

"What's Mark say about the threats?"

Sam shrugged one shoulder. He'd meant to talk to his Dallas-based partner last time he'd flown down to Dallas but then Mark announced Jodi's pregnancy and Sam hadn't wanted to intrude on his friend's happiness. And now he felt uncomfortable discussing it via email. *Oh, by the way, thought you should know, someone's taking pictures of me.* Yeah, that would make him sound a real lame-ass weenie.

"You haven't told him about them, have you?"

"Damn it, Chad, there've been a half dozen pictures in the past three months. And the phone calls—it's some kid who dialed a random number and got lucky, that's all."

"Christ, Sam, listen to yourself. You get a picture doctored so it looks like your brains have been shot out, you're getting phone calls with some mechanized voice telling you to prepare to die—"

Sam covered one fist with the other, cracked his knuckles. "If they wanted me dead they could have shot me any one of those times, but they didn't. They took my picture a couple times and made a coupla calls. Big deal."

"What about the break-in? No," Chad corrected himself. "They didn't need to break in, they had a key. And they knew the code to disable your security system so they could take as much time as they wanted. Yet here you sit trying to pretend it's...what? A kid pranking you? Some practical joke?"

Yeah, the break-in had been hard to ignore. But damn it, that meant he knew whoever it was who was stalking him. Intimately. This wasn't something he wanted to call the cops in on. He'd handle it himself. "So they emptied the ketchup bottle on my bed, and left one of those damned photos. That's it. They're not trying to hurt me, Chad."

Chad forced his shoulders down and exhaled through his mouth in a long slow blow. "Sam, if I were a client receiving these pictures, you'd recommend I wear a vest every time I went out in public. You'd tell me to change up my routine—to take different routes at different times—"

"I'm already doin' that. I check my six regularly—no one's following me. They're trying to psych me out, that's all."

Chad continued as if he hadn't been interrupted. "You'd insist I used one of our special bullet-proof limos with a bodyguard trained in defensive driving as the chauffeur, and you'd assign a team of Close Protective Officers to guard you twenty-four/seven. And if I still didn't listen, what would you say?"

Sam slumped back in his chair. "I'd ask you if your will was in order."

Chad folded his arms across his chest and rocked on his heels. "So tell me, Sam, you got your will in order?"

Chapter Three

"*Stupido!*" Rosie muttered as she picked up a ten-pound barbell.

"What was that, Rosie?" Andy Walters asked as he increased the incline on the treadmill. Considering he'd probably run about six miles, he'd barely worked up a sweat. A tad less than six feet, he wasn't the typical body-builder people expected from a bodyguard. Today's shirt had *I'm the man your mother warned you about* silk-screened across the chest, which most people meeting him for the first time would believe. Especially once they got a look at the tattoos completely covering his left arm and shoulder that made most people think he was a member of Hell's Angels instead of one of the highest level operatives in Hauberk. But if they talked to him they'd discover he was a soft-spoken man who didn't swear, didn't smoke or drink and had manners that would stand him in good stead at Buckingham Palace.

"Just talking to myself, Andy."

Five minutes later she was muttering again.

It wasn't as if Sam Watson even knew she was alive. All right, maybe he knew she existed, but she doubted he realized she was female. *He's your boss. You know you shouldn't get involved with people you work with—it's trouble with a capital T.* Yet she couldn't stop watching her boss. Couldn't stop fantasizing about him. Especially after the night he'd escorted her to one of Washington's finest restaurants. Pity he'd only taken her to dinner because she'd made the winning bid at the bachelor auction. It's not like it was a real date or anything. But a girl could pretend.

At least when he pulled the car in front of her apartment, she hadn't blurted out how sexy she found him and revealed how horny she was by inviting him to come up to her apartment. Instead she'd fled. Like a coward.

Not that he would have come up to her apartment if she'd asked. All the photos she'd seen of him showed him beside tall leggy blondes with names like Cynthia or Allison or Lee-Anne— not short Puerto Ricans named Rosalinda who had hair resembling Lisa Simpson's if she didn't wrestle it into a bun every morning. Look at that night—she'd dressed up in her sexiest little black dress and he'd barely given her a second glance, if he even bothered with a first one. No, she was his employee, nothing more.

And then this morning—she'd proven herself a total airhead. She'd been hitting the target until he walked into the firing range, and then she started hitting snow. It's not that he'd said anything or made a noise, it was his cologne, that wonderful dark scent of cedar and amber he wore. She would have known he was there if she'd been blindfolded. It wasn't right that a man could smell so good.

Instead of concentrating on her target, she'd imagined commanding him to strip off his clothes. Slowly. First she'd have him shrug off his shirt to reveal that rock hard stomach and chest that she'd often admired in Hauberk's private gym. Have him turn around, maybe even bend over so she could admire his ass. *Ay bendito*, that man had the best ass of any man she'd ever seen.

Her tongue darted out to moisten her lips as she imagined him kneeling in front of her, ready to do her bidding, his cock pendulous between his legs. No! Bobbing high against his abdomen. If it matched the rest of him, he was probably as wide as her wrist. The ache in her pussy increased exponentially, her panties now drenched at the thought of him suckling her nipples, his full lips feathering down her belly until his tongue lapped at her labia, taunted her pulsing clit. He'd probably be an expert in making a woman come with his tongue. Then she'd lay back and feel those muscular thighs between hers as he pounded her into the mattress. All the while he'd murmur to her softly in French, or growl at her in German. She'd heard he spoke six languages, four fluently. Body parts always sounded so much sexier in a different language.

Then he'd strolled over to her and wrapped his hand around hers as he corrected her grip. His touch, combined with the strength of his rigid muscles of his thighs pressed against her body, had scattered her wits.

To make matters worse, less than an hour ago, he'd once again proven his disinterest, or worse. She'd stepped on the treadmill—of course the only one free had to be the one right beside his. Less than two minutes later, even though the meter on his treadmill showed he'd only run three miles instead of his usual five, he'd slung a towel around his neck and walked away.

No, Sam Watson didn't just walk, he prowled like a lion. And not just any lion, Samuel T. Watson was Mustafa himself, the king of the pride, right down to the deep voice. It was a good thing he'd left when he did, because when she'd attempted to peel off the sweatshirt she was wearing over her tee, the treadmill rocketed her into the wall behind her like a sling shot flinging a pea. She'd tried to pretend she'd intended to step off, but from the grin Andy had given her, she was sure everyone in the office would now think her the clumsiest operative of the group.

At least Sam hadn't witnessed her humiliation.

Or Kris, the newest trainee she'd been assigned. If he'd witnessed her total spazzdom, she'd never hear the end of it.

"Speak of the devil," she muttered when Kris chose that moment to walk in. His gaze lingered on her cleavage briefly, then trailed down to her legs, his grin slowly widening. "Put your eyeballs back in their sockets, Campbell."

He grinned, a wide crooked smile. "It's the drool that's the problem. I swear you need to hand out bibs when you're working out, Rosie." As usual he wore a pair of faded tan shorts, and the ubiquitous blue T-shirt with its gold Hauberk crest. "You going to need a sparring partner later?"

She glanced over at Andy as she chugged back a quarter of the water in her bottle. He was in the middle of a good sprint—he wouldn't be ready for a while yet. Pity, she wanted to figure out that leg sweep he'd used on her last time they'd paired up.

"Yes, I just want to get in a couple more reps."

By the time Kris had finished his warm ups, her foot was braced against the wall over her head as she stretched her hamstrings.

"Goddamn, woman. It isn't right that a body is so flexible."

"It isn't right that a woman should be expected to pass a basketball through an opening the size of her nostril either, but we can." She lowered her leg and flexed a few more times. "You ready?"

Kris grinned. "I'm ready to kick your butt. You ready to kiss the mats?"

As they moved to the sparring area, Rosie saw several of her co-workers exchanging money. If they bet on Kris, she vowed they were going to regret it.

Although she was ten inches shorter and a good eighty pounds lighter than Kris, she managed to flip him onto his back fairly quickly.

"Aw hell," he muttered. "I wasn't warmed up properly."

She rubbed her thumb and forefinger together. "World's smallest violin, you big baby."

"That's cold. And strangely arousing. Let's see you do that move again."

As Kris rolled to a stand, Andy winked at Rosie and called, "Hey, cougar bait, I hear you had another date with that old lady who bought you at the auction."

Kris shrugged and turned away. "Hey, Bonnie may be forty, but she's still hot. I figure it's a win-win situation."

"Just make sure when she asks to check out your gun, that you don't rack a bullet in the chamber prematurely."

Turning bright red, Kris grimaced muttered to Rosie. "Wow, he's so subtle."

He rushed her as he had before but when she moved to intercept him again, he changed directions and she found herself flat on her back, staring at the ceiling.

"Shit!" That was the same move Andy had used on her. How had he done that? She'd have to ask him. After she paid him back, of course.

A grin split Kris's face when he loomed over her. "Sorry,

Rosie, but if you want to dish it out, you gotta be able to take it too. Isn't that what you told me my first day?"

She took the hand he held out to help her up. Once on her feet but before he released her, she forced his thumb toward his wrist and wrenched his arm behind him in a classic takedown maneuver. In an effort to lessen the pain, he twisted as she'd intended and fell to his knees. She placed her knee in his back and forced him flat onto the mat where she'd been moments before.

"Cheater!" he gasped.

"Weren't you just talking about taking what you dish out?"

"Ah, Kris with his face in the mats, and Rosalinda controlling him. All is right with the world I see," a voice said from the doorway to the men's locker room.

Rosie released her grip on Kris's arm and straightened. She grinned when she saw Chad watching them. "It was like taking candy from a baby. As always."

Kris stood so fast she'd sworn someone had called attention on deck. "Heya, boss! What's up?"

"You two hit the showers and then come to Sam's office. Andy, you too. We've got some business to discuss."

Rosie raced through her shower, muttering curses under her breath as she struggled to tame her wayward hair, hurriedly drying it with her diffuser and using the silicon hair tamer she wished she'd bought stock in. Finally she wrestled it into the bun she found easiest to deal with.

"At least I won't look like a dandelion," she grumbled. She stepped into the hall at the same time Andy exited the men's change room.

He gestured back at the men's change room with his head. "Skippy's still making himself look beautiful. You want to wait for him or head over to the Sanctum?"

"He can meet us."

They'd made it as far as the accounting area when Kris jogged up behind. "Hey, you guys got any idea what this is about? Must be special though if Sam's in on the meeting, don't you think?"

"We'll find out soon enough, Skippy," Andy said. She could

hear the amusement in his voice, especially when he shook his head and muttered, "Newbies!"

Andy reached for the door to the manager's section then stepped to the side when he saw Sandy heading out.

"Heya, beautiful, what's cooking?" Kris grabbed Sandy's hand as she passed. He whirled her into what he obviously thought passed as a waltz.

Andy snorted and headed into the inner sanctum alone. Rosie would have followed but her path was blocked by the dancing duo.

"Thought any more about going out on a date with me, Sandy? I was thinking we'd go dancing, maybe enter us in *Dancing with the Stars*. We'd be good together, you and me."

"First of all, I'm not a star and neither are you, so we couldn't get on that show." Sandy laughed. "Second, one of these days you're going to do that to the wrong woman, and you're going to find yourself in front of a judge. Either being sued or married."

He grabbed his heart and staggered back. "No! Not the M word!"

"Kris, we're waiting for you," Chad's voice echoed from Sam's office.

Sandy blushed. "Sorry, Kris. I didn't mean to get you in trouble."

"It's not your fault, Sandy," Rosie said. "Kris's day isn't complete unless he causes at least one melodrama." She gestured to Kris who grinned in return. "Come on, mat-kisser, let's find out who we're protecting this time."

Chad greeted them at the door and told them to take a seat. Andy had made himself comfortable on a loveseat at the far end of Sam's office, leaving the two visitor's chairs empty. While Rosie perched on the edge of the farthest leather chair, Kris hesitated. He glanced again at Sam before relaxing enough to sit in the second, though even sitting, he seemed to stay at attention. Chad closed the door behind him and leaned against it, his arms folded.

Sam stood behind his desk, his back to the room, arms folded across his chest as he stared out the window. He'd abandoned his jacket on his chair. The crisp linen of his shirt stretched taut over his biceps and broad shoulders. Even though it was October, he appeared tanned. He must have had some down time in Miami, Rosie thought. His thick dark brows were longer than the dark hair he kept closely cropped - a change since the summer when he'd shaved his head completely bald. The slight slant of his eyes and high cheekbones made her wonder if there was some mixed heritage a few generations back. Perhaps some Native American? Hawaiian, maybe?

The amusement that had been in his eyes at the fundraiser had been doused and now irritation radiated from him like a lighthouse beacon.

Rosie shared a look with Kris and Andy. *Who'd fucked up and how?*

There was silence for a minute as Chad waited for Sam to speak. When it became obvious Sam intended on ignoring them, Chad nodded to himself and took a deep breath. "Sam's been receiving threats so I'm assigning you to be his personal guards."

He opened a folder from Sam's desk and handed them each a picture of Hauberk's owner in a brushed cotton shirt, and blue jeans mingling with several other similarly clad people in an outdoor setting. "It started with this photo the day after Labor Day. More arrived, each a few weeks apart."

Rosie recognized Rock Creek's Carter Barron amphitheatre. Which meant any one of several thousand attending the annual Blues Festival could have taken the picture. The next picture was one of Sam jogging on a residential street. A circle had been drawn in red ink over his chest.

Chad handed them more pictures. The first was a high quality photograph that could have been taken by a professional. The next two were grainy. But all had red targets drawn on his chest.

Kris fingered the third one, of Sam exiting the Hauberk building. "From the blue hue of this one and the pixellation, it looks like it was taken from an older cell phone."

"Or it could be blue because one of the colors of ink in the printer was running low, Skippy," Andy said.

Rosie glanced at Kris's before studying the next better quality photo—this one of Sam parking his Harley Road King in front of a large red brick Colonial building—an elite club from the looks of it. Whenever she'd seen him at the office he was in tailored suits, but in the photo he was wearing a leather biker jacket and a pair of leather pants that clung to him like a second skin. If she hadn't already admired his ass, this picture would have clinched the deal.

Andy exchanged pictures with Rosie, this one of Sam holding open the door as a leggy blonde got out of his Jaguar.

She held it up closer, wishing she had a magnifying glass handy. "I'd say this one was shot through a window. There's a reflection."

Sam whirled toward them, his jaw snapping closed, his lips tightening as he glared first at her, then at Chad. "I thought you said—"

He bit off the remainder of his comment and some sort of nonverbal exchange occurred—but about what Rosie couldn't tell. Somehow she had a feeling it was about her. Though why, she couldn't guess. Her record at Hauberk was spotless.

"We'll discuss it later, Sam." Chad handed them copies of another photo. "This one arrived last night—they broke into his place, disarmed the security and left it on his bed."

If she hadn't recognized the setting and his suit, she'd never known it was Sam, considering his face had been digitally removed and replaced with blood, brains and gore.

"Didn't they set off the silent alarm?" Andy asked.

"Nope, whoever it was knew the code to turn it off. Security tapes show a male entering through the lobby, bold as brass. Had a hood up, and he faced away from the cameras as if he knew they were there."

"So no description," Andy finished in disgust.

"We know it's probably a male between 5'10 and 6'2, no age, no hair color, possibly white but we're not even sure of that."

"Just dandy. That narrows it down a whole bunch." Andy straightened from his place on the couch, resting his elbows on his knees as he leaned in. "Didn't the guard on duty check his

ID before he let him in?"

"He was...otherwise occupied."

Andy snorted. "Tell me the idjit wasn't in the bathroom givin' himself a hand job or smokin' up."

"He said he'd left his desk to investigate the smell of pot coming from the stairwell. Says he wasn't out of sight from the front door for more than sixty seconds. I figure it was probably more like a couple minutes. In any case, we're re-examining the building's security." Chad tossed the file folder on Sam's desk, then hitched one hip on the desk. "Sam's also received threatening calls to his home phone."

"Three." They looked up as one, startled that Sam had rejoined the conversation. "You're making it sound like I've received dozens. I've only received three calls."

From the corner of her eye, Rosie saw Chad shaking his head in frustration.

"Did you recognize the voice?" she asked.

"No. It was a male, no accent that I could hear, street noises in the background but nothing recognizable." He bit the words out. "First time he talked about how he'd seen me that day and how easy it would be to take me out. How he wished he'd had his gun, then he hung up. He's gotten a bit more creative since but nothing specific about what I did to make him want to kill me." He resumed his study of the parking lot.

"What's Caller ID show?" Kris asked.

"He's using pay phones at various locations around the city," Chad answered when Sam didn't respond. "We've checked the addresses, but so far there've been no security cameras near the phones. When we dusted the phones for prints, they'd been wiped clean."

While Kris, Chad and Andy continued to discuss who might have that information, and how easy it might or might not be to find, Rosie let the conversation flow past her and observed Sam ignoring them all. He had eschewed protection for three months, and even now stood in front of a window, a clear target. Was he trying to prove his invincibility? That he wasn't afraid?

His eyes scanned the rear parking lot, the field beyond.

Alert. Aware. But not an ounce of fear.

Maybe he was being driven by guilt. Did he have a death wish? Because if he did, that would make her job that much harder.

She glanced back down at the photo of the leggy blonde. What she wouldn't give for another eight inches in height and blonde hair. She'd tried peroxide once, but it wasn't worth the trouble, not with her complexion. But maybe she should consider it again if that's what it took to get Sam Watson's attention.

In the reflection of the glass, his eyes met hers. She wanted to look away, but couldn't, the darkness of his gaze drawing her in, compelling her to keep the contact. There was heat in his gaze, need.

"With all due respect, Mr. Watson, may I ask you to move away from the window? If someone is watching, you're presenting a good target right now," Rosie said, glad to hear her voice was steady.

There was a moment's hesitation before Sam sat in his chair. Something flared in his eyes before he veiled his expression.

No, not guilt. Frustration at having to place his life in someone else's hands. Sam Watson was a pride-filled ego-driven walking pile of testosterone.

I'm not letting this whacko get you on my watch, buddy. Better a hit to your ego than your life.

As if sensing her challenge, Sam leaned back, lowering his chin to his chest. His gaze dropped from hers and made a leisurely perusal of her chest before slowly travelling a reverse route and catching her gaze once more.

Ready to burst into flames, she focused on his lips and imagined them kissing her breasts, his teeth nipping and catching her nipples, suckling them. His fingers flexed, drawing her attention. What would it feel like to have those long fingers caress her bare skin, blaze a trail down her stomach, down to that aching area between her thighs and stroke her clit, pressing deep inside—

"—you think, Rosie?"

Rosie blinked and looked at Kris, who nudged her with his knee. He was staring at her as if she'd grown a third eye in the middle of her forehead.

"Don't you agree?" he asked as if repeating a question.

Agree? To what?

"Yes, I do," she quickly answered. So unprofessional, her conscience lectured. Your boss needs a bodyguard, not a lover. Besides, she had an unbreakable rule about never dating co-workers. A glance at Sam and that one tilted eyebrow told her he knew exactly what she'd been thinking about instead of work. "Who else knows the security code of your condo?"

"Me," Sam said with not a little irritation. "My cleaning crew, and it's probably on file somewhere here in case of emergency—Sandy may have it. The IT guys possibly could access it."

"I hate to say this, but it's looking like an inside job." Andy set the photos he'd collected on the desk. "I think we should look at Hauberk employees—those who might have received a bad report, or have recently quit."

"Goddamn it! It's *not* a Hauberk employee." Sam laced his fingers together, clasping them so hard the nail beds were white.

"Andy's right, Sam. We can't rule anybody out at this time," Chad said quietly. "Very few people have access to your private phone number. Even less to your security code."

Rosie recognized the Voice of Reason coming out in him, and heard the steel behind it as well. As much as Sam Watson was bucking the truth, Chad wouldn't let him ignore it.

Go Chad.

"They could have pretexted the phone number from the goddamned phone company. From security at the condo. You know how easy it is to get information—they phone up and pretend they're me, or my mother, for Christ's sake." Sam took a deep breath and continued in a more normal tone, though his smooth southern accent had disappeared.

"Damn it, Chad. It's not an employee. Not one of mine. You know everyone has to go through background checks." He swiveled his chair around to the window again, his head resting on his thumb and forefinger at his temple. "It's not an employee."

She wanted to reach over and lay her hand on his but knew she couldn't. Instead she sat back, considering the ramifications that it might be someone they worked with. The idea that someone she worked with might wish ill of their boss was terrifying, especially given the capabilities and backgrounds of some of her co-workers.

Chad cleared his throat. "We'll assume Sam's safe while he's inside this building. Besides if anyone did try anything, there'll be enough people around to stop whoever it is."

If it was one of them, Sam might be safer out of the office.

"Outside of the office, I want you to treat this as a high-level protection assignment. We have no idea what to expect— watch for a sniper, a close attack, or even a bomb."

Sam cursed—not low enough to be said it was under his breath, but loud enough to let them know Chad's suggestion annoyed him.

He shot a look at Sam who sighed and nodded his head once. "I want at least two of you with him from the moment he leaves this building to when he walks back in the next day. You escort him everywhere he goes. Don't forget to check his mail every day and make sure there are no nasty surprises in it. Don't take anything for granted."

"You can do that, Rosie. Real guys don't check the mail." Kris grinned and stuck out his foot until his toe bumped hers.

Sam shot out of his chair so fast that his chair bounced off the wall behind him. He leaned across the desk, grinding his fists into the desktop. "Ms. Ramos is one of Hauberk's top CPOs. She deserves your respect, not your sexist bullshit. You hear me?"

A flush rose up Kris's neck as his lips pressed together so hard they turned white. "Yes, sir, Mr. Watson."

Chad cleared his throat. "Why don't you three step out for a moment?"

Kris stood, his naval training showing in his rigid posture. From a movement of his hand, Rosie would have bet he was forcing himself not to salute as they left the office.

Chapter Four

Chad followed them out, closing the door to Sam's office behind him. "Rosie, Kris, you guys go on over to my office. Andy? You got a minute?"

Leaving the two men, Rosie followed Kris into Chad's office beside Sam's and set the door against the jamb so they couldn't overhear whatever Chad was saying to Andy. When she finally sat, she didn't feel the need to perch the way she had in Sam's office.

His fingers flexing and releasing at each turn, Kris paced the five steps of the office.

"I'm sorry, Rosie. I didn't mean anything. I was just joking about you checking the mail."

"I know you were, Kris."

"Do you think I should go back and apologize to Mr. Watson? I don't want him to think I'm a slacker." He glanced back at the door to the executive office, his body angling as if he was about to do exactly that.

"I don't think that's such a good idea. He's a bit too wound up right now—let Chad get him cooled down."

"Yeah, I guess." Kris passed three more times before he paused halfway across the office, stabbing his fingers through his hair. He'd let it grow out from the high-and-tight he'd had when she'd first met him, and now his mahogany hair flowed around his fingers in thick waves. Normally she would have found it attractive. But for some reason, a certain almost-shaved head was more appealing to her right now.

Ay bendito, she shouldn't be thinking of her boss that way.

Not since he was now her principal.

When Andy came in and shot Kris a glare, Kris walked to the window and stared out, reminding Rosie of Sam's posture earlier. After a few moments, he said, "You guys know I didn't mean anything with that crack, right? I was joking—I'd never let anything happen to you or to anyone. I'd take a bullet for any one of you."

"Yeah, we know, Skippy, but your timing sure sucks." Andy hitched a hip on the windowsill. "You need to control that case of diarrhea of the mouth you're afflicted with."

"Either of you hear anyone griping about Sam in the locker room? Or over at Charley's?" Deciding a change of subject was in order, Rosie named the bar a lot of the operatives frequented to shoot the breeze and a little pool during the long slow stretches.

Chad walked into the office and threw the file folder of photos on his desk. His tie had been loosened and twisted askew, the top button of his shirt loosened.

"Okay, listen up, folks. Considering we think it might be someone inside, I think it best if we try to keep this on the QT. As far as I know, before today, only Sam, Sandy and I knew about the pictures and the threats. So if anyone mentions anything about either—consider them a suspect."

After they all agreed, Chad stared at the two male operatives. "I'm making Rosie the lead op on this case."

The urge to stand up and cheer at her first supervisory assignment warred with the heavy burden of leadership that crushed her shoulders. Every decision she made, every order she gave would be witnessed by none other than the owner of Hauberk himself. Someone who had the power to override her anytime he wanted. Someone who had the power to fire her. But why her and not Andy who had more seniority?

"Either of you got a problem with that?" Chad continued.

Andy gave Chad a thumbs up as he winked at Rosie.

Kris shrugged. "Hey, no problemo here, boss. Her ass will be a lot sweeter to kiss than lardbutt's over there."

"Check the attitude, Campbell." Chad unlocked his top drawer and removed another folder and handed Rosie a piece of paper. "I've arranged to sublet an apartment in Sam's building so you can keep an eye on him at night. This is a letter the owner of 1202 faxed over giving us access to his apartment. With that, building security should give you the spare set of keys the owner left with them. There's also the security code to his place in there so you don't set it off. Sam's in suite 1201, you'll be beside him in 1202—he'll have to go by you to get to the elevator."

"Or if someone's trying to get to him, they'll have to get past us first." Rosie nodded her approval.

"Exactly. Kris, I want you to install extra cameras in the main hallway—I've already secured permission from building management. Set up a system in your apartment so you can monitor them. You'd better change the codes too. Whoever it was that broke in knew them. Let's see if we can prevent that from happening again. Can you get everything working before tonight?"

Kris returned to his attention-on-deck stance. She needed to remind him he wasn't in the navy anymore. "Yes, sir."

"Andy, John Lake over in IT has configured a laptop so you can monitor the security system in Sam's apartment. That way you'll know immediately if he hits the panic button."

"So John knows about the op?" Andy asked.

"Only that I asked you to keep a personal eye on Sam's system because of the break-in."

"But you trust us?" Kris asked.

"I already checked your schedules. None of you could have taken some of those pictures—you were out of D.C. on assignments when at least two of the pictures were taken."

"Wow, thanks for the vote of confidence, boss." Okay, maybe Kris remembered he wasn't in the navy still after all.

"Why don't you guys head over to Sam's and get started on those cameras. I'd like to talk to Rosie privately for a few minutes."

"I'll grab the laptop from the Nerd Brigade and meet you out in the parking lot, Skippy." Andy snagged the letter from Rosie as Kris unfurled himself from the chair.

Once they were alone, Chad leaned back in his chair. "I

want your team to see if they can find any patterns of when the pictures were taken compared to who might have been off duty. Check the personnel files, see if there's any reason someone might have a grudge, that type of thing. I've cleared your access with Personnel—they think you're helping me do annual assessments so they shouldn't hassle you."

"I hate to think it's someone inside Hauberk."

"I'm hoping you'll be able to rule out that possibility. I've also arranged for you to have access to any cases Sam was involved in from the time he started with Hauberk. If you have any questions and Sam or I aren't available, you can ask Sandy."

He opened the folder he'd tossed on the desk earlier, and removed a half dozen sheets of paper. "This is Sam's schedule for the next month."

Rosie scanned Sam's appointments. "He's got a fundraiser tomorrow night, a black tie event at the French embassy Thursday. A speech in Annapolis Friday, an event on Saturday morning, a literacy fundraiser Saturday night." She flipped the page and tried to stop her jaw from dropping at the number of functions he was attending. "Next week he's attending a party in Annapolis, a speech over at Explorer's Hall, three more fundraisers—including ones for the Democrats *and* the Republicans, something at La Porte Rouge—whatever that is, an exhibition over at the Corcoran, another at the Library of Congress." Too many people, too many places. Too many opportunities should anyone want to kill him. "I don't suppose he'd be open to canceling any of these, would he?"

Chad made some weird noise in the back of his throat. When she looked up at him, he picked up a pen and began to doodle. "I, um, I think I can convince him to cancel out on a couple of those functions." He tossed the pen back in the pot and took another, cleared his throat again. "As for the rest, you can ask, but don't be surprised if he refuses. Man's determined not to let someone get the best of him. You know what they say about doctors being the worst patients? Sam's going to be our worst client."

"Men," Rosie muttered under her breath.

"It's not all ego, Rosie. Sam's got his reasons for not

wanting bodyguards. He's going to fight having CPOs to his last breath. And I sure as hell don't want it to get that far. Which means you'll need to stick to him like glue."

Chapter Five

The limo pulled into the underground parking lot and past his Jag. A sigh escaped Sam as they cruised past his Harley. The crisp October day would have been perfect to drive his Road King. Instead he was cooped up like a damned dog in the back of the limo that finally stopped near the elevator where Rosie was waiting.

Damn it, why had Chad insisted on Rosie Ramos as his lead CPO? If he'd wanted a woman to accompany him to any upcoming parties or meet 'n greets—the reason Chad had given him—why not McKee or Anderson? Neither of those women got his cock twitching like Rosie did.

The fantasy he'd had of getting her alone in his apartment hadn't included her wearing a gun and acting as his personal bodyguard. All right, maybe one had. But, damn it, if a bullet was going to be aimed in his direction, there was no way in hell he wanted the little spitfire throwing herself in its path. He'd rather have her throw herself in his bed. Go down on her knees and unzip his fly... Damn it! Damn it! Damn it!

"All clear, Mr. Watson," Rosie said quietly.

"Of course it is." Sam ducked his head and clambered out of the limo, then stomped to the elevator. Goddamn it, she'd even acquired a key to the elevator, locking the door open so no one else could use it. He ignored that it was standard operating procedure and lashed out, "You think other people might not need the goddamned elevator?"

"Better than having the door open and somebody shoot you from inside. Besides there are other elevators still available."

Her voice was so damned reasonable. Placating. Like he was some baby to be soothed out of a tantrum.

Which is exactly how he was behaving but goddamn it, his people were supposed to be protecting others. Not him.

She turned the key and let the door close, pressing the button for the penthouse. The elevator began to rise, a quiet chime announcing each floor they passed. And with each ding, Sam became more and more aware of the delicate smell of apricot shampoo and woman filling the confined area. He closed his eyes, trying not to deliberately inhale great lungfuls of that amazing scent.

As long as she was around him, he'd not sleep. Instead he'd be staring at the ceiling imagining what it would feel like to cup her breasts in his hands, to unzip her pants and nudge aside that blue thong. Imagine going down on her and tasting her honey. When she'd been in the gym doing those stretches, he'd obsessed about some of the positions she could get into while he fucked her. Then in his office while Chad had been briefing her, he'd pictured her stretched out over his desk, her legs hitched over his shoulders. And now she'd be in the next apartment, so damned available.

Damn it!

"Mr. Watson, do you have a problem with me guarding you?"

"Nope." He couldn't help that his answer sounded like a growl. He had one helluva a problem and at the moment it was punching against his zipper. He shifted his briefcase so she wouldn't see his hard-on.

"I mean, do you have a problem with a woman guarding you?"

Shit! She thought he didn't want her because she was a woman? Why not add sexual discrimination to the mix today? He exhaled and opened his eyes. "No, Ms. Ramos, I do not have a problem a female operative leading my team."

"Then do you have a problem with me personally?"

Was it a problem that he was imagining pinning her up against the wall and ramming into her until she screamed her release? How the hell did he explain that to her without getting slapped with a sexual harassment suit in addition to the discrimination one?

"If I didn't have complete confidence in your abilities, you wouldn't work for Hauberk, and Chad wouldn't have personally chosen you as team leader."

That must have been the answer she was looking for. She nodded, and her shoulders imperceptibly relaxed. "Thank you."

"I'm pis—ticked off at whoever is sending those damned photographs, and I fu—frickin' don't like having to accept that I had to ask my own people to protect me. Leaves me damned twitchy. So don't take my grouchiness personally, Ms. Ramos. It's not directed at you."

No, what was pointing directly at her was his goddamned dick.

The elevator bounced once before the doors slid open, and Sam waited for her to precede him.

Aw, crap. Now he had to watch that bitable ass of hers walk along the hallway and that did nothing to help him control his raging hard-on.

She's your employee. She's a crack shot with that Glock 11 she carries. He almost groaned as the image of her bending over on the firing range, wiggling that ass at him, had his cock so hard it hurt.

She can stomp on your nuts and have you singing soprano without breaking a sweat.

Didn't work. All his dick thought of was wrestling on the ground with her body pressing against him, over him, under him. Around him.

What was in that coffee of Sandy's today that left him so fucking horny? Spanish fuckin' fly?

As they approached the door to his apartment, the door to 1202 opened and Kris nodded. "Evening, Mr. Watson."

Sam couldn't help but notice his newest and youngest operative standing at attention, a worried frown marring that baby-smooth face of his. Aw hell. He'd stomped on that poor boy's ego pretty good earlier. Hadn't he been a bucket of sunshine today?

He stopped, and blew out a breath. "Look, Kris, I owe you

an apology. I shouldn't have yelled at you this morning. I've been..."—a festering pile of self-centered dogshit?—"under a lot of pressure lately."

Yeah, right, and if you buy that one, I've got some land in the Okefenokee for you.

"It's all right, Mr. Watson. I don't think I'd be feeling too happy if someone threatening me had access to my apartment and personal information either."

He might have bought Kris's smile if it hadn't been for the *Mr. Watson.* Unlike some of his employees, Kris had never had a problem referring to him as Sam. Or even "buddy" on occasion in the gym. *Mr. Watson* meant he still had some fencing to mend.

"Chad told me you and Walters got those cameras in place."

"Sir, yes, sir. It was no problem at all, sir."

First Mr. Watson and now *sir.* And not just sir, but the military sir, yes sir. Well, he supposed it was natural for Kris to fall back on his naval training.

"I didn't expect you'd have a problem with it, son."

Son? Son? Kris is twenty-five, you idiot, not eight the way you've just made him feel. He's not young enough to be your son.

Okay, *technically* he probably could have been a father at fourteen thanks to Becky Sue's idea of a birthday present that year. Thank the good Lord above, she'd stolen a condom from her brother Billy's bedside table before sneaking out. Not that he'd needed another condom for a coupla years after that, but if she'd not had the forethought that night, he could have been a daddy by his fifteenth birthday. But he sure as hell wasn't old enough to call Kris *son.*

"Mr. Watson?" Rosie said, touching his arm. "Are you okay?"

An electric shock jumped from her fingers and crawled under his skin in a tingle that caused his breath to hitch. He'd noticed that she was a toucher, seen her patting people's arms or hands to calm them or support them, but she'd never touched him before. His cock hijacked his thinking processes and started him imagining her tiny hands closing about Sam Junior, milking...

Shit on a stick! She's your employee, not a member of the Rouge.

"Yeah." He pinched the bridge of his nose and exhaled as he forced his mind back onto the scene in the hall. "Look, Kris, I didn't mean to imply you're not a good CPO. Chad wouldn't have assigned you to the team if he didn't have confidence in you."

Color crept up Kris's neck. "Thank you, sir."

"Sam."

"Sam," Kris repeated, his smile breaking out.

Feeling that at least one corner of the world was back on its axis, Sam headed toward the end of the hall and his sanctuary.

Rosie stopped him as he pulled his keys from his jacket pocket. "Let me get that for you."

His teeth threatening to splinter when his jaw locked down, Sam stepped back and let her unlock the door with her own key. She drew her gun and entered his apartment. Chad had reported they'd monitored the cleaning service doing their thing that afternoon, so they knew the apartment was clear. Though he couldn't fault her vigilance, it was what she'd signed on for when Hauberk hired her, but damned if it didn't shrivel his balls that she was willing to take a bullet meant for him.

The office had emptied as he leaned back in his chair, running one hand through his hair. Sam had finally yielded to pressure and accepted the detail.

His sense of accomplishment dimmed as he thought of the obstacles still in their path. When the truth came out, would he find himself out of another job? Too late to worry about it; the wheels were already rolling down the hill.

Releasing a long slow exhale, he pulled out his Berry and scrolled through the menu. When he reached the text messaging option, he entered his co-conspirators' addresses, typed *"Operation Payback Begun"* and hit send.

Chapter Six

Rosie checked the apartment and called the all clear before they let Sam enter. They'd been monitoring the hallway since they'd arrived that afternoon and knew exactly who was home and who wasn't but she wasn't going to take any chances. They'd coordinated with the Hauberk Security guards manning the front desk and had descriptions of all the regular tenants. Plus, while Kris and Andy were installing the extra hallway cameras, they'd discovered a high-pitched yapping down at 1206 started anytime someone opened a door, loud enough that they would have heard it even if someone hadn't been monitoring the cameras. The sensors on the terrace doors showed no breech, so they would—should—know if someone had scaled the wall or climbed in from another apartment. But even so, it was her job to make sure the perimeter hadn't been breeched and no one was laying in wait inside the apartment. She'd be damned if she'd slack off when her boss was watching.

Once she'd given the all-clear, Sam walked into the living room and shrugged off his jacket. He tossed it over the back of one of the leather couches. She tried to inhale a lungful of air filled with his scent without him noticing. God, just being in the same room had her wanting to rip her clothes off and jump him.

When he realized she'd shut the door with her still inside, he frowned. "You don't have to stay with me. I don't need a babysitter, Ms. Ramos."

"Until we discover who's making the threats, I want someone with you twenty-four/seven. Besides, Chad gave me orders to stick to you like glue."

A flash of his eyes told her he wished he could countermand his second's order, but his clamped jaw told her he'd swallowed his objection. God keep her from men who thought they were bulletproof.

He headed toward the kitchen she'd scoped out earlier. She couldn't help but be impressed by the granite counters, the cherry wood cabinets and the gleaming stainless steel appliances.

"You want a beer?" He opened the fridge and stared. "What the...? You didn't have to shop for me."

"Aside from a six-pack of Heineken, the fridge only contained a hunk of moldy cheddar and a half dozen boxes of take-out Chinese that were about to sprout legs and walk out on their own. I figured if we wanted to eat, I'd better order some groceries." Not to mention she'd thrown anything out that had been opened in case the prowler had tampered with them. The right poison could kill him as efficiently as any bullet.

He poked through the Sub Zero. "Chicken, cold cuts...hey, you bought pecan pie. How'd you know that was my favorite?"

She shrugged, wondering at the warm and fuzzy feeling creeping through her. "Lucky guess."

"Thank you." He lifted her hand and pressed a kiss to her knuckles. The fleeting touch zapped the warm and fuzzies to scorching flames.

There was a look on his face she couldn't quite fathom. A hungriness—not for the food she'd put in his refrigerator, but for her. It left her both excited and unnerved.

"F-for someone who has a kitchen as big as most people's apartments, and appliances my mother could only dream of, you sure don't look like you make use of it." *Ay bendito*, he'd actually made her stutter.

"It's sort of wasted on me. Unless I have someone to cook for that is. I make a mean Chicken Creole for two." He removed a Heineken and cracked it open. "So how come you're the one babysittin' me tonight, and not Walters or Campbell?"

He lifted the beer and sipped then lowered the bottle and stared at her, frowning. "Tell me you didn't agree to play a game of poker to determine who got stuck with me."

"Hardly—Andy cheats."

Sam chuckled. "He sure does—I lost almost two thousand to him before I twigged to his game. That boy's slicker than owl sh—droppings."

"I was lucky. When I first joined Hauberk up in New York, Rick Sparks taught me how to spot someone cheating. So I caught Andy dealing from the bottom on the second hand we played. I've never trusted him with a deck of cards since."

"Yeah, Rick's pretty slick too." He placed the beer bottle on the counter, turned it in precise quarter turns. "But you never did tell me how you ended up with the short straw tonight?"

"We figured it might raise some eyebrows if people found him sharing the apartment with you. Easier to explain a woman coming and going in your apartment than a man."

At least that's what she *thought* Andy had said, but he'd managed to twist and turn the conversation around in such a convoluted path, she wasn't entirely sure what his point had been. She'd given in because she knew Kris was still concerned about his joke about her checking the mail and wouldn't want to face Sam just yet. From the way her panties were starting to soak she already knew that she'd made a mistake in agreeing to stay in the same apartment with him. She'd go to sleep smelling the cologne that subtly permeated the sheets knowing the only thing separating her from him in that custom made bed of his was two thin sheets of drywall and a couple of metal two by fours. That and her willpower. Which was threatening to take up sleepwalking.

She realized he was talking and forced herself to focus. "—day and age, I don't think many people blink at two guys sharing an apartment." He lifted the beer then paused and frowned. "You sure you don't want a beer?"

Rosie leaned her hip against the counter and decided to deliberately put some space between them, mentally if not physically. "You know, earlier today Kris wondered if maybe you were trying out some new form of employee evaluation. Is he right? Because frankly, if this is all your idea of a test, I find your methods insulting."

"What makes you think it might be?"

"Drinking is against the rules for an operative protecting

their principal. Yet you deliberately offered me a beer—twice."

"It's not a test. I was trying to be hospitable—it's how my momma raised me. My daddy taught me to look after myself—which is why having you—anyone—babysit me while they're waiting around for someone to try to take a potshot at me sticks in my craw."

"That's precisely what Hauberk hired me to do. It's understood that we're agreeing to protect our principals by whatever means necessary."

"Yeah, well...if it comes down to taking a bullet for me, don't."

"I'm supposed to let them shoot Hauberk's owner and president?" She crossed her arms and waited for him to answer.

He lifted the bottle to his lips and hesitated, his gaze dropping down to her cleavage and the three buttons she'd left undone.

Her nipples hardened into tight buds that pushed against the thin fabric of her T-shirt. Yup, agreeing to stay with a man who could make her so horny just with a look was a major logistical error.

He muttered something under his breath that sounded rather like "death of him" but she couldn't be sure. Her theory about him having a death wish started niggling again. Had he done something he was ashamed of? Did he feel he deserved a bullet for whatever he'd done?

"How will you protect me if you're dead? I'm not the president with over two hundred agents who can jump in if one falls. If someone shoots me, you'll follow standard Hauberk procedure—keep yourself safe, and get me the hell out of Dodge. You can get me medical care once you're clear of any danger." He finished his beer and stashed the empty bottle in a bin under the sink then stalked out to the living room.

Once he'd flipped on the large flat screen to a football game, she knew it was time to change tactics. She wandered around the apartment, waiting for a commercial break before picking up a picture of a woman with similar golden skin and high cheekbones. She already knew who it was, she'd been through his file, but wanted to keep him relaxed. Hoping to project a casual manner, she asked, "She's pretty, who is she?"

"That's my little sister, Sarah." His defensiveness dropped, pride filling his voice. "She graduated medical school last year and is doin' her residency in Atlanta."

"And this lady?" She picked up the picture of a Hawaiian woman in traditional Hawaiian garb with dark hair and high cheekbones, and Sam's beautiful smile.

"That's my momma." His entire face softened as he looked at the picture. "After Pop died, she moved back to Hawaii." His brow creased. "If she calls, don't tell her that you're here to protect me, all right?"

"She'll get upset?"

Sam snorted. "More likely she'll get on a plane and come here to try to run the detail herself. She was a nurse with the Army—served in 'Nam for two tours—that's where she met Pop. I swear she's a mind reader because you can't get away with anything when she's around."

The next picture was one of Mrs. Watson and a small boy with a full head of black curls. Before she could ask, Sam sneered. "Yeah, that's me. And if you say how cute I was, I'll kick you out."

"I won't." But she wanted to.

He ran a hand over his stubble. "And don't tell me you'd like me to grow it out because I'm tall enough as it is without lookin' like someone parked a goddamned poodle on my head."

Rosie couldn't help but laugh as she moved along the mantel and picked up the next picture. Sam in leather pants and motorcycle jacket, standing by a black and chrome Harley, the Washington Monument in the background. It was the look of adoration on his face as he smiled at a curvy redhead wrapped up in his arms that had caught Rosie's attention when she'd first seen the picture earlier that day.

"That's Jill Hoskins." A bleak look crossed his face as he turned his head to stare out the window. "She died two weeks after that picture was taken."

Carefully setting the picture back on the mantel, Rosie murmured, "I'm sorry."

"Yeah. So am I," he replied even quieter, one of his hands rubbing idly at his chest. After a moment, he hit the remote and unmuted the television, focusing on the scrimmage instead.

She waited until halftime before speaking again. "Has Chad told you about Troy loaning us one of his operatives to help out?"

"Yeah, Scott Phillips." Sam's scowl and something that sounded like it would be a particularly filthy curse in what might have been German. "If anyone should be on vacation, it's Scott. Instead Troy sics him on me. Do him a favor—give him a pile of files to check out or something. Keep him busy, will ya? He sits around with nothin' to do, he'll drive himself crazy second-guessing himself."

Without another word, he stalked from the kitchen and headed down the hall to his bedroom. Obviously she needed to take a look at Phillips' file herself and find out why he deserved a vacation. A burnt out operative definitely wouldn't help protect Sam.

Thirty minutes later, a rhythmic noise had her peeking around the door. Wearing only a pair of shorts, Sam was working out on a rowing machine. His shoulder muscles rippled and his thighs bulged as he hauled on the pulley. Rosie stood in the doorway, entranced by a bead of sweat as it rolled down his forehead and slid down his neck.

The play of his muscles as he worked out made her imagine his chest flexing, his arms planted either side of her head. She'd dig her fingers into those broad shoulders, feel his strength as he held himself above her. When he drove into her, she'd wrap her legs about his, feel the power of his thighs as he whipped her into an orgasmic frenzy.

He's your boss, her conscience hissed. She fled to the safety of the living room, wondering if she was fleeing Sam, or the strength of her desire.

You're just horny, she reminded herself. *It's been almost a year since you've been with a guy and now you've got the man of your dreams at your fingertips. You've been on a starvation diet and he's a delicious hunk of cherry chocolate cheesecake.*

Forty minutes later the sounds changed and the whir of the treadmill started, followed by a regular thumping that gradually sped up as his feet pounded on the belt. An hour more had passed when she heard the shower turn on in his bathroom.

She found herself prowling along the floor-to-ceiling windows like a panther trapped in a cage. He'd be naked, those four showerheads in his expansive bathroom pounding his back with steady pulses of hot water. Water that would cascade over his chest, sluice down his belly and over his cock. A cock she wanted to—STOP IT!

When the water shut off, she turned her back to the room and pretended to focus on the lights of the city. But once he stepped into the room, the lights faded and all she could see was the reflection of Sam. Wearing only a pair of navy sweats and a towel wrapped around his neck, he prowled across the room to stand directly behind her. The broad expanse of his chest was still visible in his reflection for the top of her head barely cleared the base of his sternum.

"The view is beautiful, isn't it?" he said softly. Except he wasn't looking at the panorama of the city, he was looking at her reflection.

"Y-yes." It took every ounce of her willpower to continue facing the windows, not to turn into the chest that formed a wall at her back, not to touch the scar down the middle of his chest, or the star-shaped bullet wound just to the left and ask him about it. She'd once asked, but no one, not even Chad, would tell her the story of who'd put it there. She closed her eyes and forced herself to breathe slowly.

Closing her eyes only made her awareness of him worse. It let her focus on the warmth that flowed from him, enveloping her in a comforting blanket. While he hadn't put on any more of that wonderful cologne he wore, she was aware of a scent underneath the smell of the soap he'd used. Every man she ever met from now on would be compared to the man standing directly behind her.

Her breath left her in a whoosh when he placed his hands lightly on her shoulders.

"You look like you've had a tough day, Ms. Ramos. You need to relax."

Heck he didn't even have to touch her, his voice alone could melt her bones and turn her into a puddle of goo at his feet. When his fingers massaged her shoulders, she couldn't help but lean into his touch.

"That's it, Rosie. Just relax."

Her breasts felt heavier, warmer, the fabric of her blouse tightened over her nipples longing to be touched by the fingers that caressed her neck.

Her Berry rang, a unique ring she'd assigned to Chad's number. Crap! How had she forgotten that she was not only Sam's employee but his bodyguard?

Employee, not lover. *Remember his type.* Tall, lithe and beautiful. And if she added the news clippings and photos of his last girlfriend to the equation, rich.

She straightened her shoulders as she removed her Berry then, without looking at Sam's reflection, took a half step sideways and fled to the kitchen. "Hey, Chad, what's up?"

When she returned, she found Sam sprawled on the couch, one foot on the floor, the other propped up on the coffee table. He patted the cushion beside him. "Come here, Rosie, let me finish that backrub."

"I'm here to protect you, Mr. Watson. Not to relax."

His lips tilted up in a half smile that she knew so well. "You don't mind if I relax though, do you?"

Something about the way he asked had her on alert. Nothing he said ever meant quite what she expected. "It's your home, Mr. Watson."

"My name's Sam."

"I think while I'm guarding you I'll stick with Mr. Watson." She had to keep that formality or she'd not only fall into his arms but crawl into his bed.

One eyebrow arched up. His fingers drummed on his thigh a couple of times before he reached for a box by his foot on the coffee table and withdrew a cigar. "Since this is my house, I'd say that you should abide by my rules."

His rules? "Why don't I just call you *My Lord* or *Master*."

His gaze dropped to her cleavage, which swelled over the arms she'd folded across her chest, and his smile widened. When he looked up at her, something hot and dark flared in the back of his eyes. "If I'm your master, I guess that makes you my slave."

His sense of humor was well known, but the look on his

face told her that he wasn't joking, and the powerful undercurrent in the conversation left her floundering for sure footing. "Slavery's outlawed in this country."

"If you only knew." He trimmed the end of his cigar then picked up a book of matches and struck one, holding the flame to the cigar's tip.

Her feet touching bottom once more, Rosie raised her chin and looked him square in the eye. "While I am staying here, Mr. Watson—"

His brows clamped together in a frown of displeasure. "I thought I told you to use my name. My Christian name."

Arrrgh! "Sam then! The point is, I have a few rules of my own."

"I'll just bet you do." He gestured with his cigar to the couch again. "Why don't you make yourself comfortable while we discuss your rules?"

"I prefer to stand, thank you." Ignoring his raised eyebrow, Rosie paced in front of the fireplace. "You've made it very clear you don't like having bodyguards, but you have to remember that you are the owner of Hauberk—if something happens to you there will be a lot of people out of jobs."

"I'm quite aware of that." His thumb and index finger rolled the cigar in what she knew was an unconscious gesture, she'd seen him do it so many times before. Yet she found herself entranced by the motion of the glowing tip. "You were telling me your rules?"

She jerked her attention back to his gaze and saw the look of amusement on his face. Damn it, she had to stay in control. "As your lead op, it's up to me to ensure your safety as well as the future employment of your employees. So first off, you do not answer your door—that'll be my job. I'll be screening your phone calls as well. Whenever you leave the apartment, you will wear a bulletproof vest and we will take one of the company limos. You will not attempt to leave—" She held up her hand when he opened his mouth to speak. "No, Chad warned me that you might try something sneaky. If you try to get past us—past me, I will recommend that you be stashed in one of Hauberk's safe houses and kept under armed guard. And Chad'll agree." He would, she'd already discussed that possibility with him.

"Now, I want you to guarantee me that you will not try to go anywhere without one of the team with you."

"You'd trust me if I agreed?" His voice deepened.

"Yes. You're a man who honors his promises. Now, will you give me your word not to go anywhere without me, Andy or Kris with you?"

He tipped his head and drew a long puff on his cigar. After he'd exhaled a wreath of smoke into the air, he nodded and raised his left hand. "I promise to let you answer the door and the phone, and I promise to stay in the apartment while you're with me."

Chapter Seven

Before she could point out to him that he'd raised the wrong hand, or question the way he'd phrased his promise, her cell phone buzzed, and two seconds later there was a knock at the door.

Checking her cell, she found a one-word text message from Andy confirming the identity of their visitor. As she hurried to the door, she glanced over at Sam who crossed his feet on the coffee table and took another long drag of his cigar.

A king of the castle ensconced on his throne as his lackeys hustled around him. Yet there was no sense of entitlement about him. No smug satisfaction. So why did she have the feeling she'd fallen into some sort of trap?

Even though she knew who was on the other side, Rosie checked the flat screen monitoring the camera they'd mounted outside. Their visitor's identity confirmed, she opened the door.

"Hi, Sandy, what brings you here at this hour?"

Sandy stepped into the foyer and gestured to Kris who trailed behind her carrying two bankers boxes.

"Chad asked me to bring over the files of clients we've had for the past two years—he figures there might be something in them about Sam's stalker."

"Where do you want 'em?" Kris asked.

Rosie jumped when Sam spoke from directly behind her. "Why don't you take one box back to your apartment? Rosie and I can start going through the other box here."

How did such a large man move so quietly?

Sam relieved Kris of the top box, but before he could

disappear down the hall to his study, Sandy stopped him. "Oh and, Sam? Chad wants you to give me your Blackberry—he wants to give you a new number. John is loading some program on my computer to catch anyone going into my address book."

"Hang on a sec, I'll get it for you."

Sam headed to his office while Kris ambled back to what Rosie now thought of as their temporary headquarters, leaving her alone with Sandy. Rosie made small talk, but noticed that Sandy kept shuffling her feet and not meeting her gaze. "Sandy? Is something wrong?"

"It's just... I'm surprised you're..." Sandy glanced down the hall, her bottom lip caught between her teeth. "Forget I said anything."

"Something's bugging you, Sandy, I can tell. So spill."

"I'm just didn't expect to see you at Sam's place, that's all. I figured you'd be monitoring the cameras and Kris or Andy would be here." Sandy shrugged and shuffled closer to the door. "You know it's nothing. Really. I shouldn't have said anything."

"Sandy?" Rosie fixed her with a glare. "You knew I was heading the team, so why are you surprised I'm here."

Sandy's gaze darted toward the hallway again to make sure Sam wasn't nearby before she leaned in and lowered her voice to a whisper. "When Sam and Chad were discussing who to assign to the team and Chad said he wanted to assign you as lead op, Sam said he didn't want you guarding him."

Rosie stiffened as her pride in being named head of his team evaporated in a red haze. How had she forgotten the look on his face, or how he'd snarled at Chad when he'd realized she was in on the meeting? That feeling she'd had in the elevator hadn't been an illusion. "Was it me personally he objected to, or any operative?"

Sandy's gaze dropped briefly, darted back to the door. "Sam said..." She took a deep breath. "Sam said he didn't want you guarding him. He was fine with Andy and Kris."

He'd lied to her. Outright lied.

Oblivious of the flames about to erupt from Rosie's ears, Sandy kept talking. "Sam didn't want to have any bodyguards at all—you should have heard them arguing, I've never seen

Chad get so riled up. But he was definitely against having you on his team."

"Here you are, Sandy." Sam walked into the foyer and handed Sandy his Blackberry. "Thanks for runnin' those files over. Make sure you expense your mileage. And don't let Chad make you work too late tonight, you hear? There's nothing that can't wait until tomorrow."

"It's no problem at all, Sam." As Sandy gave Rosie a hug good-bye, she whispered, "Don't make a big deal about it, okay? He's a guy and you know how guys are."

Hitching her purse up on her shoulder, Sandy fled the foyer, leaving Rosie shaking.

No wonder he kept offering her a beer—he'd been trying to find a way to get rid of her. If she'd accepted, she'd have given him grounds for dismissal.

Sam wandered toward the kitchen. "I was fixin' to make some dinner. I could grill us some chicken and toss a coupla sweet potatoes in the oven. We could finish it all up with that pecan pie you bought." Normally she found the way he pronounced pecan more like pehcawn sexy, but now his drawl shredded her nerves.

"No, thank you." Rosie turned her back on Sam and marched to the spare bedroom. She pulled her suitcase from the closet, tossed it on the bed.

"Is there a problem?" Sam said from the doorway.

"Not at all." She grabbed the clothes she'd put in the top drawer and tossed them into the suitcase.

He leaned his shoulder against the doorframe, his forehead furrowing. "Then why are you packing like there's a four alarm fire on the floor below?"

"I've decided to switch off with Kris or Andy. We'll all be happier that way." Well, she wouldn't be. Goddamn, when would men realize that just because she was only 5'1 and didn't have a penis didn't mean she couldn't provide proper protection or run an effective op?

"Happier? You wanna tell me why you think I'd be happier with them? What bee crawled up your— What'd I do to send you running like someone tied a bottle rocket to your tail?"

She whirled, her arms held rigidly at her side. "Oh, let's see, you wanted someone else protecting you, not a little bitty woman who wasn't a former Navy MP or D.C. City cop or CIA spook. And then when I asked you earlier if you had a problem with me being on your detail, you lied to me. Outright lied! I've put up with a lot of crap, Mr. Watson, but I don't tolerate lies. You don't want me guarding you, fine. But you should have said that when I asked."

"I didn't lie. I never said I didn't want you protecting me because you were a woman."

"But you told Chad you didn't want me assigned to you, didn't you?"

"Yes, that part's true. But—"

"*Ay bendito.* I knew it." She advanced on him. "Just because I'm short doesn't mean I can't take you down—just ask Kris or Andy. Just because I'm a woman doesn't mean I'm not a damned good shot. I've been trained in counter-surveillance, and bomb disposal."

"I know that, I—"

"Just because I've never worn a uniform or carried a badge doesn't mean I can't guard you. I've been on details guarding an Oscar winning actor while he was making that movie down in Savannah and got him to safety when the barricades failed to hold back hundreds of screaming fans." Then the asshole had expected her to put out in the limo. "I've protected those three country music singers—did I mention how much I hate country music—and let's not forget the gentleman from Saudi Arabia with his three wives and sixteen kids, or the dozens of women from the Safe and Sound program."

"I know you're good at your job. That wasn't why I wanted someone else."

"Ha! So you did want someone else. You admit it."

"Yeah, I already admitted it. But—"

"But you don't trust me to protect you." She closed the cover on the suitcase and zipped it.

"I trust you. But—damn it! I wasn't objecting to you because you're a woman, Rosie. Well, yeah, it's sort of because you're a woman. Aw, hell, you're reading this all wrong."

"For all your bullshit about equal opportunities, it's still just bullshit. You want to be a big macho he-man who guards the 'little woman' but God help you now it's the other way around."

"Rosie—Ms. Ramos—"

"I'll stay until Chad can get someone else over here to replace me, but then I'm out of here. And not just this assignment but D.C. I refuse to work for someone who doesn't respect my abilities. I'll expect you to approve my transfer first thing in the morning. Because if you don't, then I'll file a lawsuit for sexual discrimination." She stopped talking, the words clogging her throat. Oh Lord. Fifteen minutes ago, she was feeling so proud and now she was about to walk away from the job she loved.

"Goddamn it, I don't want you to leave Hauberk, Rosie. I didn't want you guardin' me because I can't guarantee I'll be able to keep my hands off you!"

The breath whooshed from her lungs. Of all the excuses he could have given her, that was one she wasn't expecting. A blast of heat, of desire, filled her veins, headed straight for her nipples, her pussy. "You—"

"You drive me crazy, woman!" Heavy hands landed on her shoulders, spun her around. "All you have to do is walk by and I get hard. I'm so hard right now it hurts."

A glance down proved him correct.

Her traitorous eyes refused to return to his face, instead they sent a message to her knees to drop down to the floor, to her hands to cup him, caress him, free him. Her traitorous tongue flicked out and licked her upper lip in anticipation of taking that impressive erection into her mouth. Luckily enough, a part of her mind retained just enough control to override those urges.

"All I can think of is getting you out of those clothes and beneath me, Rosie. I know that you could slap me with a sexual harassment suit just for saying that. But it's true." He muttered something about the difficulty of herding cats—whatever the hell that meant—then moved closer, the heat from his body like a blast from a foundry. "I can tell when you've been in a room by the scent of your shampoo. That's all it takes to stop my brain from workin'. Then my dick takes command."

Just like her pussy heated and creamed whenever she smelled his aftershave. Or heard his deep chuckle floating through the office. Just like her breasts ached watching him roll his cigar between his fingers, wishing it was her nipples he was touching.

So why did her chest hurt hearing him say what she'd fantasized about for months? Because he was lying. For all his smooth words, he was trying to find some lame ass explanation to weasel out of having her as his lead op.

"That's why I asked Chad not to assign you. Not because I don't trust you to guard me. But because I don't trust myself to leave you alone." His voice dropped an octave. "I want you, Rosie. And not as my bodyguard."

"I don't...I don't believe you." Why wouldn't her knees support her? What had happened to all the oxygen in the room?

"You want proof?" He pulled her until her breasts mashed into his chest. Before she knew it his lips were pressing against hers in a hard hungry kiss.

His tongue lightly stroked the seal of her lips. One of his hands cradled her head, holding her in place, his thumb toying with the skin below her ear, rhythmically stroking, calming her. His other hand kneaded her behind, pressing her against his erection. "Do you feel what you do to me? Do you believe I'm not lying when I say I want you?"

The hoarse entreaty melted all her objections like they were snowflakes at a Fourth of July barbeque. The moment she relaxed, he slipped his tongue between her lips. As he plundered deeper, he made a sound deep in his throat, of approval, of desire, of need. His hand dropped from her neck and slid to the front, brushing the side of her breast.

When his thumb flicked across one nipple, it was her turn to moan.

"Rosie," he whispered. He moved the hand cupping her behind to between her thighs, his fingers stroking her clit through her jeans, setting off a firestorm of sensation. "Do you know how many times I've imagined going down on you, how I've wondered what your sweat cream tastes like? Did you know that after I watched you doing your stretches in the gym this morning I had to go back to my shower and pretended my cock was inside your pussy instead of my own palm."

While her head was screaming to run, reminding her of the thousand ways this would come back and bite her in the ass, her hips arched into his touch.

She wasn't aware he'd moved at all but she found herself laying down on the bed, with him kneeling over top of her just like she'd fantasized. Except this was real. She hoped it was because if it was a dream, her vibrator would need a new set of batteries by morning.

To her surprise, her blouse gapped open, exposing her lacy beige bra.

When had he undone her buttons?

He broke their kiss, his warm breath heating the side of her neck, the roughness of his beard abrading her skin. A tug at the clasp of her bra, and he exposed her breasts, their cinnamon nipples cinched into tight points.

"Baby, you're so beautiful." His tongue laved one, then the other in a tender stroke. Seconds later he latched onto one and pulled it into his mouth, suckling it deep.

This wasn't supposed to be happening. She had to stop him. She had to... Oh, sweet Lord, it felt so good.

Her fingernails dug into his shoulders when his fingers unsnapped her jeans, drew them down over her hips. His fingers, long and blunt, snaked beneath the thin band of her thong and teased her labia apart, setting fire to her as her juices drenched him.

One finger penetrated, stroked deep inside her while he sucked harder on her breast. Another finger joined the first.

The hell on him stopping, she had to help him. She had to have him inside her. All of him.

He was murmuring now, telling her what he wanted to do to her, what he wanted her to do to him. Things she'd never before thought she'd wanted. Things she'd never considered. Things she now had to try. With him.

The heat built as his fingers pressed deeper, his thumb whisking over her clit. The room darkened as she squeezed her eyes shut, concentrated on the sensations building within her.

She arched her back, moaning as he teased her, tormented her by bringing her to the edge before slowing his movements, taking away the precipice she wanted to plunge over.

"Please."

His lips left her breast and feathered over her stomach. They lingered on the spot right above the thin patch of hair before tasting first one hip, then the other. Her breath left her in a rush when his lips fastened onto the spot his thumb had been avoiding. His teeth rasped over her sensitive clit, his tongue licking on either side. Slow and then fast. Her body tensed as everything focused on where he touched her, inside and out.

"So sweet, just like I knew you'd be." His words set a vibration through her tissues that rebounded until they touched the aching spot teased by his fingers.

She pushed his head back down and changed her "please" from a request to a demand.

Whether he touched her with his tongue or his thumb she never knew but the full body orgasm that erupted drove her breath from her and sent every muscle quivering.

She drifted off the bed, out of the room, floated high in the sky, among the stars that exploded on the back of her eyelids and left her to flutter back down to the soft silken covers beneath her.

Chapter Eight

Rosie's sigh as her body relaxed was a soft caress and a damning slap to Sam's conscience.

"Damn." He retreated several steps, one broad hand splayed over his temple briefly before dropping it. "God damn, I'm sorry, Rosie. I didn't mean to take it that far."

Her eyes shot open and with a look of horror on her face, Rosie grabbed the pillow and covered herself as she bent over and retrieved her pants from where they'd fallen to the floor. He noticed she carefully kept her face averted. "You said you've been fantasizing about me. Did you mean it?"

Uh oh. The breathy murmurs had changed to crisp speech; she sounded like a lawyer questioning a hostile witness. Was he about to face a lawsuit? Not that he could deny what he'd just done to her—he'd definitely shattered the employer/employee boundary.

"Have you really been fantasizing about me?" she demanded again.

"Yes."

She pulled on her pants, her head bent over as she fastened the clasp at her waist. "Does that explain why Miss Stewart and you are no longer together?"

"Nope. Cynthia and I...well, let's just say we were never exclusive." *Tread carefully, Sammy, Rosie's not ready to know about the club or its members.* Not that he could tell her if he wanted to without permission from the board.

Rosie slanted him a strange look as she fastidiously did up every single one of her blouse's buttons, including the three she'd left undone when she'd first met him at the limo. "So why did you keep seeing her?"

Because Cynthia was a damned good fuck who let him enjoy some of his kinkier preferences while he fantasized about another woman didn't seem to be the right answer.

He realized Rosie was holding her breath, realized what she was asking.

"You're askin' why I never approached you before."

She gave him a stiff nod.

"I'm your employer. I couldn't treat you as anything other than an employee without risking a lawsuit." Until tonight when his dick definitely had taken control of his brain.

"Is that honestly why you told Chad to assign someone else?" When she finally looked at him, he was surprised at the anger spearing out of her eyes.

Oh yeah, this was no wilting lily waiting for a man to validate her existence. She hadn't let whatever had happened just now distract her the way it had him.

He shouldn't have let his frustration get the best of him, he shouldn't have taken her the way he had. Hell, he shouldn't have kissed her, even that was way over the line. But he didn't regret it either. His fantasies hadn't come close to matching her in reality. She'd tasted like strawberries and rain and heaven rolled into one enticing package.

He wanted to see her eyes unfocus again. And often. Now. Without thinking, he stroked her cheek. "Believe me, baby, I wasn't objectin' to you guardin' me because I think you're not good enough. I know you're one damned good protective officer."

With precise movements, she tucked her shirt into her pants. "Then we'll forget this happened. I'll tell Andy and Kris one of them will be staying with you from now on."

She was out the door and in the foyer before her words penetrated the haze of his lust.

Forget this happened? She could do that after the full-body orgasm he'd just given her? He scrambled from the bed, having to fight his way out of the comforter that had tangled about his feet. "Hell no, we won't forget this happened."

The front door was just closing behind her as he reached

the foyer. He yanked it open and stalked into the hall following Rosie. "You think I'm gonna just let you walk out of here after what we just did?"

He pulled up short, shutting his mouth when he saw Kris and another man standing in the hallway by the door to 1202. Kris's eyes went wide, then his lips pressed together until they were nearly white. His scowl deepened, and he muttered something under his breath. Though Sam couldn't hear what he said, he had a pretty damned good idea the newbie had just lost any respect for his lead op. Or more likely him. The other man—Scott Phillips, the guy Troy had assigned to the cause—went from a look of surprise to a carefully blank look. From beneath lowered lids, his eyes narrowed as he assessed Sam, lingered on the woody Sam was still sporting.

Rosie's hands clenched as she slowly turned back to face him. She stabbed her fist toward him, one finger pointing at the door to his penthouse. "You. Get back in your apartment."

"Rosie—Ms. Ramos—"

"Now! And lock the door behind you."

Aware of the two men watching them, Kris with overt hostility, Sam considered grabbing Rosie and pulling her back into his apartment where they could continue the discussion in private. Until he saw her move into a defensive position as she anticipated his thoughts. He settled for a dignified retreat.

Rosie waited until she heard the deadbolt click before turning back to her co-worker. Co-workers if the man carrying the khaki duffel bag was who she suspected.

Kris cleared his throat. "Hey, I guess I should introduce you two." He hooked a finger in Scott's direction. "Scott Phillips, I'd like you to meet our lead op—Rosie Ramos."

"Pleasure to meet you, Miss Ramos." Phillips hefted the duffel and headed toward her, his eyes flickering down. "You might want to, um,"—he waved his fingers over his chest—"check your buttons."

A glance down at her blouse revealed she'd misbuttoned

her blouse and a large gap had displayed her bra to all and sundry. Aw, crap! She wheeled around and hurriedly redid the buttons. When she turned around Scott had disappeared into the apartment.

"He'd just arrived when..." Kris waved toward Sam's door. The questions she knew he wanted to ask hung so heavy in the air she needed a forklift.

"Kris, about what just happened—"

Kris held up his hands though he spoke through clenched teeth. "Hey, if you and Sam are having an affair, it's no skin off my back. What happens in Vegas stays in Vegas, you know?"

Except it wasn't Vegas, and she'd just lost the respect of two of the men she needed to respect her right now. Not to mention her self-respect had just taken a nosedive, especially since ninety-seven percent of her body was screaming at her to march right back into Sam's apartment.

"Look, we're not having an affair." No, she'd just let her boss strip her naked and go down on her. It wasn't an affair when the pleasure had been so one-sided, was it? Didn't it take her returning Sam's attentions for it to be a proper affair? Which she would have done—willingly, eagerly—if Sam hadn't pulled away. If she hadn't walked away.

A second passed, then another before Kris spoke again, "Did Sam...he didn't force himself on you, did he?"

She looked up in surprise, and saw Kris's jaw was locked, a fierce look in his eyes. He wanted to protect her, she realized. For all his joking and tricks, deep down he was the stereotypical knight in shining armor.

"Did he hurt you?" he asked again. "Did he threaten you, or your job?"

Hurt her? He'd told her he'd fantasized about her the same way she'd fantasized about him. Right before he'd given her a mind-blowing orgasm. Which definitely hadn't hurt. Well, okay, maybe her ego hurt that he'd pulled away and apologized. But that wasn't exactly something she could confide in Kris. Or anyone.

When she didn't answer, Kris headed for Sam's door forcing her to grab his arm. "Kris, stop. We got in an argument over his schedule and how we're going to protect him. You saw how he was fighting it this morning. It was just more of the same."

Though she couldn't speak for Sam, it was as far from normal as possible for her. The whole scene in that bedroom seemed more like a dream than reality. But she hadn't decided if it was a fantasy come true or a nightmare in the making.

Kris hesitated. Then, even though he knew she wasn't telling him the truth, he relented.

"Listen, I know I said I'd take the watch tonight, but could you stay in Sam's apartment instead?"

"Sure, Rosie, anything you want."

He ducked into their apartment, emerging moments later with a beat-up gym bag. He glanced over his shoulder when he reached Sam's door and knocked on it. From the look he gave her, she had a feeling he knew it wasn't Sam she didn't trust, but herself. That she was tempted to walk back into the lion's den and meow.

As soon as the lock clicked open, Kris opened Sam's door and shut it behind him.

Muttering about her own idiocy, and flinging curses toward Sam, Rosie fled into the safety of 1202. Phillips' duffel was just inside the door, though she couldn't see him.

Andy looked up from the laptop. "Hey, Rosie. I sent Scott to crash in the second bedroom with Skippy since they'll be drawing opposite shifts. He looked pretty beat—I figured we could bring him up to speed later, right?"

Her feet slowed in the middle of the room. *You walked out to save your job. So stop being such a pathetic zombie.* "Yeah, that's fine. There's, um, been a change of plans and Kris is staying with Sam tonight."

"Oh." Andy frowned. "What happened? I thought you'd decided you were drawing that detail?"

"No, I think it's better if I co-ordinate things from here."

"Had a fight already, huh?"

"No. Not really." She flopped into a chair. What should she do now? It was only a matter of time before Scott or Kris told Andy what had gone on, and then she'd lose control of all three. "Sorta, I guess."

"Hmph. Pity. I was kind of hoping you two would hit it off." And then he shocked the hell out of her. "You know you and Sam would be good together, don't you? I mean, you guys make a good couple."

When she finally gathered enough air to speak, all she could gasp was "What?"

He tilted his head and quirked a grin at her. "Come on, you've got the hots for him—everyone in the office can see it. And Sam—well, he's obviously into you. Besides, I heard you paid seventy grand for him at that auction. You wouldn't have bought him for that type of change if you weren't interested."

Her mouth flapped open and closed a few times before she could think clearly enough to answer. "That was a favor for Jodi Rodriguez," she said slowly, referring to Sam's Dallas-based partner's wife. "She made some agreement with Sam when he was in Dallas last summer. It was her money I was bidding with. Or maybe Sam himself paid. All I know is it wasn't coming out of my pocketbook."

That another woman had driven the bidding to such a frenzied height and cost Jodi so much had left her mortified. Especially when Jodi insisted that she go out with Sam as stipulated by the auction rules. Not that anything had happened, no matter her fantasies. "Besides, he's my boss. Not to mention my principal. You know it wouldn't be good to allow myself to be distracted."

One of his shoulders slowly hitched up then dropped. "All I'm saying is that if you have a chance to find love, you should grab it, you know?"

"It's not like that." Sam had never mentioned a word about love. He'd asked if she felt what she did to him, but that was physical. And she had enough experience to know that lust was vastly different than love.

"Oh. Like I said, that's a pity." He pushed his chair back and stood. "All right, let me go move my stuff from the master bedroom and tell Scott about the change in plans. You wouldn't want me walking around buck naked in the morning now, would you?" He knocked on the door then walked in. "Hey, Scott? Change of plans, buddy."

Rosie sank back into her chair. There was no way she

could stay on as lead op after this. Her threat to request a transfer had just become a necessity. Hopefully the rumors that would undoubtedly rage like a California brush fire wouldn't reach wherever she landed. She pulled out her cell phone and hit the speed dial. While she waited for the phone to connect, she watched the monitor showing the four cameras in the central hall Kris had set up earlier. The one aimed at the elevators showed the door opening and an older lady stepping off, a yappy white spotted terrier pulling at its leash.

Mrs. Margaret O'Mara of 1206. No threat to Sam. The woman turned to the right and walked to the apartment at the far end.

The ringing switched to an automated voice mail system. Once she'd heard the beep, she drew a deep breath. "Chad, it's Rosie. There's been a...development. If you could call me on my cell as soon as you get this." Though she knew Chad had her on speed dial she recited her number anyway.

While she waited for him to phone back, she read through a couple more reports and noted who was where on the spreadsheet she'd started earlier that day, ruling out three more agents as possible suspects. At least she could say she'd contributed something to the detail before she left.

Twenty minutes later, the computer screen showed the elevator doors opening again. Chad. So he'd decided to see her in person rather than talk over the phone.

It was going to be tough to face him, but she supposed she owed him that much for believing in her enough to put her in charge. At least it was better than an impersonal email. *Hey, thanks for putting me in charge, but I'm going to turn tail and run because my boss can make me come with his tongue.*

Keep cool, stay calm. She squared her shoulders and took a deep breath, laying a hand on the doorknob. *If he doesn't grant your request for a transfer, then tell him that he can expect a letter from her lawyer.*

She opened the door without trying to fake a smile. She knew she'd fail.

"Hey, Chad, come on in."

Chad nodded once. "You all right, Rosie?"

A half-hysterical laugh came from her. All right? Where did she even begin to start?

He tilted his head as he looked at her. "The reason your call got dumped into voice mail was I was on the phone with Sam."

Why did she not find that surprising?

"He said that he's worried he gave Campbell and Phillips a wrong impression about you. And he's worried he upset you. So do you want to tell me what happened?"

"No." She pinched the bridge of her nose when a bellow of laughter echoed down the hall. Andy. Probably hearing what he'd seen out in the hall. Great. Her humiliation was nearly complete.

From the sounds of it, Andy was busting a gut in hysterical laughter.

Something smashed. Crap, hopefully it wasn't that big antique mirror over the dresser. Or if it was, she hoped it had fallen right on Andy's head. And maybe Scott's too.

Chad stalked to the bedroom and threw open the door. "You mind—" Whatever he said from there she lost when he closed the door behind him. Less than thirty seconds later, he returned, shaking his head.

"What did they break?"

"Andy dropped a vase. I told him he's got to either find a replacement or I'll take it out of his next paycheck." Chad stopped in the middle of the room and jammed his hands in his pockets, rocking on his heels as he watched her. "So, you going to tell me what happened?"

"Look, Chad. I appreciate you putting me in charge of this op, but I'm afraid you're going to have to replace me. I want to transfer to another office—maybe Miami or Chicago."

Somewhere far from D.C. and Sam Watson. She'd move to Spain if they had an office there.

"Sam said to expect that. He's instructed me to do anything you ask, to tell you he'll give you a good recommendation, pay for your moving expenses, whatever you need."

Probably worried about getting sued. But could she sue him when she had been a willing participant?

"Thing is, I don't want to transfer you. Not without knowing what happened to make you want to run."

"Then I'll quit, and you can discuss it with my lawyer." Her eyes burned, matching the fire roiling in her gut.

"Why do you need a lawyer, Rosie?" A muscle in his jaw twitched as he ground his words out. "Did Sam hurt you? Because if that mofo did, I'll take him down myself."

"No, he didn't hurt me." What did it say that all these guys thought Sam was capable of rape? Did he have a history of violence that she didn't know about?

"I wish you'd trust me," Chad said softly. "Not a word you tell me will be repeated. Scouts' honor." He held up three fingers and smiled, something that took about ten years off him.

She started to say she'd rather not, but realized that if she did see a lawyer, she'd have to describe—in graphic detail— exactly what had happened and he'd find out anyway. Screw the lawyer. "Just replace me, Chad. Please don't make this harder than it already is."

Chad sighed and gestured her to sit on the couch. After she'd settled in place, he sat on the chair across from her and placed his right ankle on the opposite knee. He leaned back and regarded her for a few moments. When he spoke, his voice was gentle, not demanding. "You know, I think I can guess what happened tonight. Sam finally admitted he's attracted to you, didn't he?"

"Finally?" Her voice dropped to a whisper, sounding as tiny as she felt. What was it with everyone insisting Sam was interested in her? He'd not made a move toward her on their date. Tonight was...an aberration, that's all.

"Sam's been interested in you from the first time he met you. Yet in all that time, he's never made a move on you. He's never acted inappropriately. He's never used his position to his advantage over you, has he?"

"No, he hasn't."

"And even though he's interested in you, he won't push you if you're not interested in him." His ankle dropped to the floor and he leaned forward, resting his elbows on his knees. "But you are interested in him, aren't you?"

"No! No." Even she could hear the weakness behind her denial. She jumped up from the chair and faced the window, hoping he couldn't see the blush on her face.

"Rosie, when Sam's in your line of sight, you put out every sexual non-verbal message ever documented—you touch your hair, you straighten your clothing, you cross and uncross your legs, you even lean in his direction—standing or sitting. And this morning—in the firing range—as soon as you realized he was there, you bent down and waggled your butt in his face."

"I was pulling up my socks!" Oh, Lord, she'd tried to be so cool, tried not to broadcast how attractive she found Sam yet Chad could read her as if she had *Horny for Sam* tattooed on her forehead.

Chad shook his head. "Okay, then how about later when we were talking in the office about the photographs? Don't try to tell me your mind was on our conversation. You were watching Sam—your pupils had dilated, your breathing pattern shallowed and quickened. You were so turned on Kris had to physically touch you to get your attention."

She buried her face in her hands, trying to hide the blood that rushed to her face. When she'd first joined Hauberk and started training in New York, the head of the team had said she had a transparent face. Rick had spent hours teaching her to mask her emotions but obviously she was still easily read. She should have realized that others, especially a former FBI agent would be even more skilled at reading her.

"Admit it, Rosie," Chad continued, "you're just as attracted to Sam as he is to you. And that scares the hell out of you, doesn't it?"

"I'm not scared." Try terrified.

"Sam's one of the good guys. If you've said no, he'll back off. I guarantee it. He's not going to hold a grudge; he's not going to sabotage your evaluations or put you in harm's way." He leaned back in the chair, hooking one arm over the back. "But why is the idea of him being interested in you making you run? Is there something in your past I should know about? Some old boyfriend you've got hidden in your closet? Most women are flattered..." He paused. "Is that it? You think he's just out to add a notch to his bedpost?"

"Maybe." *Yes.*

"I don't think he is. Sam's held off on his attraction for you too long if he was trying to play you like that."

"Perhaps. I don't know. But he's not only my boss but my principal now and every rule about guarding a client is that emotions interfere with providing good protection."

"Normally I'd agree that a relationship could get in the way. But in this case, I had my reasons for putting you in charge." He held up his fist and unfurled one finger. "First, you're a better protective officer than you give yourself credit for. I wouldn't have put you in charge if I didn't think you capable. " Another finger unfurled. "Second, you have an intuitive sense of who to trust and who not to—and people will tell you things they wouldn't tell me. Third, you have a way of getting people to do what *you* want them to do instead of what they want to do. And that's a crucial skill for whoever is in charge of guarding Sam. I know him, he sets his mind on something and he's bound and determined to do things his way. Got him in trouble a couple times at Quantico. Luckily for him it usually worked out in his favor. If I put Walters in charge—or Phillips—Sam will override them."

"But he won't me?"

Chad shook his head. "I don't think so. I think it's important to him to prove his confidence in you. He won't want to embarrass you, or worry you. He'll argue with you, loudly and often, in fact I think he gets off watching you get angry. But when it comes down to it, he'll do what you tell him to do."

"So you want me to use his attraction to me to keep him in place." So she'd gotten the leader's position thanks to a strange form of sexual discrimination. She had to use her feminine attributes to keep a man in line. Oh, brother.

"I want to keep Sam safe and I'll use any weapon at my disposal to achieve that. Because not only is he my friend, but without Sam Watson at the helm, Hauberk won't survive and we'll all find ourselves out of jobs. Which brings me back to your request for a transfer.

"I need you, Rosie. The entire Hauberk company needs you. I'm not telling you to sleep with Sam. I'm not telling you to put up with anything he says or does that makes you feel uncomfortable. You have my permission to slap him in the face or knee him in the balls if you have to, though I doubt Sam will give you a reason. It won't affect your performance review, I promise. So my question to you is—will you stay on as lead op?"

When he checked the text message, he started chuckling.

"What is it?" his wife asked as she accelerated up the ramp to the I-35E out of Dallas. "There a problem?"

"No. No problem. Just a little project I set into motion is finally coming together."

"Oh. That's good." She shot him a look sideways. "Anything I should know about?"

"Nope. Better that you don't."

"Plausible deniability?"

"Something like that." Sam Watson had just put himself in a very uncomfortable position over a woman. Just like Sam had put him in a few months before. And he was going to enjoy every single minute of that smug bastard's downfall.

Chapter Nine

The next morning, Sam walked into the kitchen and found Kris sitting at the counter, eating the remnants of an omelet. Kris put down his fork and narrowed his eyes. "So you decide to fire me yet? Say I was insubordinate or some such?"

"Nope. You're not fired. I appreciate that you were protecting a co-worker. I'd expect nothing less of a Hauberk employee."

Kris hesitated, then nodded. "Just don't forget that warning I gave you last night. I know a half dozen other fellas who would be equally peeved if you were to mistreat Rosie."

"Hard to forget a threat to have a part of your anatomy used as a cat snack."

While he was pouring himself his first cup of coffee, Sam remembered how Kris had stalked into the apartment the night before, kicking the door closed with his foot. "If you ever touch Rosie, or any woman, when she doesn't want you to, I'm going to hunt you down, cut off your dick and feed it to the lions at the zoo. You hear me?"

Sam had stilled, his insides freezing like he'd swallowed five buckets of ice cubes. Had she told them he'd forced her, assaulted her? She'd never told him to stop—she'd even returned his kiss, told him what she liked, encouraged him. He would have stopped if she'd said the slightest word. But then again with his 6'5 compared to her 5'1, no judge or jury would find it hard to believe she'd felt threatened.

At least Chad had stopped in after talking to Rosie, and told him she'd agreed to stay as lead op. But it hurt like hell when Chad had told him her conditions. At the end of the assignment, Rosie would be transferred to the Miami office and he'd never attempt to see her again.

His impulsive action last night had not only failed, it had exploded in his face in catastrophic proportions. He was surprised the whole event hadn't shown up on someone's seismograph.

When the doorbell rang, Kris sauntered out of the kitchen.

"Heya, Phillips," he heard Kris say. "I thought Andy was driving today?"

"He's off doing some errand for Chad, so Rosie sent in the A-team which means you're stuck with me today, Junior," Phillips replied, his words clipped. "Mr. Watson ready to roll?"

"Hey, boss? You ready to go?" Kris called.

Sam grabbed his laptop case. "Just as long as we're not stoppin' off at the Zoo," he muttered to himself.

As he approached, Phillips stepped into his path and got so close Sam could tell he'd used Scope that morning instead of Listerine. "Rosie said you two got in an argument last night, but we both know she was lying. From the way her hair was all mussed up, I figure you put some moves on her." He paused as if waiting for Sam to defend himself.

Sam didn't.

"But see, I don't think you got to finish what you started, whatever it was, because you were still sporting one helluva boner when you came chasing after her. And since Rosie refuses to say anything, I'm gonna give you the benefit of the doubt. This time. But I'm warnin' you here and now, whether you're my boss or not, if you ever touch that little lady when she's not willing, I will rip off your balls and shove 'em down your throat. We clear?"

Kris grabbed Scott's arm. "Hey, back off—"

Shaking his head, Sam left his two operatives to bicker in his foyer and stalked down the hallway. Just what he needed, some whackjob was stalking him, his lead op wanted a transfer or else she'd file a sexual harassment suit—justifiably so after the way he'd behaved the night before, and his two secondary CPOs who were supposed to be guarding him were threatening to a) feed his dick to the lions, and b) let him choke on his gonads. Goddamn, why didn't he just stand out front with a target on his chest and hope whoever was gunning for him put him out of his misery?

He stifled a sigh and punched the button on the elevator, concentrating on watching the numbers over the elevator light up on their slow journey to the top floor. Until he heard the lock to 1202 snick open. He didn't have to turn to know she was there, the air got lighter while the band around his chest tightened.

The elevator dinged and the doors opened. Despite his resolve not to look her way, his head turned as he walked toward the elevator. His steps faltered when he saw her in a pair of red plaid flannel pants, and a well-worn pink T-shirt. Dark smudges under her eyes revealed that she'd not slept any better than he had. But he'd bet she hadn't lost sleep fantasizing about him the way he'd been about her.

"Good morning, Ms. Ramos. Will you be coming into the office this morning?" Where we can talk this out? Because I sure as hell don't want you movin' all the way to Miami.

"Good morning, Mr. Watson. I'll be in later—I've a meeting with Chad." Her voice was cool and collected. And far too distant for his liking. Hands off, it said with no room for misinterpretation. Trouble was, his dick didn't want to listen. Maybe he'd ask to be driven straight to the zoo after all.

"Make sure you stop into my office—I'll tell Sandy to interrupt whatever I'm doin'."

Before she could respond, Kris stepped in front of Rosie, blocking Sam's view. Kris was trying to protect Rosie, just like he would have—should have last night. "Let's go."

Phillips stepped into the elevator and punched the button for the garage. There was an uncomfortable silence on the ride down. Kris got into the driver's seat of the limo while Phillips sat upfront and raised the barrier between front and back, leaving Sam isolated. Twenty minutes and innumerable turns later, Kris's driving becoming more aggressive with each corner, they finally pulled into the visitor's parking by Hauberk's front door.

When he walked into the outer office, Sandy greeted him

with a cup of coffee. "You look tired. You've got bags under your eyes."

I might have slept better if you hadn't told a few tales out of school, sugar. "Why don't you come into my office?"

She trailed him into his office and sat down, flipping her notebook open, ready to take notes.

He closed the door behind her and sat at his desk.

"You've got a meeting at—"

"Yeah, I know. We'll get to that in a minute. Right now I'd like to discuss what you said to Ms. Ramos last night." The blood drained from Sandy's face and her eyes went wide, making him feel like he was about to shoot Bambi.

"Thanks to your little jaw session last night, you nearly cost me a damned good CPO, and you exposed me—and Hauberk— to a potential sexual discrimination case."

Sandy stared at the cleft in his chin but didn't say anything.

He jammed his elbows on his desk as he leaned forward. "When I hired you last year, I told you that I expected that what was said in my office, anything that crossed my desk, was not to be discussed with anyone. Yet last night when you came to my place, you felt it necessary to mention a discussion—a private discussion—I had with Chad. A discussion that you had no right to mention to Miss Ramos or anyone else."

Sandy's bottom lip started to quiver, then her eyes flashed and she straightened, her head held high. "I'm sorry, Sam. But Rosie's a friend of mine and she had a right to know she was being discriminated against based on her gender."

He pressed the heels of his hands against his eyes. Focus, damn it. Although she may have been looking out for a friend— a loyalty Sam couldn't fault—Sandy had disclosed a private discussion with someone she shouldn't have and that could be fatal to one of his employees if she talked to the wrong person in the future. Which meant he still had to make his point, even though he'd been just as much to blame for what happened last night.

"I wasn't asking for a replacement because Ms. Ramos is a woman. If you had a problem with a decision of mine, I expect you to talk to me first. So if I discover you've *ever* discussed what is said in this office with anyone again, I will be forced to terminate your employment. Is that clear enough for you?"

Her backbone rigid, she nodded. "Yes, sir."

"Good. Now let's get back to today's schedule. I know I've got the meeting with Chad and that Parman fella this mornin', but what else is on the agenda?"

The rest of the morning fell back into its normal routine, Sandy confirming his appointments, discussing what needed to be done with the mail, and a thousand other pieces of paper she'd piled on his desk.

She was back at her desk, and Sam was plowing through his email when Chad walked in and shut the door.

"Sandy doesn't look too happy."

"Had to pull the big bad boss routine on her about what she said to Rosie last night."

Chad made a noise in the back of his throat. "About last night..."

"I appreciate you convincin' Rosie to stay. You think she might sue?"

Chad pursed his lips. "Hard to tell. Depends upon how you behave from here on in, I suppose. You let your dick lead you down the garden path last night, didn't you, Sam?"

Oh, God, another lecture. What body part would be threatened this time?

"I know you're attracted to her, but are you deliberately trying to scare her off?"

"Aw, hell, Chad, I wasn't trying to frighten her. I'm attracted to her like the proverbial moth to the flame."

"You fly into that flame and we'll all go up. And last night you got more than a little singed. You want to tell me exactly what happened?"

"Nope." He curled his fingers around his ballpoint, bending its stem. "We'd been talking—everything was cool between us. Then Sandy shot her mouth off and suddenly Rosie was all riled up. Damn, Chad, she's so fuckin' hot when she gets angry, so beautiful and I..." He pinched the bridge of his nose, trying to block the memories of dragging her against him, kissing her, tasting her, trying not to remember the soft moans and pants she'd made as she'd come around his fingers. "Yeah, I fucked up big time."

"I wouldn't apologize to her quite that way, if I were you."

"I'm hoping the couple dozen lilies I just asked Sandy to send might help. I don't want to put her in a position of feeling like her job's in jeopardy." Or her life.

A raised eyebrow gave him Chad's reply. "Sam, Rosie's a smart, intuitive woman. Half the guys here have wet dreams fantasizing about her. But you can't jump her bones like she's one of your subs at the club. Cook her dinner. Put on some soft romantic music, watch a movie on that movie theatre you call a TV—and not *Die Hard 4*, all right? A chick flick like *Sleepless in Seattle* or some tearjerker like that. Underneath that prickly exterior she deserves to be pampered."

"What are you now—a damned matchmaker? And by the way, right back at you—I haven't seen you dating much since Lauren left."

A muscle in Chad's jaw twitched telling Sam he'd hit his target. "That brings me to my next point. Thalia asked me to remind you about the club's board meeting at Cooper Davis's party next month."

"Aw, hell. I'd forgotten about that." The headache that had been a shadow behind his eyes now felt like he'd been hit with a fifty pound anvil. One the blacksmith was still pounding with a sledgehammer.

"I'll give her a call and confirm." At least it meant he'd have something to do other than jerk off to the memories of Rosie's pants and moans.

Thankfully the cameras installed in his place didn't record anything unless he hit the panic button. Otherwise whoever was monitoring it would have gotten an eyeful of him whacking off.

Chapter Ten

The two-dozen lilies Sam had sent filled the air with a sweet fragrance. When they'd arrived, Rosie had fingered the handwritten card that came with them. The practical side of her said she should keep it should she need proof if she filed a lawsuit for sexual harassment. Her romantic side urged her to tuck the card away in a favorite novel, along with one of the blooms. She'd split the difference and tucked it into the forensics book she'd brought with her in case she found herself with nothing to do.

"Hey, Rosie?" Kris called through the closed bedroom door. "Sam's ready to go and Scott's waiting in the limo out front."

"Thanks, Kris, I'll be right there." A quick check in the mirror confirmed she was presentable. At least her make-up covered the dark circles left from not sleeping the night before. A night spent staring at the ceiling remembering every touch of Sam's lips and fingers. She glared at the bed as if it were responsible for her fantasies of him being beside her, over her, in her.

She closed her eyes and took a deep breath before looking at her reflection again. Why couldn't this have been a casual event where she could have worn her gun and bulletproof vest beneath a jacket? But no, of course tonight's fundraiser was black tie and all the women attending would be wearing designer dresses. She'd tried to convince Chad that she shouldn't try to blend in, but let everyone know she was there as Sam's guard.

He hadn't bought it, of course. Instead he'd made a phone call, and two hours later, she was the proud owner of a stunning apricot off-the-shoulder Valentino courtesy of Hauberk Protection. Between the sleek design that highlighted the smooth skin of her neck and her cleavage, and the shimmering skirt with its slit high up on her thigh, she felt as if she were on a red carpet runway. She swished this way and that letting the silky fabric swirl around her legs while telling herself she was simply ensuring that the thigh concealment holster wasn't visible.

Satisfied with her reflection, and feeling somewhat a fraud, she opened the door.

Kris wolf whistled. "Whoa momma, that dress is hot." He made a little circle in the air with his finger. "Come on, baby, shake your moneymaker for me."

"Bite me." But she gave Kris an appreciative glance of her own. He'd left the top two buttons of his crisp white shirt undone, the V exposing a tantalizing glimpse of the hair matting his chest above the beige bulletproof vest. Pity she didn't go for hairy guys. She rethought her preferences when he moved from the doorway and his black pants hugged his ass. If she knew how to wolf whistle, that ass deserved one.

Andy snickered under his breath. Damn, he'd caught her ogling Kris. "Don't forget your tie, Skippy."

Kris rolled his eyes. "It's in my pocket. I'll put it on in the limo. You ready, Rosie?"

At her nod, Kris knocked on Sam's door while Rosie teetered her way toward the elevator and inserted the key to bring it straight to the penthouse. If it came down to a footrace, she'd have to kick off the four-inch stilettos the store had sent to accompany the dress. She'd never be able to justify spending her paycheck on a pair of Mahnolo Blahniks, but now she had them on, she was in love.

Of course the sparkly triple teardrop diamond earrings and matching pendant Sam had sent over had to go back at night's end. He'd probably convinced some jeweler to loan them to him for the night the way the stars did for the Oscars. She had to admit, although she'd initially thought all the bling overkill, once she'd put on the dress, the diamonds made the outfit. It wasn't as if the earrings, pendant or even the tennis bracelet dangling on her wrist would stop her from pulling her gun.

Same with the touch of perfume she'd dabbed behind her ears. They were simply window dressing, letting her fit in with his crowd.

Before Kris could knock on Sam's door, it opened and Sam filled the doorway. When their eyes met, a snapping electrical current snaked between them, bound them for a long minute. Kris and his excellent ass disappeared. All she could see was Sam in his crisp white silk shirt, magnificent black tux and shiny Guccis.

Accompanying him tonight, especially wearing a dress that let her feel so feminine, was a bad idea on so many levels.

"Evenin', Ms. Ramos." His smooth southern accent washed over her in an intimate caress.

"Mr. Watson." While she congratulated herself on her cool neutral tone, she wondered if he could see how hard her nipples were beneath the thin fabric of her dress. Could he smell her arousal or sense how wet she was getting watching him stroll down the hallway toward her? She had to pinch the inside of her forearm to remind herself that she was supposed to be guarding him, protecting him from whoever might want to harm him, not indulge in her own sexual fantasies.

When she followed the two men into the elevator, she concentrated on her reflection in the shiny metal of the elevator doors, working hard not to reveal how turned on she was getting just by his fragrance. What was that cologne he wore? Whatever it was, it permeated all her senses and left her knees weak.

It took every ounce of control not to wrap her arms about his waist and bury her nose into his chest. As the elevator descended, she let her eyes drop, glancing askance at his hand hanging casually at his side. His thumb fiddled with a gold band he wore on his pinkie, twisting it this way and that. Remembered those long talented fingers as they'd thrust into her until she'd seen stars.

Sam shifted, his arm grazing her breast. When she looked up, she realized he was using the metal in the doors to watch her. The edges of his lips curled up as their eyes met.

Before she could look away, Kris stepped between her and the reflection and the elevator glided to a stop. The doors opened and Kris scanned the foyer before allowing them to exit.

"Evenin', Max. You workin' late tonight?" Sam shrugged on the jacket he'd folded over his arm. Damn, none of the men tonight could match him, Rosie decided, watching the wool hug his shoulders. And though Kris's ass was damned good-looking, Sam's eclipsed it. She stifled a giggle. Could one moon eclipse another?

Max placed a slip of paper in the book he was reading and closed it. "Yes, sir, Mr. Watson. With Mr. Miller wanting two people to guard the desk now, they were a man short, so I volunteered."

"How's your son doin'?"

A pained expression flickered across Max's face. "They measured him for a new leg yesterday. They say he'll be able to walk without a limp with the prosthetics they have these days. But it's..." Max cleared his throat. "He's doing a lot better knowing Cindy and little Max are taken care of."

Sam nodded. "Glad to hear it. You be sure to let me know if they need anything more, okay?"

"I sure will, Mr. Watson. And thanks again."

She followed Sam out the door, scanning the street as he climbed into the limo. Kris held the door open for her, waiting until she'd sat in the seat facing Sam. She'd deliberately chosen not to sit beside him, but now regretted it. Having to face him was worse. She looked out the back window for a tail as the limo pulled into traffic.

"What happened to Max's son?" she asked two blocks later.

"His Humvee was hit by a remote controlled IED in Iraq. Took off his left leg below the knee."

From the sounds of it, Sam had taken care of his family— probably monetarily, but Rosie would have bet he'd arranged a lot more. Flights, daycare, housing. Anything they'd needed that they couldn't get through the Armed Forces.

Damn, why couldn't he be a sonovabitch she could despise?

Another block passed before Sam broke the silence. "You didn't come to my office today."

"There wasn't a need." She'd made sure to stay away from

it, especially after Sandy had given her the cold shoulder.

"From the way you're avoiding looking at me, I'd say there was. You wanna take a kick at me or something?" He glanced down at her feet. Did he realize she'd raced out and had a pedicure—something she seldom indulged in? "Those stilettos look like they're plenty sharp enough to do some damage."

She crossed her feet at the ankles, shifting them to the side as she told herself to ignore the silly thrill that he'd noticed her shoes. "They aren't very practical, but my cross-trainers wouldn't have gone with the dress."

Sam pulled a cigar from his pocket, looked at it and then stuck it back in its place. "I wanted to apologize for my actions last night, Rosie. I can only plead temporary insanity and throw myself upon your mercy."

"Thank you." She tucked an errant hair behind her ear, then clasped her hands together in her lap when she remembered how Chad had said the night before about her putting out non-verbal signals.

Sam stretched his arm across the back of the seat. "But I meant what I said. I would like to get to know you better."

"Considering I'm in charge of your protection, I think it would be inappropriate for us to pursue any sort of relationship." Damn it, why couldn't he have said this three months ago?

His brows together in a dark slash. "You're not the only one guarding me. Walters, Campbell and Phillips won't drop the ball." He leaned forward, resting his elbows on his knees. "I promise I won't force you to do anything, Rosie. How our relationship progresses will be entirely up to you. But you can't deny there were sparks between us last night. Just give me a chance to prove myself."

Should she give him a chance to fan the flames that threatened to ignite into a wildfire? But when he walked away, and he would when the fire burned out, she'd be a pile of ashes. "I'll think about it."

Three more blocks passed before she broke the silence. "I never thanked you for arranging the loan of the jewelry."

"It looks good on you." He settled back in the seat and

folded his arms over his chest as his eyes flicked down her, lingering on her cleavage.

It was possible he was examining the necklace, but she was pretty sure that wasn't his main focus. That knowledge and the heat in his expression, sent a hot shiver in a slow crawl across her breasts until they ached.

"That dress certainly highlights all your...attributes."

The air thickened until she felt like she was six feet underwater. Her hand smoothed her skirt over her knees. "I feel like a fairy princess, though I don't know how much use I'll be protecting you tonight without a vest. You're wearing one under your shirt, right?"

He leaned so close the tendril of hair that had sprung free fluttered over her ear when he spoke. "I have the feelin' I'm gonna need to be keepin' the men away from you tonight, Rosie. You're so beautiful—no man in their right mind could fail to notice you. But then again, nothin' would look beautiful on you."

Rosie searched for some way to answer his double entendre. Eventually she gave up and settled for staring out the window, watching the lights and buildings as the car climbed the ramp onto the beltway. But no matter how hard she tried, she couldn't ignore his blatant examination.

Not once the rest of the ride did he take his eyes off her. By the time the limo pulled up in front of the hotel, she felt like a bug under a microscope. Or the proverbial mouse trapped between the cat's paws. Only this cat was a tiger. A tiger with long fingers that had caressed her with an unrivalled skill and full lips that she wanted tasting her. Everywhere. And somehow she didn't think real tigers sported such impressive erections.

Chapter Eleven

Sam waited for Rosie to get out of the limo before he moved. It wasn't that he was trying to be gentlemanly, but he needed a few moments for his raging hard-on to deflate. His cock had been waving like a goddamned flagpole ever since he'd first seen her standing in the hallway wearing that dress. It had taken every ounce of willpower not to bury his face in her breasts.

He snuck another glance at her legs, which she'd primly crossed at the ankle for most of the ride. There should be a law against concealing legs like those in the cargo pants she normally wore. When she made a little sigh, his gaze shifted back to her face. It wasn't as if he'd never seen her wearing makeup before but tonight she'd done something that made her eyes appear as large as a fawn's and added a bright red lipstick to full lips that screamed *fuck me*.

As she shifted to get out of the car, the fabric strained over her cleavage, threatening to reveal the bounty it concealed. When she stepped out, her ass wiggled in front of him like she was a toreador with a bright red flag and he was the charging bull. Instead of relaxing, his cock hardened until he could feel every tooth in his zipper.

Once he finally emerged from the limo, he couldn't help but notice Kris's glance down and raised eyebrow nor Phillips' expression of amusement. Damn it, why did his employees have to be so damned good at noticing details?

He made a mental note to cancel as many of his evening engagements as possible. There was no way he was going to be able to keep his hands off her if she insisted on accompanying him wearing anything other than the bulkiest sweaters and loose jeans. Even that probably wouldn't keep him from getting hard, he'd probably still picture peeling them off her.

The fundraiser was a standard D.C. schmooze session of senators and congressmen. Mingling amongst them were the ubiquitous bejeweled society matrons who were there to impress others with their philanthropy but in private couldn't care less about the charity needing their donations.

While Phillips stayed behind with the limo, Kris and Rosie kept close to Sam's side, discreetly checking that no one approaching him was armed or meant him harm. He found himself regretting that they'd banned smoking in the building several years before because no matter where he went, a subtle scent of apricot, and some new scent she wore—L'air du Temp?—floated over him.

Glasses clinked and voices murmured, nearly drowning out the bluesy quintet entertaining that evening. He pressed through the crowd, glad-handing the occasional former client or possible future ones.

He was about to suggest he'd put in enough of an appearance when he heard someone calling him. He turned around and came face-to-face with a familiar pudgy, freckled face. Since he'd guarded the man's father during one of his first assignments for Hauberk, the man's hair had receded into the standard male pattern baldness horseshoe, and at least forty extra pounds now padded his short frame. But Sam knew discretion landed more contracts than honesty. "Mr. Tompkins, you're looking good. What brings you back to D.C.?"

"A combination of love and hard work. I finally made VP of Bennett Enterprises which means they transferred me to the Head Office." Tompkins's chin waggled like a turkey's wattle as his head bobbed in excitement. The man looked twenty years older than his mid-thirties, yet acted like a teenager still.

"So who's the lucky lady, anyone I know?"

Tompkins pointed to a familiar blonde standing a few feet away talking to a Senator from Louisiana. "Lee-Anne, honey, come meet one of my friends."

The tall blonde turned to face him, a cool, practiced smile not reaching her eyes until she recognized Sam. But behind the smile, Sam could see the calculations going on in her head. "Actually, lambkins, Sam and I are already acquainted. Sam's a founding member of the Rouge."

While congratulating them both, he made a mental note to send her a reminder that the Rouge was not to be discussed in public.

Shaking her hand was like shaking a dead fish. He knew some people suffered from arthritis and so kept their touch light, but this woman had no excuse. Especially since he'd seen her wielding a bullwhip.

He preferred the firm handshake Rosie had been giving people all evening. The tiny hands that constantly gestured when she spoke. Hands that would firmly wrap around his cock and stroke him to completion. Something he suspected Greg would never experience from his fiancée. Cock-and-ball torture was more Lee-Anne's style. There was no doubt as to who would be the Dominant in this relationship.

Lee-Anne's eyes darted to where Rosie stood beside him, scanning the crowd. One thin eyebrow arched up in question. "I've been wondering why we've not seen much of you at the Rouge. And now I see what's been taking up so much of your time." She flung her long blonde hair over her shoulder in a move she must have practiced in a mirror to perfect and held out her hand. "I don't believe I've met you before, dear. I'm Lee-Anne Bennett, a friend of Sam's."

Now there was an overstatement. Although as a board member he'd agreed to Lee-Anne's membership at the Rouge, he hardly considered her a friend, more like an annoyance to be avoided when he met her at the club or anywhere else. "Lee-Anne Bennett, meet Rosalinda Ramos. Rosie is a Close Protective Officer with Hauberk."

"It's a pleasure to meet you, Miss Bennett," Rosie said. "Although I believe we met at the Women's Shelter bachelor auction a few months back."

Aw crap. That's right, Lee-Anne had driven up the bidding that night and cost Jodi 70K.

"I remember." Lee-Anne's voice dripped icicles. "You don't mind if I borrow Sam for a few minutes, do you, dear? I have some private business to discuss with him." Lee-Anne turned her back on Rosie and wrapped her nails about Sam's biceps in an attempt to draw him away. Once she realized he wasn't about to move, she lowered her voice until he could barely hear her over the quartet that was now playing a rousing rendition of Aretha Franklin's Respect. "She's not acting properly submissive—if she gives you any problems, feel free to call me to help train her."

Like he'd let Rosie get anywhere near the Ice Bitch. Although he suspected that Rosie might be just the one to teach Lee-Anne the effective use of a single-tail. "As I said, Rosie is my employee, not my sub."

"Darling! A man with your...appetites can't go too long without eating now, can he?" She lowered her voice even further. "Enough about her. I'm sponsoring Greg for membership this year. I take it there should be no problem with getting approval from the board?"

"His application will be viewed as objectively as every other applicant for initiation, but I know of no impediments." Though Greg might wish to withdraw his application once he got a glimpse into Lee-Anne's sexual proclivities. Or maybe he already knew but was willing to sacrifice his pride and dignity for a corner office.

Lee-Anne hmmed and tried another tack. "But you will be there, won't you, darling? I'd love for you to participate that night."

Sam shook his head—his neck was so stiff he thought even the band could hear his bones cracking. Even if he had been planning on it, he would have made himself unavailable for whatever humiliation she had planned for Tompkins. "I won't be attending this year's Gala."

"What happened, did your itty bitty slave convince her master to wear the dog collar for once?" Lee-Anne's lips smiled widely, though anyone carefully watching would see her eyes were daggers formed of ice. Damned if he didn't prefer the fire in the chocolate brown eyes of the woman beside him. "You aren't turning into a switch, are you, darling? Because if you are, perhaps you might be open to letting me tie you up in the grotto for me to play with."

"If you ever mention the club in public again, or what goes

on there, I'll blackball you myself." But the thought of Rosie wearing his collar as he led her through the halls at the Rouge had his cock hardening—especially when he pictured her breasts overflowing a leather corset he'd have made to match. Or stretching her face down on the bench he had in his suite, her ass glistening with lube as he fucked her tight rosebud entrance.

Sam placed his wineglass on the tray of a passing waiter, then clamped one hand around Rosie's waist. "I think it's time we blow this popsicle stand, Ms. Ramos."

"I'm supposed to be guarding you, not the other way around," she protested as he wound through the crowd to the front door.

"I'm the one wearin' the bulletproof vest and you aren't, so go with me on this one, will you?" He shrugged off his jacket and placed it around her shoulders, then slid his hand back around her waist. Using his jacket as cover, his hand moved up until his fingers brushed the side of her breast.

When she tried to pull away, the hand on her back held her firmly in place. "Mr. Watson—"

"Why are you back to bein' all formal? You say Mr. Watson and I look around for my daddy. My name's Sam." The movement of her walking in those killer stilettos had her nipple rubbing against his index finger. The soft flesh quickly pebbled and peaked. Damn she was responsive. "It's real easy to say. Just one syllable. Sam. Say it, Rosie. Let me hear you call me Sam."

"S-Sam."

A shot of smug male satisfaction filled him. "I like the way my name spills from your lips, Rosebud."

"Rosebud?"

His Georgia accent thickened, along with the heat in his eyes as he smiled. "You're beautiful"—he leaned in and made a show of sniffing her—"and you smell delicious. And you keep yourself wrapped tighter than a bug in a rug in July. So I'm figuring you're a rose just waitin' to blossom."

Forcing herself not to focus on the burgeoning heat in her breasts, in her pussy, she managed to gather herself when their limo stopped in front of them. "Be warned, Sam. This rose has thorns."

Sam waited until Kris had closed the door behind them before he replied, "Hmm, sounds like a challenge. And I have to tell you, Rosie, I do love a challenge."

"I thought we'd already discussed how our…dating wouldn't be a good idea."

"I can't ignore the attraction I have for you. And from the way you reacted yesterday, the way you're reactin' now, I'd say you're attracted to me too." He cupped her jaw, his thumb tracing back along her bottom lip, the touch an electric caress. "So I'm thinking maybe we could come to some…accord?"

"An accord?" She sounded like a parrot, incapable of doing anything but echo what he said. What was it about that thumb of his that was causing her brains to short circuit?

"An agreement so we can explore our mutual attractions." He shifted and leaned over her, his lips hovering above hers.

All she had to do was stretch her neck a fraction of an inch, a millimeter and he'd kiss her again. Make stars appear with those magic fingers, that talented tongue.

He'd agreed to back off when they'd left the limo, and now he was a bloodhound on the scent of a bitch in heat. What had changed? The blonde—Lee-Anne Bennett. That's what this was about. He didn't want her. He just wanted an available pussy because he was between blonde bimbos.

"I'm in charge of your protection, Mr. Watson. Entering into an affair with you could be considered unprofessional." More to keep herself from leaning up for that kiss than to encourage him, she moved to the rear-facing seat.

Three intersections had passed before he spoke again. "How about if I agree that I'll not touch you or give any indication that we're a couple while we're in public?"

She closed her eyes and shook her head. "It's not enough. Besides you're not going to be alone even when you're at home—Andy, Kris or Scott will be around."

"They're discreet. They have to be in this job. And if they're not they'll find themselves transferred to Troy McPherson's group where he'll assign them to Timbuktu for the rest of their careers."

"I've worked hard to get where I am—I'm the lead op and I don't want people to think I got the position because I'm sleeping with the boss." She frowned. "I didn't, did I? Get this job because you want to sleep with me?"

"No, if you care to remember, I told Chad *not* to put you on the team. For precisely that reason."

Why did things have to be so complicated? Why did he have to be, not only her principal but her boss?

"What do you say, Rosebud? Can we come to an accord?" he asked as the limo stopped at a red light.

"I'm...flattered, Sam. But I respectfully decline your proposal and I'd appreciate it if we didn't discuss it anymore."

"All right."

She started to breathe a sigh of relief until he added, "For now. But I reserve the right to try to convince you you're making a mistake."

Oh, good Lord, she'd just made herself a target. A challenge to be conquered. "You mean you're going to try to seduce me?"

"As long as you realize your job's not at stake. And you acknowledge that—" he dropped his voice, "—you've been thinking about how I made you come with just my tongue."

Ay, he'd found a way to suck the air from her lungs and set her heart racing again. "N-no. I..."

One of his eyebrows quirked up in a challenge.

She shot a glance over her shoulder to ensure the divider was up all the way before whispering, "Oh, all right, yes, you've got a very talented mouth, I admit it. But you won't be able to change my mind." She hoped.

He leaned back, stretching one arm along the back of the seat. "Rosebud, I'm fixin' to romance you so good that before this assignment's done, you'll be the one seducin' me."

Chapter Twelve

Without looking, Rosie placed the personnel folder she'd just finished checking on the stack piled in the middle of the dining room table. When her fingers brushed across a set of knuckles, she looked up. Fire burned in the back of Sam's eyes as he left his hand beneath hers.

Ever since the fundraiser, Sam had made good on his pledge to *romance her*. It had started when three-dozen long stemmed roses were delivered first thing the next morning. It continued when she'd gone into the office and opened her locker in the gym changing room and discovered the tennis bracelet she'd worn to the fundraiser. John Lake arrived mid-morning and plonked a brand new laptop with all the bells and whistles on her desk and told her it was hers to keep. Later that afternoon, she'd gone to the firing range, and discovered a new Sig Sauer in her gun cabinet. It was when she'd gone to the parking lot to run an errand, and found a brand new Lexus in place of her ten-year-old Honda that she'd marched into Sam's office. Slamming the bracelet, gun and car keys on his desk, she'd informed him that she couldn't be bought, bribed or otherwise purchased.

Grudgingly, he'd taken back those gifts, but insisted she keep the laptop and gun—somehow convincing her that she'd need them as his lead op. And the flowers continued to arrive each morning until every room in the apartment now contained a vase and Andy couldn't stop sneezing.

She forced herself to pull her hand back, moving it to the pile of unchecked personnel folders. No matter how much she told herself she could resist him, the electricity between them crackled and hissed like a living entity and she knew the barriers she had erected would soon crumble.

Would their affair burn bright but fast, ending quickly? Or would it be a long, smoldering fire?

As if sensing her disintegrating walls, Sam stood, "I'm gonna go get a drink." As he walked by, he leaned down and whispered in her ear, "Chicken."

Each night since the party, he'd made a point of coming to the apartment to help wade through the folders of potential suspects. They'd divided the files into five piles. Scott flipped through the bodyguards' records from the Hauberk Protection section while she and Kris cleared the employees who worked in the Security Services unit. That pile had been huge, since they had hundreds of security guards in the various apartments and businesses around D.C. Two smaller piles of the alarm systems technicians and the Information Technology geeks still had to be tackled. They ruled out as suspects any employees who were not in town when the photos or phone calls had been made, but gotten into quite a discussion about whether to exclude those who hadn't had bad reviews. Meanwhile, Andy and Sam examined Hauberk's client files for someone who might want revenge.

"Here's a guy who could be a suspect," Scott said. "Barry Germaine—he got fired about six months ago. Anyone know anything about him?"

"Yeah, I remember him. He only worked here about six months, if that." Andy looked up from the chair where he'd draped one leg over the arm. "But Sam didn't fire him, Chad did."

"Might not make a difference. To most people, Sam's Hauberk. What did he do?"

"Chad caught old Barry smokin' up with one of his principal's teenage sons and hauled him into the office. After he'd reamed him out, he escorted Barry to his locker to clear out his stuff. That's when they found a crap load of marijuana, ecstasy, crack. You name it, he had it. Bastard had been dealing on the side. Chad called in the police who took Germaine away in handcuffs. Last I heard he was still awaiting trial for possession with intent."

Rosie had to agree when Scott put Germaine's file in the "suspected" list, commenting that Germaine made a damned good suspect.

"Would Barry have had access to Sam's home phone number when he was here?"

"No, he didn't," Sam answered from the doorway. "Besides Mr. Germaine is currently residing in the Eastern Correctional Institution for the next few years, courtesy of the State of Maryland."

When she glanced over at Scott, she saw the elevator doors opening on the monitor. Mrs. O'Mara stepped off, her brown and white fox terrier jumping in circles around her. Though Scott had turned the sound down, she could hear the dog's excited yips echo down the hall.

Kris pushed away from the table. "I need a break. Who's up for pizza?"

Four sets of hands went up. "But no anchovies this time, Kris," Rosie insisted and Scott argued over the addition of pineapple to the ham Andy had requested.

Sam was in the middle of adding his request—extra feta cheese and hot peppers—when the phone they'd linked to Sam's line rang. "Got a number—says it's a pay phone."

He read off the number slowly as Andy typed it in to his computer, before he hit the connect button. Within five seconds, he raised his hand and pointed to the receiver, mouthing, "It's him."

While Andy traced the call, Kris ensured the recorder had started, and Rosie listened in on the extension, scribbling the text of the conversation into her notebook.

Less than a minute later, Sam hit the button and disconnected the call. "Same guy—usual threat."

"Looks like it's another payphone in Chevy Chase." Andy shook his head. "I've texted the location to Chad—he's sending a team to that location, but the guy'll pro'ly be gone."

Rosie patted him on the shoulder. "Maybe there'll be some witnesses or a security camera this time."

A voice echoed through the room when Kris replayed the

recording. A raucous background noise of laughter and country music made the message hard to hear, especially since the speaker spoke very quietly. "Did you think those four CPOs you have can stop me? You can surround yourself with all the armed guards in the world, but I'm better than any of them. I'll be there when you least expect it."

"So we know he's watching you still," Rosie said after they'd replayed it a half dozen times. "But there's nothing unique about that voice—no unusual phrases. No accent. Nothing that would identify him. Maybe when we track the location, there'll be witnesses."

"He could be using a spoof card," Andy reminded her. "Make us think he's in one place when he's somewhere else."

"Except the phones are wiped," Scott countered. "Which means even if they didn't use it to make the actual phone call, they'd have to clean the receiver at some point right before hand and someone might see whoever it was."

While they waited for Chad's team to get back to them, Kris ordered the pizza. When it arrived, they took it into the kitchen, where Rosie perched on a stool at the breakfast nook beside Sam. Andy ate standing so he could monitor the hall cameras at the same time. Scott plated a couple slices and disappeared into the bedroom.

"He's got to be one of us," Kris said suddenly. "Or a client at the very least, someone who knows how we work."

Rosie felt some relief when Sam looked just as confused as she felt.

"The caller," Kris explained. "He called us CPOs. Not bodyguards the way a normal person would."

Andy tossed away his third crust of the meat lovers' pizza he'd insisted upon, having won the pineapple debate. "Don't jump to conclusions, Skippy. Any one reading the Hauberk website knows that's what we're called. Besides, most companies call their employees CPOs these days."

"Okay," Kris persisted. "So how about when he said he was better than us? Maybe it's someone who wants to make Hauberk itself look bad to future clients. Maybe we should be looking at Hauberk's competition."

"Could be. Or maybe it's an ego thing," Andy suggested, grabbing another slice. "You know, like that movie where Clint Eastwood is a secret service agent and John Malkovich is out to kill the president."

"Man, Rene Russo was hot in that movie." Kris shook his hand as if he'd been burned.

When Kris and Andy started debating which movies got the details of bodyguards and police work wrong, Sam shoved his plate away and stalked out.

Rosie hurried after him out of their apartment and down the hall toward the elevators. "Sam, wait. You agreed you'd not go out without one of us with you."

His fists clenched and unclenched before he faced her. "Look, Rosebud, I've played this game for over a week now. I've cancelled appointments that I shouldn't have, I let you guys answer my door like you're my goddamned butlers, and I've been driven around in the limo like I'm Miss Freakin' Daisy. Christ, when we're out somewhere, Campbell and Phillips even follow me into the bathroom when I have to take a—" he swallowed what he was going to say, "—leak. And where's it gotten me? Nowhere. That sonovabitch is still out there laughing at me. Well, no more. If he's watching, I'm damned well going to draw him out."

"How? You going to stand on the sidewalk and put a target on your chest and yell *shoot me*?"

"If that'll end this, I'm willin'."

She grabbed his arm, feeling the tenseness of the muscle beneath her fingers. "You aren't seriously going out there, are you?"

He ran a hand back and forth over his head and heaved a sigh. "No. But damn it..." His hand moved from his head to her cheek. "There's only one other thing I'd rather be doin' than giving in to this SOB. You thought anything more about that accord, Rosebud?"

Her head tilted until her cheek rested in his palm. "I can't, Sam. I like my job, I like working at Hauberk. If you and I have an affair, when it ends, I'll be out of a job." When he started to protest, she straightened her head and took a half step back, leaving his hand hovering mid-air before he dropped it a second later.

"I'm not one for casual sex. If I have an affair with you, it'll turn into something more and you'll...well, you're the boss, so I'll be the one looking for a new job." She paused, waiting for the ache that had started in her heart to ease. "I'd have to leave Hauberk, Sam. I couldn't stay. No matter how much you say my job isn't on the line, my heart is. And I'm not willing to lose either."

"Who says it would have to end?" He stepped closer, but didn't touch her. He didn't have to. Her body was so aware of him it swayed toward him. Her lungs tried to fill up with that scent of him, imprinting it indelibly because one day she knew she'd never smell it again.

"Affairs always end, Sam." And in her experience, they never ended with them being just friends.

"Maybe I want more than an affair, Rosie. Maybe I'm lookin' for the long term."

Her eyes closed on their own. He was so smooth, so convincing. She wanted to believe him, but she also knew his history—she'd been checking him out along with the other employees. No one she'd interviewed could remember Sam Watson dating a woman longer than four months since he'd been with Hauberk. And he hadn't committed himself to a longer term relationship with her, he'd simply said "maybe."

It would end.

The door at the far end of the hall opened and the fox terrier streaked toward them, yapping its head off. The connection between them broken, Rosie stepped between Sam and the open door, her hand on her gun.

Mrs. O'Mara appeared in the doorway, and peered at them over her coke-bottle glasses. "Oh, it's just you two. Come back here, Georgie, you naughty boy. I'd told you it wasn't anything to worry about."

As the old lady closed the door behind her, Rosie headed back toward 1202. Knowing he was watching, counting on it, she accentuated the roll of her hips. "So how about we go back in and see if we can find who's been taking those photos?"

He heaved an overly dramatic sigh. "You think I don't

realize you're tryin' to distract me from goin' out and finding my stalker?"

"Is it working?"

"Hell, yes."

Chapter Thirteen

The next night Sam didn't appear for their usual research session. Instead he bypassed their door and headed straight to his apartment. Andy gave her a shrug and trailed him while Scott ducked into their apartment. Ten minutes later Scott sat across from Rosie, burying himself in the files piled on the dining room table.

Dark circles ringed his eyes—evidence of the nightmares he denied having but they all heard every night. Not a surprise. After Sam's cryptic comment, she'd read Scott's file. He'd spent three months as a hostage of some obscure group in Colombia, escaping through hostile terrain with tales of brutality that had everyone worried about those left in the camp. When he'd been cleared medically, Troy and Sam had both tried to convince him to take some time off, he'd refused and so ended up on her team.

For the next hour, she and Scott slogged through more of the Hauberk client files, while Kris finished going through the Security Guard files. She placed the last of her current pile on the table and rubbed the back of her neck against the ache that was forming. "I'm not finding anything. How about you?"

"Nothing concrete." Kris picked up the list he'd made. "Got a few trainees who might be bitter because they washed out of the Protection Agency program and ended up guarding buildings. And there are a couple who got fired who might qualify but from what I've seen of their write-ups they couldn't find their dicks with a magnifying glass."

"Guess that makes you a suspect, too," Scott said with a grin. "I found a few possibles in the client files, but one's left the country, one's dead, and the other hired some hot shot firm out in California to guard them. So I can't see they're viable suspects."

Before she could reply, Rosie's Berry chirped with a familiar double tone announcing a text message had arrived. Sam.

Table 4 2 set in 1201

She shook her head and went back to the list of employees working for the Security Guard division. Five minutes later, her Berry chimed again. *Chicken Creole.*

"Is there a problem?" Scott asked.

"No, it's just Sam wants me to eat at his place tonight."

Kris, who had buried himself in yet another folder, looked up with a hopeful expression on his face. "What's he cooking?"

When she told him, he closed the file. "Hey, if you don't want it, I'll go. I've got dibs."

"Be my guest—"

Before she could finish, Kris dashed to the front door and slammed it behind him.

A minute later, her Berry chimed again. *Not Kris. You.* On the heels of that message came another. *Clothing optional.* ;)

Sheesh! That one didn't even warrant a reply.

The front door opened and Andy stomped in, obviously grumpy as Kris trailed him. "Sam says to get your butt over there before the champagne goes flat."

"Champagne, as if," she muttered. "He doesn't have any. All he has is Heineken."

"Yeah, he does," Scott said. "He asked me to pick up a couple bottles of Dom Perignon this afternoon."

"Kris, why don't you go into the kitchen and toss one of those frozen cannellonis Rosie bought into the oven. Scott..." Andy paused. "Shoot, just leave us alone, will you? I want to have a private word with Rosie."

Some sort of unspoken communication passed between the two men. Scott nodded and headed to his bedroom as her Berry rang again.

Apple Crumble & French vanilla ice cream 4 dessert.

What had he done? Called her mother to find out her

favorite dessert? And vanilla ice cream, how ironic. If ice cream was a metaphor for sex, vanilla certainly described her love life lately. She had a feeling Sam's would be Rocky Road.

"When are you going to admit there's something between you two?" Andy asked quietly.

"You know the rules say operatives can't get romantically involved with their principals."

"Oh, screw the rules." He groaned as he flopped onto the couch. "Come on, Rosie, you gotta give the rest of us poor shlubs some hope."

"I'm not willing to risk my job for a couple of nights of..." mindblowing sex, but she wasn't about to say that, "...fun. Because at some point it'll end and I'll be out of a job."

He leaned forward, resting his elbows on his knees. "Or you could end up Mrs. Rosie Watson, mother of 2.4 kids and part owner of Hauberk. You're using the job as a shield, Rosie. Since when did you sprout a yellow stripe on your back?"

"It's just..." She rubbed her face with her hands. Day by day, hour by hour, Sam had been chinking away at her armor until the barriers she'd thrown up were tissue-paper thin. "It's just Sam's so...Sam, you know?"

"Larger than life? I thought women liked that type." He leaned back, sprawling his legs wide, his arms stretched along the back of the couch. "You're not usually a coward, so what's the problem?"

"He's...he's not like any other man I've ever dated before," she said slowly. He makes me feel things with an intensity I've never felt before. He makes me want to do things with him, to him, for him I've never considered with another man.

Whenever she felt any of her other lovers gaining any modicum of control over her, her claws came out and they ended up running away with their tails between their legs. But for some reason she couldn't fathom, all her need for control fled around Sam.

"Can't say I know many people like him, so that makes sense." He rubbed his thumbs across his eyes. "I have to be honest, Sam's got his kinky side, but I don't think he'd ever ask you to do something you weren't willing to do. He's not a big bad wolf who's going to tear you apart. Besides I get the feeling you could wrap him around your little finger if you tried."

What the hell did *Sam's got his kinky side* mean? But before she could ask, he eyed her suspiciously. "You haven't got some hang up about sex, have you?"

She plopped onto the couch beside him, her legs unable to support her. Her face felt like someone had just set a flamethrower to it. "No. It's not about sex."

No, sex with Sam Watson would be off the charts of the Incredible Scale. Look at the orgasm he'd given her with only his tongue and fingers. Her pussy started creaming just at the thought of his cock filling her.

One of side of his mouth hitched up. "I'm just saying I think you could trust Sam not to overstep whatever boundaries you set, you know?" He gestured to her Blackberry which was buzzing again. "Besides, he's only asking you to dinner."

With her as dessert.

Trouble was, now she didn't know if she'd simply become a challenge to be conquered. A rose to be pruned, enjoyed until the blossom faded, and then tossed aside and replaced with a new flower. She buried her face in her hands. "It's not just dinner. It's more than that." *It's my whole life. My job. My home. My heart.*

"You have a chance at love and you're kicking it away like it's an old tin can when the rest of us…" Andy trailed off. "Well, the some of us have it yanked from us, you know? And we'd give anything to grab it and hold onto it."

She grabbed the only lifeline she could find. "I don't know."

Andy pushed himself to a stand. "Just think of it as your downtime. Pretend you went to bed early and let me look after things here. The place is secure—nothing's going to happen. If someone wanted to take a pot shot at him, it'll be somewhere public. Otherwise they'd have already gotten to him."

"But it's my—"

He pulled her to her feet and marched her to the door. "Go have dinner with Sam, Rosie. And if you two don't hit it off, come back here."

Her Berry beeped again. *Trust me. Please.*

It was the *please* that unraveled all her arguments, that had her walking down the hallway.

Just as she lifted her hand to knock, the door opened and Sam stood there, filling the doorway.

"About that accord..." she whispered.

Chapter Fourteen

The smug smile she was expecting never appeared. Instead he bent down, brushing his lips over hers in a feather-light touch before pulling back and leading her by both hands into the foyer. He closed the door and pulled her close, cupping her cheek.

"Are you sure 'bout this, Rosebud? 'Cause I don't want you saying I pressured you later."

No, she wasn't one hundred percent sure, but there was no way she was going to stop whatever rock had just started rolling down the hill to perdition. Not after she'd had a sampling of the bliss he could bring her. Besides, Andy was right, she had a shot at happiness, something she should grab with both hands. She'd had enough of all the *coulda-woulda-shouldas*. Even if their affair only lasted one night, she wouldn't—couldn't—turn away now.

When she nodded, he slid one hand down to her bottom and lifted her until his erection nestled in the cradle of her hips. She felt a quiver of trepidation mixed with a tidal wave of lust. That thing wouldn't just fill her, it would overfill her. And she wanted every inch of it deep inside.

Could he feel how her heart raced or hear how her breathing caught in her throat? Could he smell the moisture drenching her thong at the thought of him going down on her again? Of her going down on him?

He shifted his grip, sliding one hand beneath her knees, lifting her, then carried her into his bedroom. As he laid her on his bed, he kissed her again, the tip of his tongue seeking entry.

With a soft sigh she parted her lips. He tasted of champagne and spice, of power and strength. Intoxicating. Potent.

She stroked the thick length of his tongue with hers, mimicking what she would do to his shaft. A moan started deep down inside her chest when one hand slipped under her sweatshirt and cupped her breast. Through the lace of her bra, his fingers played with the sensitive tip, soothing, inciting. A flick of his fingers, and her bra no longer formed a barrier. Heat streaked over her skin everywhere his fingers touched like a fiery brand. She lifted her arms to help when he pulled her sweatshirt and bra over her head.

"Oh, baby, you're so beautiful." Lowering his head to her breast, his tongue lapped her nipple, her back arched, pushing the taut peak into his mouth.

"Do you remember when you were in my office the day this all started?" he asked softly, his breath a caress over her bare skin.

She nodded as she slid her hands up his chest and over his shoulders, feeling the strength that held him rock solid above her.

"Did you know I couldn't turn around because I had a hard-on?" Similar to the one that pushed into her belly.

"Or that when you were watching my reflection in the window, I was wondering what your creamy little pussy tasted like?" His breath whispered over her neck sending a shiver wiggling down her spine. "And once I'd had a taste of it, I craved more."

Was that really why he'd not turned around? He'd been fantasizing about her the way she had been?

He'd undone her cargo pants and slid them off her hips in a move so smooth she hadn't realized what he'd done until the cool air rippled over her thighs.

When one of his fingers dipped beneath the thin band of her thong, her hips arched, bringing her clit closer to his fingers. He barely touched her yet her pussy ached, so close to orgasm she felt ready to implode.

"So silky and wet," he murmured. "That night—after I made

you come with my tongue—did you wonder what it would be like to have me inside you?"

"Yes." She'd not slept until she'd dragged out her vibrator and driven herself into a frenzy imagining it was him inside her.

Lust, that's all it was, she'd told herself. She'd been in a dry spell and someone was finally paying her a little attention. That's why she was all hot and bothered and ready to orgasm with a single touch. Besides, he was a guy—all guys wanted pussy no matter where they got it. And she was a woman who needed what he had because no matter how many times she used her vibrator, its cool silicone could never replicate the sheer heaven of hot pulsing cock.

One of his fingers parted her labia, and thrust into her. Another joined it and he curled them, tickling her upper wall until she squirmed beneath him, panting. "You're ready for me already, aren't you, baby?"

As ready for him as he was for her from the feel of the hard length battering her belly. She slid her hands between them and undid his fly, pushed aside the fabric.

None of her previous lovers came close to the size of his cock. Cream drenched his fingers as she thought of how he'd feel inside her body. She reached down and wrapped her fingers around his dusky head, slid them down to the base nestled within a thick thatch of dark hair.

He'd thrown back his head when her fingers touched him. His hips pumped, driving his shaft along her palm once, twice. Then his fingers wrapped around hers, stilling the motion. "Slow down, baby, we've got all night."

She attempted to lift one eyebrow up the way he had earlier but failed and settled for a mocking grin instead. "What's the matter, stud, you only good for one time a night?"

"No, but I'd rather come in that pretty pussy of yours instead of your hand." His lips touched hers again briefly before he shifted, kicking off his jeans. Seconds later, he dropped his shirt onto the floor.

She examined the surgical scar down his sternum. From the placement of the star-shaped wound in his left pectoral, she was amazed that he was still breathing. How had it not hit his heart?

"It turn you off? You want me to put my shirt back on?"

From the way he pulled away, from the coolness of his voice, she realized someone in the past must have rejected him for it. Stupid woman.

She pressed a kiss lightly to the surgical scar. "Nope. I'm just thinking how lucky I am you're still alive. Now shut up and kiss me again."

With a fierceness he hadn't shown before, he swooped down on her, trapping her body beneath his. By the time he pulled back from the kiss she'd demanded, her heart was pounding in her chest. But from the timpani hammering against the palm she'd flattened over his heart, he wasn't unaffected either.

"Baby, if you're gonna say no, now's the time to say it, because I don't think I'll be able to stop once I get inside you."

"I don't want you to stop."

He reached into his bedside table, pulled out a silver packet and tore it open then rolled into position. Within seconds, the sheathed head of his cock nudged her entrance. To her surprise, he hesitated as he looked where their bodies would join.

"What's wrong?" Her mind raced at all the possible reasons he might reject her. Did he suddenly realize she wasn't his type and regret inviting her? Did he think he didn't have to go through with it now he had her here?

"Nothing's wrong, baby. I'm just admirin' the view."

"You say the nicest things." She curled her hand around his neck and pulled him down to her until his forehead rested against hers. "Now put that bad boy inside me."

Still, he hesitated.

"Now, damn it!"

That earned her a grin. "Pushy little thing, aren't you?"

Fed up with his delaying, she wrapped her legs around his hips and pulled him closer, pressing the tip of his cock inside and squeezed her muscles once before loosening them and pressing him further.

"I should warn you," she murmured into his chest as he pushed into her. Not for the first time, she cursed her lack of height. Just once she'd like to be able to look a man in the face while they made love. "If you get off on women screaming when they come, you've got the wrong woman."

"Oh, Christ!" he groaned, his arms shaking. "I already know that. And don't worry, even if you screamed the loudest you could, no one could hear. The room's soundproofed...shit, you're so tight..." He panted and pressed an inch deeper.

While she knew he was trying to give her time to adjust, her body couldn't wait any longer. Her heels drove into his buttocks as her back arched. "Fuck me, damn it!"

"Shit! Baby, I'm sorry, I don't mean to hurt you but I can't..." In a single thrust, he buried himself so deep inside her she swore he was about to come out her belly button.

Holding himself off her by his elbows, he pistoned into her, grinding against her clit. Her fingernails dug into his shoulders, holding on for dear life. The world outside ceased to exist, all that mattered was here in this room, on this bed. The scent of his sweat, the sound of his balls slapping against her ass, the bed rocking, faded as the heat in her core sharpened. Her back arching, her body imploded dragging him with her.

Hours later, she snuggled against him, her breath even as she slept. She felt like a tiny kitten beneath his fingers, her bones frail, crushable beneath his great weight. Yet she'd made love as fierce as a tiger. As she slept she muttered something and frowned. Using his thumb, he smoothed the worry line from her forehead.

"There's no reason to worry about anything when I'm with you, baby," he whispered. "I'll take care of you."

Except by being with him was she now a target?

He'd have to make sure that no one outside of his team knew they were a couple.

She murmured again but didn't fully wake. He pressed a kiss to her cheek then nuzzled her neck, murmuring sweet nothings. Instead of waking so he could make love to her again, she relaxed and drifted back to her dreams.

No kissing her in public, that was for sure.

The sheet he'd covered them with had drifted down and left one breast bare. Very lightly, he cupped it, rubbing his thumb over the nipple, marveling at how it puckered even while she slept.

No holding hands or touching her in public either.

Damn, this was going to be tough.

To his surprise, her hand splayed over his belly, then slid down. Her fingers wrapped around his half-erect cock. He glanced at her face and saw her heavy-lidded eyes watching him.

Even though it was past midnight in November, her smile turned the room into midday in July.

He bent down and kissed her, his tongue teasing her lips, coaxing them open so he could taste her again. She was so sweet and yet there was a fire in her that drew him to her to bask in her heat. He trailed his lips over her cheek and down her neck to a spot just below her ear where he sucked and nipped until she moaned and arched her breast into his hand.

Where before he'd taken her quickly, now he took his time to get to know her body, to discover its secrets. Like how she loved one side of her neck being kissed but not the other. And how her nipples pebbled and peaked with a mere touch of a fingertip. Again and again he'd return to her mouth, to sample her kisses, before returning to explore the rest of her body.

When he finally allowed himself to taste her sweet, creamy pussy again, her quiet moans and sighs were better than any screams of pleasure.

And when he'd rolled onto his back, pulling her on top of him, his magnificent spitfire took him into her body without hesitation and rode him to oblivion.

Chapter Fifteen

As she had since they'd begun their accord as she insisted on calling it, Rosie met the limo in the underground garage and accompanied him to the penthouse where they'd spend the rest of the night. Hopefully, Sam thought, in the bedroom.

He'd agreed to cancel most of his engagements. It hadn't been much of a concession on his part, not only would it keep her safer, it gave him unlimited access to her body. And since she'd moved back in with him, he'd made it a point to leave work on time. Why chain himself to a desk when he could make love to her on his bed? Or in the bath? Or on the floor in front of the living room fireplace?

He hung back, letting her take the lead and Andy trail him. It wasn't a sacrifice—he enjoyed watching the tips of her tattoo peek out from her jeans as she walked down the hall. He'd traced the butterfly tattooed on the small of her back the first night she'd fallen asleep curled up beside him, and researched it the next day. A Blue Morpho Butterfly. Did she realize that Morpho was an epithet for Venus and Aphrodite? How appropriate.

That first night of their accord, he'd gloated that she'd come to him, seeking acceptance into his realm. He'd thrilled when her lips parted to let him plunder. He'd exulted when she'd begged him to fuck her, digging her tiny heels into his ass and clutching him to her.

But her orgasm, her body clenching his cock, milking him, had been a transcendental experience that left his body shaking, and his wits scattered. Each time he'd made love to her after that, she'd taken him to heights he'd never flown before.

She'd been a delight—quick with a retort yet other times soft spoken. Quick to arouse, yet slow to satisfy. Demanding, yet willing to concede him the lead on occasion—which was more often than not. She'd also been a challenge because he sensed a part of her holding back. A hidden core, a secret place he wanted to reveal, to explore, to conquer. But it was time to start introducing her to what life with him meant. Something he had to be very careful to do without losing her trust.

Once Rosie gave the all clear that no one had entered the apartment, Sam shut the door behind him, locking Andy out. As he pulled off his tie, he shifted until he'd trapped her against the door.

Time to see if she would stick it out or cut and run.

"You up for a little game tonight, Rosebud?"

"Ye-e-s." She drew out her agreement so the word contained three syllables. From the way her tongue swiped across her lips and her hand touched her hair, he could tell she was at the very least curious if not outright aroused. Maybe she'd been here thinking about him all day the same way he'd been thinking about her.

He dragged his tie over her fingers and up her arm, drew it across her forehead. "In case you haven't realized it, I prefer things in the bedroom spicy rather than sweet."

"I don't mind a little jalapeno, but why do I feel you're talking hallucination-inducing habanero spicy?"

Locking his hands together beneath her behind, he lifted her until she could look him in the eye, then he kissed the tip of her nose. "Maybe because you're getting to know me."

"As long as you don't tell me you want to dress up like a baby and have me mother you. Because, I just am not into that."

He snorted. "No, that's not my particular kink."

She narrowed her eyes. "You're not planning on bringing another woman in, are you? Because if you are, I'll kick your ass from here to California. I'm fairly liberal, but I'm not about to get it on with a woman just so you can get off."

Damn, he loved her sass. The things he could teach her,

show her. What a thrill it was going to be watching her learn to submit, teaching her how to let go of all the rules society had crammed down her throat.

"No women. Fine. But you shouldn't knock something 'til you've tried it."

"Uh-uh." She rolled her eyes. "Why is it guys are so big on threesomes? Why do you get off on watching two women going at it? How would you feel if I asked another guy to join us? How would you feel watching me blow him?"

He started to say he had no objection at all, even hoped she'd agree to such an arrangement, but then he tried to imagine having to watch another man touch her breasts, her sweet pussy, watch her lips close around another man's cock. Nope, not happening. Not in this lifetime. "You're mine, Rosie. No other man is ever going to touch you."

What the hell was that all about? He understood when Mark had gotten angry in the summer, but Mark loved Jodi enough to make her his wife, though the idiot hadn't seen it until he'd been tied up and helpless. That was the whole point of that night. So why was he reacting like a green-eyed monster about having a ménage with Rosie and another guy? He hadn't felt this way since...Jill. Damn. Nope, that was SO not happening.

"I'm my own person, Sam," Rosie said stiffly.

"Never said you weren't. Far as I'm concerned, while I'm with you there are no others for either of us. Agreed?" He hadn't given anyone that promise in a long time. What the hell was he doing?

"If I didn't agree, I wouldn't be here with you." She wrapped her hands around his neck and cocked her head to one side, her bottom lip caught between her teeth. "Now, tell me. What's your big kinky secret?"

He took a deep breath, knowing she might turn around and walk out the door with the next statement. "I'm a Dominant, Rosie."

He almost missed her whispered "You're tellin' me."

Damn, she hadn't understood. All right. Time for a little showin'. Because tellin' definitely would have her runnin' out the door. "Do you trust me?"

"Yes, of course." A puzzled look crossed her face, and her voice tinged with caution.

"Would you let me blindfold you?"

"Oh, is that all you're talking? Sheesh, here you are making me think you're into something kinky, and all you're talking is about blindfolding me? Spicy he says," she muttered. "That's not even comparable to black pepper."

Her quick response told him she'd probably been blindfolded during sex before. Good. Though curiously, he found himself jealous that she had allowed another man to control her.

When she'd wound down and stopped grumbling, he asked, "Would you let me tie you up?"

A wicked grin lit her face. "As long as I get to tie you up and have my way with you the next time."

His cock twitched and hardened. If she only knew the challenge she was presenting, and how it was stronger than any chemical aphrodisiac. "We'll discuss that. Later. But for now..." He tossed her over his shoulder and carried her into the bedroom, ignoring her curses.

Once he'd set her down at the end of his bed, she asked, "Do I need a safe word?"

"You know about them?" Maybe she'd already dabbled in his world. That would explain her acquiescence. Was he playing things too cautiously?

She shrugged "I'm not a vestal virgin, you know."

Yeah, he knew. And thanked his lucky stars for it every night she stayed with him. So how far should he push her? "What types of things have you done, Rosebud?"

A delightful blush crept up her neck and over her cheeks. "Not as much as I think you have, but more than I'll admit to my mother. So what else were you thinking of doing tonight, I mean besides tying me up and blindfolding me?"

What he wanted to do got ramped down from what he would do tonight. It was too soon to jump right in introducin' her to his lifestyle. "I may gag you." The corner of his mouth twisted into a smile. "Though I think I won't want to do that for a while. That smart mouth of yours is quite amusing. And very—" he leaned down and caught her bottom lip between his teeth, bit it lightly before releasing it, "—very tasty."

"Is that all?" She seemed disappointed.

"You will not speak unless I ask you a direct question. Any time you do speak to me, you must call me Master. And respond to..." he considered her sub name, "...Princesa. If I tell you to do something—or not do something, you'll obey me."

"Oh, puh-leeze." She pushed her hand against his chest. Did she just stomp her foot? "So you want to be the big bad stud warrior while I play the poor helpless captive who must do your bidding. That's not very original—all guys fantasize about that."

Okay, let's take it the next step, see how she responded. "When I ask, I'll expect you to stick that pretty ass of yours up in the air and let me fuck it without a murmur."

She shuddered. "Ugh. I've tried anal before, Sam, and it hurt, so I don't think I can agree to that."

He frowned. "Didn't your partner prepare you first?"

"Do you mean use a lube? Yeah, he did, but it still hurt like hell. Since you're way bigger than he was, I'm not about to let you stick that bad boy of yours up my ass."

As much as he was flattered at her assessment of his size, he'd had the same concern. Even when he'd fucked her pussy, he'd worried about tearing her. At least she'd taken that matter into her own hands so he hadn't had to worry for very long.

The anal play being put on hold was a definite—he forced himself not to snicker—bummer. But she hadn't completely ruled it out at least. Maybe she'd allow him to slip an inflatable butt plug into that beautiful puckered opening, gradually increase the size, let her body adjust to the intrusion.

"Let's start with the blindfold and restraints for now." He decided not to tell her that he'd want to spank her or even flog her one day. He'd have to work her up to that idea.

"You can choose a safe word if you want, but I don't think you'll need it." Not tonight. But one day soon she might.

"*Cochino,*" she responded before he could finish his sentence.

He snorted. "Is that your safe word or an assessment of my

character?"

She grinned, a bright mischievous smile that lit up the room.

Dayam, his apartment had been so dull without her in it. So had his life.

"Could be both. But for now we'll say it's my safe word. So do you want me to undress before you blindfold me? Or do you want to undress me?"

"Ditch your blouse and pants, but leave your bra and thong. I want to take them off myself." He pulled a red silk scarf from his drawer.

"Okay, so it's a little kinky, but it's still pretty vanilla." But despite her protests, she shivered when he tied the blindfold in place. He had others he could have used that would be more effective, but he figured she might freak if he brought out his leather hoods at the get-go.

He lead her to the chair by the window "Stay there. And don't remove your blindfold." Once she'd given him her assurance she wouldn't peek, he ducked into the walk-in closet and opened the panel concealing the safe room he'd had privately constructed and outfitted for his personal needs. He'd been thinking about his plans all day, so it didn't take longer than a minute or two to select the restraints he'd require, along with a couple other toys.

When he returned, Rosie's legs were sprawled open, allowing him an unimpeded view of her stroking one finger beneath the thin matching thong. The sight of her pleasuring herself nearly had his tongue hanging on the floor and his dick ready to shoot a load prematurely.

Should he tie her face up on the bed? Or should he have her standing, her hands tied to the upper ring of the bedpost so he'd have access to more of her body? And oh, man, did he want as much access to her body as he could get.

Lying down—because he was definitely going to fuck her and that way he wouldn't have to move the restraints later. Even if he wanted to put a wedge pillow under that tiny ass of hers, the restraints would move up the iron posts with little problem. Yeah, that still left him a whole range of possibilities. He dumped his equipment on the night table, then flipped off the duvet and lifted her to her feet.

"Lie down on the bed, Rosie. Face up."

"Yes, Master," she said in a breathy Marilyn Monroe impression. He palmed the hard-on that throbbed at the title. If she only knew how he'd fantasized about her calling him that.

Once she was in place, he ran his hands down her calves, gently massaging her tiny feet. Hmm, ticklish. Interesting. Normally she was only ticklish after they'd made love. He fastened the restraints around her ankles and spread open her legs so he could attach the cuffs around the iron end posts. He stepped back and examined his handiwork, admiring how her lips glistened on either side of the thin black string of her thong. "You're already thinkin' about what I might do to you, aren't you?"

He sure was.

"I'm guessing," Rosie said with a beatific smile, "that it's going to end up with you riding me, pounding Big Sammy into my pussy and making me see stars the way you did last night. And if I'm really good, you'll let me ride you, the way I did yesterday morning. Which, by the way, was extremely enjoyable."

He smiled at her new nickname for his dick. Definitely better than Sam Junior. And she'd guessed correctly; he was intending to end the night that way, but not before he'd driven her to her own fulfillment once or thrice.

Should he have her arms stay straight over her head or spread out in an X? Straight for now, he decided. "Stretch your hands above your head, Princesa."

Looping the other ends of the restraints through the iron bars of the headboard, he buckled the leather straps around her wrists. Although they'd hold her for now, the bands were loose. He'd have to buy some slightly smaller. Or add extra padding inside.

Finished, he sat on the bed and waited. Watched. Appreciated.

Her hair spread in wild abandon over his pillows. It would leave her wonderful scent embedded in them so he'd be reminded of her when he slept. Though her eyes were covered by the silk scarf, her mouth formed a natural bow, her bottom lip protruding slightly more than her upper lip. He bent over and brushed a light kiss on them. She arched up, attempting to capture him, but he pulled away without saying a word.

With her arms over her head, her back was slightly arched and her breasts lifted in invitation. Should he take her bra off now or wait for later?

Decisions, decisions.

Later, he decided. There was a lot to be said for delayed gratification.

"Well?" she said after he'd sat there for a few minutes more. "Aren't you going to do something?"

Vixen.

He stood and prowled around the bed, planning each move he'd make.

"Sam?"

Impatient vixen.

Picking up the ostrich feather, he dragged it up one bare foot. As he'd expected, she squirmed, trying to move her foot away. So he treated the other foot to the same attention.

"Sam! Stop dragging things out and fuck me, damn it!"

Very impatient vixen.

"You have been told not to speak unless I give you permission." He spoke sharply, as if he were commanding one of Hauberk's new recruits who had just screwed up.

She stuck her tongue out at him. He had to swallow a snicker, nearly choking himself in the process. God, she had such fire.

For the next twenty minutes he teased and tickled every exposed inch of skin with the feather. If any other sub had cursed him and pleaded with him and tried to top from the bottom the way she did, he'd have ball gagged them long before. But he couldn't do it. There was something so refreshing about her. So intriguing. So challenging.

He switched the feather for a flogger, and let the leather tails trail over her shoulders, then down her breasts. He flicked open the front clasp on her bra, then enjoyed watching her nipples pebble at the cool air, he swirled the leather straps over her until she was panting. To her credit, and his disappointment, she didn't twitch or make a sound.

Goose bumps raised down her arms when he slid the thin tails along her stomach. Her hips arched when he dragged them across her mons and let them dangle over her labia. The artery on the side of her neck betrayed her rapid heartbeat when he touched the tip of the braided handle between her thighs and rubbed against her thong. She gasped when he slipped it inside her, rubbing the balled end so it would caress her most sensitive spot.

"Oh, and Rosie? You can't come unless I give you permission."

"Bas—" Her teeth clenched together a she swallowed the insult.

Her fingers wrapped around the straps holding her in place, her hips arched up as she tried to move with the whip handle, press it deeper. He drove her until she was about to slide over the edge. Just before she could orgasm, he removed the faux dildo.

"Damn it!" she snarled. "Let me come."

"Nope. And if you talk again without permission, I'll leave you tied up without you for the rest of the night."

He stepped away, letting her consider his threat as he stripped off his clothes. Taking his time, he poured some oil with a light coconut fragrance into one palm then coated both hands with it. Starting at her toes and slowly sliding up her legs, he gently massaged. If he'd done this first, she would have been completely relaxed, but now she was a quivering mass, her breath short desperate gasps.

He slid one finger along her labia, causing her hips to jerk off the bed. Damn, she was so ready. With a quick motion, he snapped the string on one side of her thong and stripped it from her.

"Lift your hips up, Princesa."

When she did, he slid a wedge-shaped pillow beneath her and knelt between her thighs. The moment he touched his tongue to her, she exploded, cream running down her sweet slit and pooling on the pillow.

He shook his head in mock dismay. "Oh, baby. You're not allowed to come unless I give you permission."

"Fuck. That," she panted. "Why on earth would I ever need to stop an orgasm? Most guys are happy if a woman has one at all."

"I'm not most guys."

Before he thought about what he was doing, he was seated hilt deep inside her. He groaned as the last of her orgasm caressed his rigid cock.

Damn it, when he had lost control? He'd planned to make her come at least three times before he allowed himself inside her. And yet here he was, buried balls deep in the little spitfire.

Right. So they'd both have to exercise some control. Which he'd never do in this position from the way his hips were working in concert with his now pulsing cock. Damn it!

Using every ounce of determination, he pulled from her.

"Saa-a-am!" Yup, three syllables. "Fuck me, goddamn it!"

In less than twenty seconds, he'd released her from her restraints. Before a minute had passed, he'd picked her up and sat in the chair, settling her knees on either side of his thighs, his erection trapped between them.

She didn't need to be told what he wanted, she wanted it just as much. With a wiggle, she impaled herself on his cock.

"Lord almighty," he groaned, sliding his hips a bit further along the chair's pillow and then arching them. He grabbed her hips, stopping her from moving, then pulled her so she was resting her head against him. When she protested, he shook his head. "Don't move. Not yet."

"Did I hurt you?"

"God, no." How could he explain? If she'd wrapped his cock in a Tensor bandage it wouldn't have been as tight as her pussy was around him. He could feel her heartbeat pulsing against both his cock and his chest.

Despite his request, her body undulated, in tiny motions at first. Then she pulled back and grabbed his shoulders, grinding her pelvis over his. She was so beautiful, her eyes closed, her hair hanging wild about her shoulders, her nipples hard buds sticking out proudly. The tiny sensual ember he'd sensed in her blossomed into a full conflagration of sexuality.

He dipped his head, and caught one of the taut buds in his mouth, suckling hard. Her pussy immediately clamped on his cock and her movements doubled in their fury. His fingers caught the other nipple between them, rolling, tweaking until she shuddered her completion once more.

It took every ounce of his control not to take the leap with her, but he managed to stop his climax. Just.

"You didn't..." She looked at him in confusion.

"I will."

As she relaxed against him, he held onto her hips and held her in place as he began to move inside her again. A long slow stroke until her pelvis met his. He pulled back until only the head of his cock was within her. Another slow stroke had her panting.

She lifted her head. Her fingers dug into his shoulders as she matched his movements, lifting herself when he pulled out, and lowering when he plunged deep. Joy and pleasure filled her beautiful eyes, mesmerizing him. They moved together, in wordless communion, their tempo growing faster and faster, the walls of her pussy caressing him, kissing him.

And then she leaned down and did the unthinkable. She whispered, "Come for me, Sam."

His cock exploded at her command, his hips bucking as his brains fled along with his come.

Chapter Sixteen

"What's the matter, not sleeping well?" Chad asked. "I only ask since that's the fourth time you've yawned in—" he checked his watch, "—oh, a whole twenty minutes."

Sam held up three fingers pressed closely together. "Read between the lines, buddy."

"I take it things are going well between you and Rosie?" Chad leaned back, lifting his leg so one ankle rested on the opposite knee. Why was he looking so smug?

"Oh, yeah." When she was around, he found himself unable to take his eyes off her, his hands off her. His cock out of her. He still hadn't figured out how she'd managed to turn the tables on him and make him come on command like a goddamned sub. For the first time in his life, he realized how little control he had in a relationship. Rosie held the power. She would forever be his mistress, with him the submissive. The slave desperate to be allowed entry to his mistress's glorious realm.

He'd never been so terrified. Or so aroused.

"Earth to Sam. Come i-i-in, Sam."

He opened his eyes—when had he closed them?—and saw Chad watching him, smirking.

"Why are you here buggin' me anyway?" he grumbled, pushing his chair further under his desk to hide his erection. Damned thing was jutting so high his pants looked like a circus tent.

"Thalia phoned me—she's worried about you."

"What's she worried about this time?"

"She's worried because she sent you the final list of

initiates two weeks ago and since you're supposed to have returned them a couple days ago, she's worried the Gala may have to be cancelled if you don't get your ass in gear."

"Oh, shit." He grabbed his mouse and scrolled through his emails. Yup, there it was. His brains were so scrambled from this affair with Rosie that he wondered what else he'd missed. He opened the document she'd attached and scanned the short list of names. "Only five initiates this year?"

"Hey, times are tough—besides, there are only so many people who can afford the initiation fee."

"True." He tapped his finger on the mouse again.

Joseph Loudon was sponsoring some woman from England as a casual member. Didn't matter how often they used the damned place, they still had to fork over the full million. He just hoped the woman wasn't a gossip or a looky-loo. He made a note to check out the security report his people had done.

Plastic surgeon Peter Harrison was sponsoring his latest mistress, and had received his wife's blessing. Considering he'd agreed to let her sponsor her lover at last year's Gala, it wasn't as if she could object.

Congresswoman Janssen's husband, the host of a reality television show that had past its peak a half dozen seasons ago, was forking over his million to ensure unlimited access to his wife's publicity assistant. Why Janssen didn't just come out of the closet and admit he was gay, no one could figure out. Lord knew, it would probably help his ratings these days. Then again, maybe the good congresswoman knew her husband preferred men and decided to open her reportedly tight fist on her pocket book to keep it quiet. Especially considering her platform during the last election had targeted alternative lifestyles. Hmm, maybe her husband's preferences had fueled that fire. It didn't matter one way or another to Sam—his share of the money would help the women's shelter open another house in Alexandria.

Ms. Kinson was sponsoring her latest boy toy, some faded rock star she'd met in Bermuda. This was her fourth initiate, wasn't it? Nope, her fifth—he'd forgotten the half-her-age actor she'd brought in two years before. You'd think she'd caned him from the way he'd burst into tears the first time she'd used a deer skin flogger on his pasty white ass in the grotto during his initiation. She'd retracted her sponsorship immediately, to all the other club members' relief.

And lastly, Lee-Anne Bennett was sponsoring Greg Tompkins. Who, if Sam's suspicions were correct, might also find himself tempted by the congresswoman's assistant, with or without Lee-Anne's blessing.

Would he be sponsoring Rosie at the next Gala? She'd enjoyed the bondage he'd used on her the night before, but she still thought it was a game, not realizing it was his lifestyle. And considering the end result, if he took her to his private suite, who would ultimately end up shackled to the St. Andrew's cross? Her? Or him?

"By the way," Chad interrupted, "Thalia's still under the impression you're going to be at the initiation Gala. You forget to cancel?"

"Aw, crap!" He picked up the phone and stabbed the speed dial for the club.

Warm water pounded Rosie from four sides as she stood in the shower. As her aching muscles attested, living with Sam Watson for the last couple of weeks was better than any exercise in a gym.

The threats had slowed down, they'd only received two the week she'd moved in with Sam, and a single photograph the following week. She'd started to wonder if Sam would disband the team since it had been so quiet. But then another photo had arrived the week before, and there'd been two more phone calls, threatening Sam if he showed up at several events he'd planned on attending. Luckily enough, he'd listened to her recommendations that he cancel and had spent the evenings hanging out with her in his apartment. Until tonight's party, which he refused to cancel. But it was in a security-controlled building and Chad said he'd been through the guest list and there'd be no security risks amongst the guests.

Still, she'd have to remind the team to stay vigilant.

She closed her eyes and tilted her head back under one of the sprays, luxuriating in the heat of the water. In her own apartment, the water would have long since cooled. Reaching blindly for the shelf where she'd balanced her bottle of shampoo, she encountered a wall of flesh.

With a gasp, she opened her eyes and saw Sam.

He reached over and changed the angle of one of the showerheads so it was no longer spraying directly at his hips. Then he captured her hand and wrapped her fingers around his already hard cock. "On your knees, Rosebud."

Without hesitation, she slid to her knees like a supplicant.

His cock jutted proud and straight from a thick nest of black curls. Tipping her head back so she could watch his reaction, she licked the very end, then swirled her tongue around the bulbous head. Dark heat flared at the back of his eyes as he buried his fingers in her hair and tightened his grip.

She took hold of his hips and closed her lips around his shaft, using her teeth to lightly scrape down its length, while her tongue alternately compressed and caressed his foreskin. When she sucked lightly, he exhaled in a hiss. Wrapping her hand around his base, she took his entire cock in her mouth.

God, she loved sucking him off, loved the power she felt when his cock pulsed beneath her tongue. Loved the taste of his come as it leaked from his tip. Her free hand drifted between her legs, played with the swollen bud of her clitoris until she neared orgasm herself.

She sucked harder, letting his hips drive his cock over her lips. With a hoarse cry he tried to pull out but she tightened her grip on his hip and let a raw sound at the back of her throat vibrate him until he erupted in her mouth. She swallowed repeatedly until he finished, then delicately licked off the last drops of come from his shaft and sat back on her heels.

"I love doing that for you," she murmured.

Sam reached down and lifted her to her feet, pulling her to rest against him. "I love you doing it for me." His voice was husky, as if he'd been shouting for hours.

He picked up a bar of soap and worked up a lather then cupped her breasts in his palms. Although she'd already washed herself thorough, she stayed quiet, enjoying the attention as he soaped up every single inch of her body. The bubbles swirling down the drain, he leaned her against the wall and went down on his knees in front of her.

"My turn, Rosebud." He tapped her knee so she'd spread her legs.

His fingers spreading her labia apart, he used his tongue to set fire to her clit in ways she didn't know possible. Somehow he'd gotten a hold of the soap again, as one lathered hand caressed her behind. When one finger slid down the crack of her ass and circled her anus, she tensed.

"Relax, Rosie. Trust me," he murmured against her sensitive bud, his breath hot on her flesh. His tongue started teasing again, darting into her pussy then back out and up to her clit in a rhythm designed to drive her crazy. When she'd forgotten about his other hand, one finger broached her muscles at least one knuckle deep, but no further. His other hand decided to help out his tongue as two fingers spread her pussy wide and caressed deeper than his tongue could reach.

Trapped by both hands, she squirmed in place, her brain warring with her body. It wasn't supposed to feel this good. Was it?

Who cared? All she could think of was the delicious pressure as his finger pushed deeper into her behind then was joined by another. God, she'd never felt so full. So... satisfied. So...well fucked.

Her eyes scrunched closed, concentrating on the movements of the fingers in both orifices, teasing the sensitive tissues until she couldn't draw another breath. Her muscles clenched around his fingers in an explosive orgasm that left her clutching Sam for support.

When she finally could draw a breath, she found herself draped in his lap, her head on his shoulder, the water pounding both of them on their shoulders.

Oh, yeah, she'd been having a shower.

"You all right?" He stood, lifting her with him.

"I'm fine." Better than fine. She'd heard the term boneless used before but thought it was a myth. But they were right. She didn't have a bone left in her body that could support her.

And she had to go out tonight and protect him? Talk about falling down on the job.

Carrying her like she weighed no more than a toy poodle, he stepped from the shower. Instead of taking her into the bedroom as she'd expected, he laid her on the massage table and covered her with a fluffy white towel, patting her until she was dry.

She tried to sit up but he pushed her down. He rummaged through a cabinet and returned with a bottle of oil. When he uncapped it and poured some into his palm, she recognized the coconut scent he'd used on her a few nights before.

Once again, he massaged her, from her toes to the tips of her fingers, then he turned her over and started again. His fingers kneaded and pressed, releasing the kinks in her legs and back that lingered despite the warmth of the shower.

She shuddered when he pressed a light kiss to the small of her back. "You know how I said I didn't want to...you know...do it that way?" she asked, closing her eyes that she would even consider what she was about to offer.

His hand stilled. "Yes."

"I-I've changed my mind." A shiver rippled along her body, cinching her already taut nipples against the cool leather of the bench. She turned her head so she could see him. "Is there a way we could sort of ease into it?"

The heat in his eyes flared, and a look of predatory satisfaction filled his face. "Are you sure?"

"As long as you take it slow and stop if I tell you to."

"Of course I would." He leaned over and pressed another kiss to the tattoo on the small of her back before he lifted her hips until her knees were tucked beneath her and her ass was high in the air. "Stay right here."

He disappeared for a few moments, she heard the same sound she had the night he'd blindfolded her—like a panel sliding on a track.

When he returned he had a small anal plug, along with what looked to be a supple leather thong. Where the hell had he stored that? She'd given the place a thorough going over the first day and never found any stash of sex toys. "So you keep a collection of dildos and butt plugs on hand?"

"Yeah, this is the smallest I have."

"You gonna show me this collection one day?"

"Maybe one day." He didn't sound too convincing. "I'll put this in you to get you used to the feeling of being stretched there."

Her apprehension must have shown on her face, because as he lubed up the plug, he said, "It won't hurt, I promise."

"And how would you know? You ever had one shoved up your butt?"

"Yes."

His simple answer surprised the hell out of her. She squirmed around until she could see his face, expecting to see him laughing, expecting a wink, but he was completely serious. Of course that could have been because he was concentrating on inserting that plug into her ass.

"When?"

The plug paused on its journey for a second before the pressure resumed. "Long story."

"We've got ti—" Oh, God, the entire thing filled her ass, stretching muscles that weren't used to being stretched. This was his smallest plug? She took a couple deep breaths, waiting for her body to adjust.

He smoothed a hand over her butt cheeks, then slapped one lightly. "I'm gonna make it good for you, okay? Now turn over so I can get you properly set up for tonight."

The plug shifted slightly as she did. He was right; it didn't hurt, but it sure felt weird.

After he murmured for her to lift her hips, he fastened that thin leather harness around them to hold the plug in place. At the front was an unusual pink panel that rubbed against her clit. It was slightly uncomfortable, but after she wiggled a bit, it settled into place.

"So what's the long story? We've got time."

All she received was a shake of his head. "Not long enough. You..." he leaned down and kissed her belly button, "...have to get ready for Cooper's party."

"Get ready...? But..." She gestured to the belt. "I thought we were going to..."

That predatory smile she was growing to know so well reappeared. "Oh, baby, we are. After the party."

"You mean I have to wear this thing all night? In public?"

"Yup. And I'm bettin' that by the time the party's over, you're going to be so hot, you're gonna be beggin' me to take you into the nearest corner and fuck your beautiful little ass."

Chapter Seventeen

Walking with the butt plug presented a challenge, especially wearing the sky-high silver heels Sam had insisted she wear. When the limo started, the movement of the car over the pavement caused the strange triangle at the front of the harness to rub her clit. By the time they arrived at the Georgetown condominium, every cell had been caressed and sensitized so each breath was a struggle not to come. Sam hadn't been kidding when he'd said she'd be ready to drag him into a corner and beg him to fuck her—and the night had barely started.

The limo had just slid to a stop when a valet opened the rear door. As Sam led her up the steps, Rosie whispered, "You're evil, did you know that?"

A smug satisfied smile lit up Sam's face "Baby, any time you want to find a dark corner, just holler."

They walked into a luxurious lobby with a water wall on one side and a double-sided fireplace separating them from the resident's lounge. A wave of music and chatter washed over them from farther down the hall.

Damn, she wished she'd had a chance to discover just how many people were here tonight. And had a chance to vet the guest list despite Sam's repeated assurances that they were all friends and told her not to worry about it. Of course, she had worried, but when she'd called their host, Cooper Davis had flat out refused to provide a list and told her to talk to Sam.

The concierge led them to an elegant though rather bland entertainment room.

They were fashionably late and the party was in full swing. A black grand piano and a string quartet entertained while tuxedoed staff ferried trays of champagne and hors d'oeuvres amongst the two-dozen guests. She glanced at Kris, who nodded and began a full sweep of the cocktail area. Andy had parked the limo and now mingled through the crowd, keeping a close eye on both her and Sam. To her surprise, Chad was there, greeting the guests by name which gave her some relief. If they passed his muster, they posed no threat to Sam.

Several of the people she'd met had mentioned La Porte Rouge, sometimes simply referring to it as the club, but despite her requests, neither Sam nor Chad had ever explained exactly what or where this club was so she could check it for potential suspects. Something she intended to rectify when she got home.

A woman in her forties, her shoulder-length black hair embellished by a single streak of bright red, swept up to them.

"Samuel, *mon amis*." She began speaking in rapid French and Sam replied in kind.

As she scanned the guests for possible threats, Rosie absently wondered if his French bore a southern accent.

Sam's introduction brought her attention back to the woman in front of them. "Jocelyne, I'd like you to meet Rosalinda Ramos. Rosie, this is Jocelyne Garneau."

"I'm honored to meet you, Rosalinda." Jocelyne pulled Rosie into a hug and air-kissed both cheeks. When she pulled back, she continued to hold both of Rosie's hands while gazing fondly up at Sam. "Samuel, my dear boy, now I understand why you haven't been to the club lately. She's absolutely adorable. Come, you must introduce her to Cooper."

They were spared a long search when a barrel-chested man a couple inches shorter than Sam headed toward them, a martini glass in hand. "Sam! It's about time you made it. I was starting to worry we'd have to send out the troops to fetch you."

"Coop, happy birthday! How's it feel to hit the big four oh?"

As Sam exchanged handshakes and insults with their host, Rosie stood back and assessed him. In a few years, the man's hair would be completely grey, but for now there was still a fair portion of pepper in the salt.

From what she could dig up in their files, Cooper Davis was the head of a computer networking company and had been a friend of Sam's for eight years. But she'd not been able to discover how they'd met and become friends. When she'd asked, Sam just murmured something about like tastes and kissed her senseless.

Her lips tingled at the memory as Sam introduced her to the birthday boy. When she shook his hand, his grip was firm, but held no sign of calluses, and from the peek she'd taken at his fingers, it looked like he'd recently had a manicure. Yet despite his deceptively mild appearance, Cooper Davis reminded her of a wolf sunning himself on a rock. Languid and laid back, but ready to strike at a moment's notice.

While Davis was holding her hand, her thong started vibrating against her clit. A quick glance showed Sam with his hand in his pocket. The danged thing must be remote controlled. She shot Sam a glare, which he returned with a smug smile and a wink.

It took every ounce of control to maintain a smile and keep her voice steady as she wished their host a happy birthday.

"So this is the little lady who's kept Sam away from our club." Cooper's wire-rimmed glasses couldn't hide how his gaze slid over her in a quick assessment, one that had her body adopting a defensive position though she couldn't determine why. Maybe it was how his grasp had tightened about her fingers. Or maybe it was the way his thumb caressed her knuckles in a strangely possessive gesture. "I look forward to getting to know you better, my dear."

"This is about as well as you're gonna get to know her, Coop." There was a hard edge to Sam's voice that made the hairs on the back of Rosie's neck prickle.

"You'll have to excuse these two, Miss Ramos. Neither are good with sharing their toys," a cultured voice from behind their host suggested. "Cooper, darling, why don't you get Sam and his guest some champagne?"

Rosie relaxed when their host released her hand and stepped back, revealing the speaker wheeling toward them.

"Thalia," Sam murmured as he bent down to kiss her cheek. "How have you been, my lady?"

"Very well, thank you." She stopped in front of them and smiled, holding out her hand. "You must be Rosie. Jocelyne mentioned Sam had brought you. I'm Thalia Harper, this is my husband, Spencer." She waved at the man who had been pushing her. He gave a rather old-fashioned bow. "Come with me, and I'll introduce you to our little family."

Spencer maneuvering her chair through the crush of people, Thalia introduced Rosalinda to the other guests, several of whom she recognized—one was a well known television personality, others from C-Span—at least one was a Senator, along with a couple congressmen. A tall blonde on the arm of one of the congressmen threw her arms around Sam's neck.

"Sammy, you came! I've missed you in the grotto."

Grotto? What the hell went on at the grotto? Was that another club?

A pained look on his face, Sam pulled the woman's arms away and stepped back. "Mandy, I'd like you to meet Rosalinda Ramos. Rosie, Amanda Henderson."

Where Rosie was short, Mandy was tall. Not just tall, but as graceful as a ballerina. Where she had black hair that looked like she'd stuck her finger in a light socket until it had burnt to a crisp, Mandy's long blonde hair streamed in golden waves over her shoulders and down the bare expanse of her back.

Rosie slowly released her breath so no one around them would notice her sigh. Mandy's body, like most of the other women tonight, was the epitome of surgical perfection. How could a regular gal like her compete? Especially for someone like Sam Watson.

Mandy spared Rosie her own quick assessing glance, then obviously decided she had no competition as she ignored her. "Sammy, why haven't you come to the club lately? It's not the same without you."

A brunette dressed entirely in leather complete with a steel-studded dog collar and thigh-high patent leather boots slithered through the crowd and wrapped one leg around Sam's hip and clung to him as she purred a welcome. If Mandy was a ballerina, this woman was a pole dancer with Sam the pole.

Rosie narrowed her eyes. No real boobs in the world retained their shape like that. Not unless they were supported by an underwire which the other woman obviously wasn't using considering the design of the...well, it wasn't so much of a dress, more like a series of straps concealing the important bits. Not that Rosie thought she was any slouch in the boob department, but the brunette's perky missiles could have drilled holes into granite.

"Tawny." Sam peeled the woman off him. "Where's Cooper? Isn't he your trainer lately?"

Tawny's collagen-enhanced lips pouted when he kept her at arm's length. "Coop says he needs to talk to you and I'm to fetch you."

Sam shrugged in Rosie's direction and followed Tawny over to their host. Cooper took Sam a few paces away so they could talk without being overheard. Able to keep an eye on Sam, Rosie chatted idly with Thalia, while her husband stayed two paces behind his wife. Rosie shifted uncomfortably as Spencer kept glancing down the deep swell of her cleavage and again to the thigh peeking out from the slit up her hip. From the way lips pressed together, Thalia finally noticed her husband's meandering gaze.

"Spencer, *my prince*," she put a strange emphasis on the title that had Rosie wondering its significance, "go to the bar and fetch me a glass of sherry."

Apparently whatever they were discussing hadn't taken much time, as Sam returned not five very uncomfortable minutes later, just as Jocelyne swooped in, accompanied by a gentleman in his fifties.

"Rosie, I'd like for you to meet my husband, Robert." She pronounced it with her French accent, so it sounded more like Ro-bair.

Jocelyne was in a middle of a story about Robert's photography when Sam interrupted. "Jo, you want to go rescue my operative from Tawny's clutches? He looks like he's a thermometer about to burst."

Rosie glanced over to where Kris had positioned himself by the door to the patio and saw Tawny wrapped around him like a clinging vine. Kris's already red face flamed completely scarlet when she swiped her tongue up the side of his face while sliding her hand down his pants.

"*Merde*, I've warned her," Jocelyne apologized before she left them to rescue Kris.

The vibrations created by the device in her harness stopped and started a dozen times through the evening, sometimes lasting only a few minutes, and once the entire length of a slow dance Sam talked her into. By the time the string quartet finished the last note, she was clinging to Sam, resting her head on his chest as she willed away a threatening orgasm.

Wrapping his arm about her waist, he led her off the dance floor. "Ready to go find a quiet corner yet, Rosebud?"

As tempting as the thought of finding relief here and now, she hated the thought that Andy and Kris would notice their disappearance, or worse, Chad, and know what they were doing. "How about we go home?"

Placing his fingers beneath her chin, he lifted her face and pressed a kiss to her nose. "Can't. I've got that board meeting, remember? You stay here with Andy and Kris, this'll only take about an hour."

"Stay here? No," she protested. "Where you go I go."

Even though Sam lowered his voice, she couldn't mistake the thread of authority running through it. "Not this time, Rosebud. This meeting is private so you're stayin' here."

"Where's the meeting?"

"Up in Coop's penthouse."

"Then I'm going to check it out first."

"Rosie—"

"This is not negotiable." She pulled away from him, ignoring the glances she drew. "You're not going anywhere that I haven't checked out first, and I'm not leaving you alone."

Silence blanketed the room, so his next sentence carried to all listeners, even though he spoke quietly. "You can check out Coop's apartment first, but you're not staying for the meeting."

"Sam—"

"No."

"I'm staying with you, Sam. I'm your lead op, remember?"

"Rosie, if I have to handcuff you to Kris and order him to take you home, I will."

"Right back at you, buddy." She called to Andy. "Have the

limo brought 'round—Mr. Watson is leaving."

"The hell I am." Sam wrapped his fingers around Rosie's forearm and marched her into the hall. As soon as they left, the silence in the party room rose to a crescendo of babbling whispers.

"Now you listen here, Rosebud. These people are both my friends and my business partners. They are not a threat to me or to anyone. You take Kris and Andy and do your search for bombs or what have you, but you will keep your ass out of that apartment once the meeting starts. Do you hear me?"

"As your team leader, it's my duty to remind you that you are putting yourself in unnecessary danger. One of those precious friends in there may be your stalker."

Sam shook his head. "Give it up, Rosie. You're seeing shadows where there are none."

She jammed her hands on her hips. "Excuse me for being suspicious of everyone but that's what you pay me to do. If I have to treat everyone as an enemy to protect you, I will."

"Sounds like something they say in the 101st Airborne," Cooper's voice grated behind her.

"I beg your pardon?" Rosie asked without turning around.

"Be polite, be professional, but have a plan to kill everyone you meet."

She nodded her head once. That about summed up her training.

"What's this about a stalker, Sam?" Cooper continued. "And why didn't you tell me you were having security problems?"

Sam exhaled and swore under his breath as Rosie faced Cooper directly.

"As head of Sam's security team, I need to verify the security of the room where the board meeting is being held. Plus I want to actually be in the room during the meeting."

"I will allow your team to check out the security of my apartment, Miss Ramos, but I'm afraid only members of the Board are allowed to be present during our meeting. But allow me to apologize for my attitude when you called about the guest list the other day. If I'd known you were head of Sam's detail, I

135

would have gladly given you the list." He turned to Sam. "What the hell type of threats have you been getting, Sam? Is there any link to the club?"

"Don't worry, Coop, the threat's to me specifically, not to anyone at the club."

While Sam explained about the photos and phone calls, Rosie left Kris to guard Sam and went up to the penthouse with Andy to check out the security. Once she'd given Kris the all clear to escort Sam up, she waited at the front door of Cooper's apartment as Cooper, Sam, Thalia and Jocelyne, along with five others filed past. But when she attempted to follow Sam back in, he stopped her with a glare. "I told you. You are not followin' me into this meetin'. Now go downstairs and have another glass of champagne. I'll be down in about an hour."

"No, Sam. I'm staying. I'm the head of your detail, remember? You're my responsibility."

"Miss Ramos," Cooper joined Sam at the door, "while I appreciate your concerns for Sam's safety, I cannot allow you to be a part of our meeting. If you wish to position a guard outside the door, you are welcome, but that's as much as I can allow. Club bylaws are very specific."

With that he shut the door in her face. She snarled when she heard him throw the bolt, locking her out.

Chapter Eighteen

"Thanks, Coop. I thought I was going to have to pick her up and carry her downstairs."

Chad cleared his throat. "In Rosie's defense, you know she's right about insisting one of her detail stay with you, Sam."

"I know, but she has to trust my judgment, too."

"Quite a little spitfire you've taken on there, Sammy," another of the founding members laughed. "I bet you're having fun bending her to your will. I can just picture the flogging that little lady's in for tonight."

"Yeah, can I watch?" asked one of the men seated in Cooper's living room.

"Hell, can I help?" added another.

"Easy boys, apparently Ms. Ramos is Sam's bodyguard, not his trainee." Cooper grinned at the inevitable hoots at that claim, and the jokes about what part of his body she was guarding. But he lowered his voice so they couldn't hear. "By the way, Sam, you can't tell me you're not doing her. If you ever have need of a third, call me first. I'd love to see her in action."

His growled repetition that Rosie was his employee not his slave was at complete odds with the hard-on he was sporting. Damn, he could just picture her in his private suite at the club, her eyes flashing in indignation above her gag. He'd start with the flat of his hand, nice and gentle but enough to bring a pretty pink blush to those bitable ass cheeks of hers. Then once she'd got really hot and wet, he'd switch to the deer skin flogger—*Fuuuck.* He shifted in his seat to give his cock extra room in his pants.

"Okay, people, let's get this meeting started," Cooper intoned. "Our first initiate is sponsored by..."

Sam let the discussion flow past him as he considered the challenge Rosie had issued downstairs, if she was even aware how turned on he'd been by her arguments. Would she ever be the sub to his Dom? Not likely, from the way she'd behaved tonight. Strangely that didn't bother him. A few years ago, heck a couple months ago, he might have been frustrated by her stubbornness, instead he was lovin' her sass.

"So that's the five of them," Cooper announced after ninety minutes of long hard discussion over Ms. Kinson's candidate. He settled back in his chair and stretched out his legs, crossing them at the ankle. "Or do we have six this year, Sam?"

"Nope, that's it."

"You're not sponsoring your little spitfire?"

"Come on, Coop. He'd need to get her more malleable, more submissive, before I'd approve her," Bert Fordyce suggested. "Frankly, I'd have had her on her knees licking my boots for her little display earlier. And then I'd have her sleeping on the floor at my feet for the next week until she showed proper respect."

"Maybe Rosie is a Domme, not a sub," Thalia suggested, cutting Sam's growl off before it filled the room.

Bert barked a laugh. "Not if Sam's fucking her. Tie her up and flog her, Sam. Teach her to submit like a good little slave. And if you can't, send her to see me. I'll have her begging for punishment in no time."

Sam faced Bert, his hands held loosely at his side, but never had he felt more ready to punch a man in his piggish snout than he did right now.

Cooper stood, his chair scraping on the ceramic tile when he pushed it back. "Jocelyne, why don't you and Robert escort Bert and the others downstairs and finish up the rest of my champagne?"

The rest of the members murmured their farewells, leaving Sam alone with Cooper and Thalia.

"Ignore Bert, Samuel." Thalia touched Sam's hand. "He's still living back in the Victorian ages."

Cooper nodded. "He's an ass, but he's an honorable ass

when it comes to other people's subs. He wouldn't touch Rosie if you sponsored her unless you gave him permission."

"I told you, Coop. Rosie's not my sub. And she'll never see the inside of the Porte."

Cooper and Thalia exchanged a glance. Was there something they hadn't told him? Maybe Rosie was right about checking the membership again.

Sam wheeled Thalia to the door. "I think maybe I should take another look at the club files. Make sure there's nothing there."

Cooper gave Sam a troubled look. "Could your stalker be a club member?"

"I don't know. There's no proof one way or another. But..." Sam let the rest of the sentence hang. None of them needed a reminder that it had happened before.

Sam rubbed Thalia's shoulder when she visibly stiffened. "I don't think it's any of the members, Thalia. Chad and I go through the list regularly, but it might not hurt to take a second look."

Cooper opened the door, revealing Andy standing on one side, Thalia's husband, Spencer, on the other.

Sam glanced down the hallway, surprised to find no one else waiting.

Andy shot him a wry grin. "If you're wondering where Rosie is, I tossed for who got to stay up here guarding you. I won."

Cooper's laugh echoed down the hallway. "Two headed coin?"

"No, just lucky." When Sam raised his brows, Andy shrugged. "Hey, it happens. Anyway, Rosie just about blew a gasket when you locked her out so I had Kris haul her downstairs." Andy's smile broadened. "I got a bet with him that you're sleeping on the couch tonight."

"Thanks for the heads up, but I sorta figured I would be sleepin' on the terrace tonight. Without a blanket." He shook his head. "Go get the elevator, will you, Andy? I'll be right there."

Once Andy walked away, Cooper chuckled. "I envy you, Sam. Your Rosie's going to be a helluva lot of fun to train."

Sam stuck his hands in his pockets and stared down the

hall. "She's my employee, Coop."

"So you said, not that I'm buying it for a second. Anyway, knowing that you're being threatened, if your Miss Ramos needs access to the membership files, I'll see that she gets it. She's a Hauberk employee after all, and since she's with you, I reckon we can trust her."

"I'd prefer if you didn't let her into the club. If she wants the files, ship 'em over to my office—but only the background reports, okay? She doesn't need to know that much information yet." I'm not about to let her near that place. I'm not about to lose her the way I lost Jill.

"I'm not comfortable with the files leaving the building, Sam. There's too much personal information on our members to put at risk. If she wants to look at them, she can come to the club in the mornings, when things are quiet."

Sam sighed. "If I tell her that she'll be camping on your doorstep first thing tomorrow." Somehow he had to keep her away from there. *She's your lead op. You can't stop her from doing her job. If you try to stop her, she'll just go without telling you.* "I'll send Andy over in the morning, get him to take another look at the files."

Cooper rocked back on his heels. "That works too."

Sam said his good-byes, then stabbed at the button to call the elevator even though Andy had already pressed it.

With an elegant move of dismissal from Thalia, Spencer stepped back, as did Andy, allowing her to speak to Sam privately. "Kneel down, Sam. I don't like you hovering over me like a giant. I want to look you in the eye."

When he had done as she bid, she said gently, "About your Miss Ramos—how come you have not told her about the club? About your part in it? And don't try to tell me she's simply your employee, I know better."

"Thalia, you know it's against the bylaws to discuss the club with non-members. Besides, I've only started to introduce Rosie to the scene."

But so far she hadn't shown any hesitation in accepting any of his suggestions. If he did take her there, maybe she'd take to it like a duck to Lake Arrowhead. Hmmph, the thought of other men getting a look at her delicious little body made him feel more like a wolf guarding his territory.

"Are you worried she'll think by submitting she's betraying women everywhere?"

Relieved she'd given him an excuse, he grabbed onto it with both hands. "I've not exactly broached it with her, but yeah, I can see her worrying about somethin' like that."

And if she did think that, it was likely he would be visiting his gonads at the zoo after all.

"When she comes to the club, have her come see me. I'll answer any questions she may have. I'll help her realize that exploring that side of her won't lessen who she is. Your lifestyle won't take away her control, if anything it will give her more power in the relationship."

Wasn't that the truth?

"To be honest, Thalia, I'd prefer if she knew nothing about my part in the club." Did he dare admit that he'd found the whole scene boring lately? That he'd had more exciting sex with Rosie in the past month than he had in the last several years?

"If you try to deny that part of yourself, you'll find yourself dreadfully unhappy. However, I think you may be misjudging Rosie. From what I've seen, she's a strong woman to have made it to where she has in a man's world. I think you'll find she'll enjoy letting go of the reins on occasion. Not every time, but I think you'll both be satisfied."

"To force her to accept my needs over hers will be a surefire way to lose her. You talk about my nature being Dominant, but I can't see Rosie following an order I give her without arguing. It's not in her nature to be submissive." And hell, he got such a charge out of her arguments, he'd often provoked her just to see her get angry. Why would he want to deny himself such pleasure? Or stifle her passion?

The elevator door opened, but no one moved to get into it and the door quietly swished closed.

"Sam..." Thalia stroked his cheek and smiled, "...Rosie is most likely an alpha submissive, which is what you require. She may even be a switch. You should train her to handle a flogger so she can whip you one day."

If she'd gotten out of her chair and walked, he couldn't have been more shocked. "I beg your pardon? I'm the Dominant in the relationship, remember?"

"Around any other woman, you are definitely a Dominant, but when it comes to your Rosie, I think you would willingly get on your knees and crawl across broken glass if she ordered you to."

"I—I would do no—" He'd crawl across broken glass to save her life, but just because she ordered him to? Not bloody likely.

"Sam," she interrupted, brooking no dispute. "Close your eyes."

She had to clear her throat before he obeyed her, a precursor to punishment from his training days. "Now, imagine yourself strung up between those two lovely posts in your suite and Rosie behind you holding a flogger."

Oh, Christ, his cock instantly got hard at the image. "Are you telling me I'm a goddamned switch?"

Thalia's chuckle had him opening his eyes. "No, my dear friend, you are not a switch. But there are times an alpha submissive can step out of their role and take care of their Dom. I also remember you very much enjoyed yourself when I wielded the whip on you. Or was that not come shooting out of your magnificent erection during our training sessions?"

"Sonuva—" he bit out.

"Reveal your true self to Rosie, Sam. Trust her. If she does not understand, if she walks away, she's not the right woman for you and it will be for the best for both of you if she leaves." She signaled to Spencer who quickly returned. "But I think she'll surprise you."

Sam pushed himself to stand and pressed the elevator button again. "I'll think about it."

"Bring her to the club tomorrow morning. I'll answer any questions she has and then she can look through the files. And don't forget, Samuel. Reveal your true nature to her tonight. Before someone else has the chance."

Chapter Nineteen

Rosie stomped in front of the elevator on the ground floor like a guard dog on patrol. "Tell me about that car again."

Kris leaned one shoulder against the wall and shook his head. "I saw it pull out from the building opposite Sam's and it followed us about half the way. When I mentioned to Andy that I thought it might be following us, he didn't think so. To prove it, he took the next turn and it didn't follow."

"But you said you thought you saw it again when we were pulling up here."

"There was a car that looked similar, yes."

"Kris, how many blue 1964 Shelby Cobras with a white stripe do you think there are in this town?"

"I don't know. Maybe a couple."

She'd bet one. "Why didn't either of you tell me someone might have been following us when we got here?"

"Andy told Sam and he said it wasn't something to worry about. Look, I shouldn't have mentioned it. Just forget it."

Like hell she'd forget it. She and Andy were going to go a few rounds on this one. She headed for the elevator and punched the button. "I'm going up."

"Aw, come on, Rosie. Andy's up there to make sure Sam's okay. Or don't you trust him to keep Sam safe?"

"I should be the one up there guarding him."

"They'll just kick you out. You might as well wait here."

He was right, they would. Andy would have to keep him safe. But once they got home... As she waited for Sam to finish up, a familiar, and unfriendly, face approached. *Ay ay ay,* the woman who had bid against her at the charity auction and driven the final price up to seventy thousand dollars. What was her name again? Lee-Anne Bennett. Not a threat to Sam other than those claws she sprouted last time they'd met.

"I must admit that I am surprised Sam brought you to our private munch when you clearly have not mastered the art of submission. Now I understand why he is not sponsoring your initiation this year."

Art of submission? What the heck was the woman talking about?

"As head of Mr. Watson's protection team, I am responsible for his safety—including occasionally going against what he wants if I deem him to be in possible danger."

Lee-Anne's lips thinned as she pressed them together. "While I'm sure you expect me to commend you for your vigilance, be warned, should Sam ever bring you to the Rouge and I give you a command, I will expect it to be obeyed to the fullest. Immediately. You'll not find me so forgiving."

Who'd crowned this bitch the queen of the world?

"I am not planning on being a member of your little club, Miss Bennett." If this broad ever tried something on her, she'd kick her ass from here all the way to California.

"Anyway, since it's obvious that you and Sam are involved, I wanted to ensure that you've had a medical recently and your files are on record at the club. Especially since Sam will be our third at the Gala."

Third? Third what? "I beg your pardon? Wait a minute. He's going to the Gala? He's not going, he cancelled."

Lee-Anne's unbotoxed forehead crinkled then relaxed. "I'm sure that's what he's told *you*. But I cannot imagine a founding member—especially Sam—not attending the biggest event of the year. Besides why else would he be here tonight if he wasn't planning to attend?"

Rosie rubbed her arms, trying to stop persistent tingle of the creepy crawlies under her skin. There was no damned way she was going to explain anything to this bitch, not that she waited for an answer.

"Since I've asked Sam to have a ménage with Greg and I as

part of Greg's initiation, I want to make sure I'm not going to be subjected to some..." her lip raised in a sneer as her gaze raked down Rosie, "...social disease."

Icy talons squeezed her chest until it was hard to breath. "A ménage?" As part of an initiation? What the hell was this club? Surely Chad wouldn't let Sam be a member in a sex club, especially after the scandal that had destroyed Chad's career. Even though she'd lived in New York and had been in college at the time, Chad's decision to involve the FBI in protecting members of a BDSM club without approval had been headlines in the papers for weeks. Surely he'd learned...surely Sam couldn't have been...but Lee-Anne was nodding her head.

"Yes, a *ménage a trois*. A threesome. You know, two cocks, one cunt?"

And then it hit her. Sam was planning on having sex with the Ice Bitch—after he'd told her they'd be exclusive. Rosie's mouth opened and closed several times, matching her fists.

"Sam is the premiere choice amongst the club members for threesomes. Having a founding member take part in the rites will add a certain cachet to Greg's membership. So when I decided upon what to demand for Greg's initiation, I couldn't think of anyone better for our little games that night. And that magnificent cock of Sam's." Lee-Anne dramatically fanned herself. "That's why I was so intent upon winning him at the auction. Besides what woman could resist?"

That sonuvabitch had not only lied to her about not attending this place, but he'd lied to her about being the only one. What else had he lied to her about?

Lee-Anne tapped one French-manicured fingernail against her upper lip, her light blue eyes coldly assessing. "You haven't answered my question. All club members and their partners have to regularly submit to a medical screening to ensure they're not carriers of any STDs. That way any other partnerships are not put at risk. And since you're Sam's dalliance of the day I need to know when you had your last physical. Sam's usually such a stickler about those details, I can't imagine why he wouldn't have filed your report with Thalia already."

"My medical information is private, Miss Bennett. And

since I'm not a member of your club, I feel no need to share my medical history with you." It was standard procedure to familiarize herself with her principal's medical records, in case they'd had to get him to a hospital if he'd been attacked, but thank God, she'd double checked his medical records before she'd agreed to their affair.

Lee-Anne's eyes narrowed and she grasped Rosie's biceps, her long nails digging into flesh. "You'd better not have an STD or I'll come after your ass. And here's another warning for you. Don't you dare try to stop Sam from attending—he's mine that night. I've waited too long to get him to fuck me, so if I hear one whiff that you tried to stop him attending, I'll tie you to a rack and punish you myself. And I won't be using a deerskin flogger—I'll be using a bullwhip. Do you understand me?"

"Perfectly." Rosie wrenched her arm from Lee-Anne's grasp. "Now if you'll excuse me..." Without waiting for a response, she fled through the crowds to the ladies' washroom. Once inside she closed the door to the stall and leaned against it. By the sinks, two women chattered and laughed, their lives normal, solid, while hidden in her stall, the floor tilted and heaved beneath Rosie's feet.

Dear God, what a fool she'd been. This whole time Sam had been playing her, lulling her into a sense of security and now...now she was seeing the true side of him.

When he'd murmured how she'd be the only one, she'd believed him. Of course she had, she'd trusted him. But how long would it be before he'd expect her to stand back while he "fulfilled his duties as a founding member" by fucking other women? As bile burned the back of her throat, Rosie pressed her hand to her belly and felt the leather harness he'd strapped around her. Felt the butt plug he'd convinced her was a harmless toy.

Damn him. Damn her for letting down her guard.

She waited until the other women left the bathroom then fled her sanctuary and grabbed a handful of paper towels. A minute later, both the butt plug and the harness found a home in the garbage.

A fitting place, considering they probably landed on top of her career.

Sam leaned against the limo door as Rosie stared out the window. He couldn't fail to notice how curt her answers to him had been when he'd finally found her once the meeting had broken up. Or how rigid she'd been when she'd stalked in front of him on their way to the limo. Nor could he miss how she refused to look at him now.

It didn't take her hauling off and kicking him in the nuts to know she was pissed. And not just about being kept out of his meeting. Something else had set her off.

Sam pulled a cigar from the inner pocket of his jacket and struck a match to it. He pulled on it until the end glowed red before blowing a ring of smoke into the air. "If you grind your teeth any harder, you're gonna be gummin' your next meal."

Rapid fire Spanish insults hurtled toward him. He managed to catch her calling him a *loco pervertido*. "So you mind tellin' me what's..." Hmm, shoved the stick up her butt wasn't exactly the analogy to use considering what he'd done to her earlier. Although he would lay dollars to donuts that his little toy was no longer filling that particular orifice. He amended his statement. "You mind explainin' why you're as ornery as a she-cat with a thorn in its paw? I'm guessin' it's not a general mad you're workin' on, but one aimed specifically at me?" He deliberately thickened his drawl and stretched his arm across the back of the seat as he sprawled out.

"Do you know, there are days when I think you're actually from Minnesota and the Deep South good ol' boy routine is all one big act?"

"Born and raised in Georgia. Want to see my birth certificate?" Not many people had ever noticed that he used his accent as a device to get people to let down their guard. Figured that she'd pick up on it.

Damn, she was hot when she was angry. Now how should he play this? If he wound her up some more, the sex tonight would probably be hotter than burning magnesium. When she folded her arms across her chest, he could have sworn he saw a hint of nipple peeking out from her gown. *Get your eyes back on her face, son, and wipe the drool off your chin.* 'Cause oglin' her breasts was definitely not a way to defuse this particular firecracker, whatever had sparked the fuse.

"I just had a very interesting discussion with Lee-Anne Bennett," she said. "Just how long were you planning to wait before telling me you're the founding member of a sex club?"

Well, fu-uck. As soon as he got to a phone, that big-mouthed trust fund baby would find herself blackballed for breaking the secrecy pact she'd signed upon her initiation. And then he'd track her down and deliver the good news himself, demand the five million dollars the contract quoted as penalty. She'd choke handing that much of her grandaddy's hard-earned cash over, and he'd enjoy watching every freakin' moment.

"You know what's worst of all? You lied to me."

What the fuck had Lee-Anne told her? "I didn't li—"

"Okay, you omitted to tell me the truth about the club. That's the same as lying, Sam. You're my principal, remember?" She barreled over him. "Why didn't you tell me you were planning on attending the club this weekend instead of telling me you'd cancelled? At least you could have told the truth so I could arrange for your detail to protect you."

His teeth ground together. "As I've already told you, I declined the invitation—and told 'em again tonight not to expect me." And taken a great deal of ribbing for it.

She reverted to a stream of Spanish invectives before losing steam and ending with, "But you went to tonight's meeting, didn't you? Which was about the plans for the initiation Gala? If you didn't plan on going, you wouldn't have gone tonight."

"Why the fuck are you believing her over me? And I attended tonight because the club requires a full quorum to vote upon the applicants. If I hadn't attended, they wouldn't have been able to have a vote and the Gala would have to be cancelled. That's worth five million bucks in initiation fees. I wasn't about to let the entire club down."

"Oh, excuse me. Heaven forbid that Sam Watson would disappoint his friends." Her tone couldn't have been more sour if she'd bitten into a crateful of lemons. "Oh, and by the way, one of your friends wouldn't happen to drive a blue 1964 Shelby

Cobra, would they?"

"So that's what this is about. And yes, Jocelyne drives a Cobra. You'll be happy to know she wasn't following us so much as taking the same route, since she lives in the building across the road. Is that why you're pissed off with me? Because Andy came to me and not you?"

That was a matter she'd have to take up with Andy. "Partly. I can't make good judgments to keep you safe if I'm not in the loop. But I need to know that if I tell you something isn't safe, you're going to listen to me and follow my recommendations. And tonight, you didn't listen to my recommendations about the meeting."

"Because there wasn't any credible threat. Besides, Chad was there if anything had gone south."

"That was for me to decide. I can't do my job if you're overriding my decisions about your safety, or telling my people to ignore what could be an obvious lead." She closed her eyes as she took a deep breath. When she opened them again, he knew she'd just sealed his fate. And it wasn't a thumbs up. "I can't do this, Sam. This—us—" she circled her finger between them, "—it won't work. You obviously don't respect me as your lead operative."

"You're gonna walk away? Just like that?" Damn it, the car was pulling into the underground garage already.

"I should never have agreed to this affair in the first place. So I'm going to go back to the way it was before—if that's possible. And if it's not..." her teeth tugged on her lower lip as the car rolled to a stop, "...if it's not, then I guess I'll be asking for a transfer to Miami or somewhere. I'd appreciate it if you respect my decision."

Andy opened the limo door. "Home sweet home."

Sam slumped back as he waited for Rosie to get out. Since Kris had already called the elevator and was holding the doors, they didn't have to wait. He didn't take his eyes off Rosie, but he could see in the reflection of the elevator doors that she was studiously avoiding looking at him.

As he was considering just how to gain and keep her attention, she quickly scotched his plans for any further conversation when she said, "Andy, you're going to be staying in

Sam's place tonight."

Andy stared at her for a moment then raised a brow at Sam who scowled in return. "You two have a fight or something? Because I don't want to—"

"It's all right, Andy," Sam interrupted, seeing a possibility arise and not wanting to let it slip through his fingers. "Stay at my place tonight."

Because he wasn't going to be there anyway. One way or another he was going to be in 1202. With Miss Rosalinda Ramos. Damned sure he was not letting her get away until she'd listened to him. And listen she would. If he had to tie her up and ball gag her.

Shooting a hesitant glance at Rosie, Andy nodded. "Okay, sure, boss. I guess I'll be your bunky for the night."

Maybe it was the fluorescent light that flickered overhead, but Sam could have sworn he saw a look of disappointment in Andy's expression. Kris, however, looked anything but disappointed—his lips pressed together and his knuckles turned white over the hand bar ringing the elevator.

Aw, crap. Looked like his gonads were taking their own trip to the zoo tomorrow.

The elevator jerked to a stop and the doors slid open. Phillips checked the hall then exited and waved him out. Rosie preceded him while Kris trailed along the hall. As they approached, Scott opened the door to 1202 and nodded. "Evening, folks. All's quiet here."

A glance at Rosie showed she still wasn't meeting his eye, and he knew she wouldn't change her mind about staying in his apartment that night. Especially when she slipped past Scott and disappeared.

He pulled out his keys and tossed them to Andy. "Here you go, sport. Do your thing."

While he waited for Andy to unlock the apartment, Sam cornered Kris.

"You want to tell me what the hell went on downstairs while I was in the meeting? What did Lee-Anne Bennett say to Rosie?"

"Shoot, I don't know, boss." Kris turned bright red. "All I

know is they spoke for a couple minutes then Rosie headed for the can. You came down right after that."

"All clear," Andy called.

Leaving Kris standing in the hall, Sam headed for the privacy of his apartment. Once inside, he tugged loose his tie and tossed it on the couch. It slithered along the leather and fell on the floor. "Andy, I've got a job for you."

Andy grinned. "Does it involve getting you in to see Rosie? If it does I'm in, but I don't work cheap."

"I need you to tweak the alarms both here and in 1202. Call Scott and bribe him if you have to."

He laid out his plans.

"That's insane!" Andy rubbed the latest tattoo on his arm. "There has to be an easier way. Why not just go down the hall and knock on the door? Scott'll let you in."

"Because Kris is there. And he's designated himself Rosie's protector. He'd never let me near her. I have to get her where she can't appeal to him for help."

After some discussion, Andy agreed to help him—though it cost him.

While Andy reprogrammed the security settings, Sam headed to the bedroom.

Why was he chasing after Rosie? Or was it just ego that she'd walked away first?

Because she'd brought laughter back to the apartment. Light. And now he'd had a taste of her, he couldn't bear the thought of being alone.

But that look on her face, the hurt in her eyes, because she thought he didn't respect her had him cringing. How could she not see how great an operative she was? How the other members, not only of her team, but of Hauberk, listened to her when she voiced an opinion?

If he did nothing else, he had to convince her he trusted her judgment, respected her abilities.

He changed from his suit to a pair of cargo pants and a T-shirt. Less than five minutes later, he stuck his bare feet into a pair of Nikes, and rifled through his desk to find his toolkit. Tucking his cell phone into his pocket, he opened the bedroom door to the balcony. He paused, then went back and grabbed a handful of condoms, which he stuck in his pocket and headed back outside. Though there was a good chance they'd not be needed, it didn't hurt to be prepared. His daddy hadn't helped him get his Boy Scout's badges for nothing.

Luck sure needed to be on his side for this harebrained scheme, but damned if that woman hadn't crawled into his system until he needed her like a scuba diver needed an oxygen tank.

He took a breath and swung himself onto the ten-inch-wide concrete ledge between his apartment and Rosie's fortress. Despite the buffeting wind's attempts to shove him into a twelve-storey swan dive, Sam quickly traversed the twenty feet and jumped down onto his neighbor's balcony.

No alarms shrieked. The motion sensors didn't klieg-light him. Scott didn't come running, gun drawn, neither did Kris. Guess Andy had earned that five grand he'd promised him for temporarily disabling the security system.

Of course there was some chance that someone on the ground had seen him and called the police to report a burglary in progress or a possible suicide. And there was still a chance Kris might come in, guns blazing. Or Kris had taken over the bedroom Rosie had first used and he'd find himself in the middle of a knock-down drag out. But he wasn't about to let little Miss Rosalinda Ramos slip away.

He paused outside the door to the bedroom she'd used before she'd moved in with him. The drapes had been drawn but there was only a glimmer of light leaking from the centre. Either she'd left the door open to the living room and was sitting out in the living room with Scott and Kris or she was already in bed. The image of her lying in bed, her hair tumbling over a pillow, or better yet draping over his chest, her lips slightly parted as she breathed, had his cock hardening.

Praying she wouldn't scream bloody murder when he entered—well, at least not when he entered the room, he thought with a grin—he slowly turned the latch. Locked. Good thing he'd brought his cell phone along with his lock-picking set. After ensuring Scott had taken down the security system for 1202, he set to work. It took him a few minutes before the lock clicked open.

To his disappointment, the bed was empty. But the bathroom light spilled down the hall and he heard a shower running and a woman muttering in Spanish. Even though she was cursing him, the sultry alto voice sent shivers down his spine and made his balls draw closer to his body. He shucked off his T-shirt and stepped out of his cargo pants. He reached down and grabbed a condom, then tossed his pants on a chair before he opened the bathroom door.

Chapter Twenty

Rosie dug her fingers into her scalp as she spread the shampoo through her hair. The showerheads surrounding her pounded her skin in an erotic caress—reminding her of just what she'd abandoned.

The last weeks had opened her eyes about her own sensuality, her own needs. She'd never be able to settle for the type of lover she'd had before. But would she find another lover who could bring her such satisfaction, such body-wracking orgasms, as Sam Watson?

She'd have to. She leaned her forehead against the cool tile. Even if she discovered that bitch Lee-Anne was lying about the threesome—but why would the woman lie about something like that? What would she gain?—she couldn't ignore that Sam had kept secrets from her.

A trickle of soap slid down her forehead and stung her eyes. Scrunching her eyes shut, she held her face up to one of the showerheads.

As she did, a hand clamped around her mouth and a large hard body pressed against her back, a warm steel rod sliding over the crack of her ass.

"Ssssh, don't be frightened, Rosebud. It's just me."

Once he dropped his hand from her mouth, she twisted, attempting to ignore his erection jutting into her ass but was unable to break his hold on her.

Arrogante desgraciado! "Let me go."

"Well, see, if I let you go, I'm willin' to bet you'd knee me in the crotch, and then I wouldn't get a chance to talk to you now, would I?"

He was like a pitbull with his teeth buried deep in her heart, refusing to let go as he tore it to shreds.

How had he managed to get in anyway? She'd locked her bedroom door, and the door to the balcony was similarly locked and the security system activated. Besides they were twelve stories up, it's not like he'd climbed the ledge between the two suites.

Somebody—Kris or Scott—must have let him in, the traitors. She could just picture him casually strolling past the guys, giving them a "*hey how are you*" good ol' boy smile—or worse, the I'm-about-to-get-me-some smile—while he walked into her bedroom as if it was an everyday occurrence.

Sighing, she slapped a hand against the tile and leaned away as far as he'd let her. The movement drew her gaze to their reflection in the mirror. He was buck naked, the soap from her hair sluicing over the rippling muscles of his chest, catching on the thick dark hair at the base of his...oh, man. All she could think of when she saw that thick shaft with its dusky head was how she wanted to go down on her knees and kiss it. Suck it the way she had in his shower just a couple hours ago... Oh, crap and a half! What type of woman was willing to go down on her knees for a cheating, lying scum like him?

She forced her eyes from the reflection of his cock and back to the white tile in front of her. "Go back to your place, Sam. We've got nothing left to say."

"Nope." He released her, but before she could move he planted his arms on either side of her, trapping her. "I'm not letting you get away from me until you've given me a fair hearing."

"Sam, I'm tired. I don't want to discuss this anymore."

"All right," he said. "I can think of somethin' else to do then." He picked up the bar of soap she'd been using and worked up a lather.

"Sam—I don't...I can't..."

His soap-covered hands cupped her breasts, his thumbs whisking over her nipples. She forced herself to grab his arms to stop him. If she didn't, she'd find herself giving in to him, letting him press her against the wall as he took her where she stood. Which was exactly what her betraying body wanted.

All her objections scrambled and fled when he sought out the juncture between her thighs and one long finger tickled and teased her clit, never quite touching it. He dipped his head and suckled one of her breasts, his teeth nipping at the hardened bud. Pleasure mixed with pain streaked from her breast to her pussy where his fingers continued their assault.

"Do you want me to stop?" he whispered, his breath hot against her ear.

Unable to say no, yet unable to verbally agree, she gave herself over to the sensations building deep within her. One finger, then another breached her, his thumb taking over the delicious torture outside. He drove her up until every muscle quivered with the need to release. But her brain was spinning too hard, processing Lee-Anne's proclamation along with Sam's penchant for domination and that butt plug he'd produced earlier.

"Come for me, baby. Let yourself go."

"I c-c-can't." She shook her head and opened her eyes to see a determined look on his face. He removed his hand from within her and lifted one of her legs behind the knee, pressing the head of his cock to her entrance. The bastard had already donned a condom, he was so frickin' sure of himself and her acquiescence.

"Do you want this inside you instead?"

Damn him! She should say no, but obviously her brain had no control over her mouth because she heard herself saying, "Yes."

He drove into her, trapping her between the cool tile and the warmth of his body.

Words tumbled from her lips, curses that changed to benedictions as the sensitive tissues of her pussy stretched then clamped around him, embracing him, milking him. His cock slid out until only his head remained inside her, then rammed deep until she swore she could feel him up as far as her belly button. Once. Twice.

On the third stroke, she shattered.

Her thighs and calf muscles shook when she finally lowered her legs to the shower stall floor. As if he sensed her exhaustion, Sam slipped a hand behind her knees and lifted her. He carried her from the shower. "Grab a towel, will you?"

He set her on the counter between the two sinks, and rested her against him while he wrapped her in thick terry towel she'd captured from the heated rack. Though she tried to protest that she needed to dry her hair properly, he grabbed another towel and rubbed it over her hair. Then he picked her up again and carried her into the bedroom.

"I didn't come in here to do this, you know?" he said as he lowered her onto the king-sized bed. After settling her in the middle, he slipped in beside her and pulled the covers over them both. "I meant when I said we need to talk. But then I saw you in the shower and... I did tell you how crazy you make me, didn't I?"

He tried to wrap an arm about her waist and pull her toward him but she pulled away and made a show of fluffing up the pillow as far away as she could get. She smoothed the covers over her, even tucked them in around her body as if they could offer her protection.

"You never did tell me how you got in here. And why *are* you here? I thought I'd made myself perfectly clear in the limo that we're through."

"I came in through the balcony."

She closed her jaw that had dropped open. "Are you insane?"

"It was pretty cool, actually. You know some women would be swept off their feet that a guy would put themselves in danger like that for them."

"And the rest of us would be calling the police to report an intruder." She couldn't decide which group she was in yet. "You're wasting your time, Sam. There's nothing left to say. I'll stay as your operative until Chad can assign someone else, but no more sex."

Way to stand up to him on that one, Rosalinda. Say no after you've fucked him.

"I'm not prepared to just walk away from what we've got,

Rosie."

Why was it so hard to believe him? Oh, yeah. Because Lee-Anne had taunted her about how Sam would be fucking her on the weekend. "Lee-Anne told me about your club, Sam. I know about the orgies and the racks and the floggers and the bull whips."

"Damn it, Thalia was right." She had a feeling she wasn't supposed to hear that part. "All right, I'll take you to the club tomorrow morning, so you can see for yourself that it's not as bad as you think."

"Not as bad as I think? It's a sex club, Sam."

"I seem to remember you tellin' me about how you and your high school sweetheart made out on the Staten Island Ferry. That's called exhibitionism. I saw that little vibrator you've got stuck in your suitcase. That's called auto-eroticism. Don't even try to tell me you weren't turned on when you were blindfolded and bound because my dick told me otherwise. And shall we discuss your penchant for fellatio?"

"I don't care if someone likes sex where people might see them. I understand the thrill factor in that." It was the ménage part that she didn't care for, not if the partners had agreed there'd be no others in the relationship. "This isn't about what goes on at the club, Sam. It's about how you didn't tell me about your membership in the club in the first place. That you deliberately withheld information that as team leader, I should have had in order to properly protect you. As I said in the car, it's about your lack of respect for my job."

"I'm sorry. I didn't tell you because I didn't think it was a viable lead. Club members are given a thorough background check as well as a psychological examination. I think you're a great team leader. I wasn't trying to disparage you that way, Rosie. Honest."

The wind deflated from her sails and she sagged back against the pillows, chewing her thumbnail. Despite her argument that it wasn't about what went on at the club, if she was honest with herself, it was a deal breaker. She wasn't one who could share someone she loved, share Sam, with another woman. Oh, crap, she loved him. How had that happened? And when?

She groaned. "Oh, God, Chad's a member too, isn't he? Lee-Anne said you were the premiere partner in threesomes. Please tell me you wouldn't have expected me to do him too."

Anger flared in the back of his eyes. "I could never share you with another man, Rosebud."

"Oh, I see. I'm not allowed to be with anyone else, but you can fuck whoever you want."

"What? I've n—"

"You said that as long as you were with me there were no others for either of us." She threw her hands into the air then grabbed the comforter before it slipped off her breasts. Suddenly she felt incredibly naked, incredibly vulnerable. "But what did you mean? As long I'm...what? In the same room? In the same building? Did you mean that as soon as I wasn't around, you could fuck whoever else gave you a boner? Do I need to go down to the clinic for an STD test?"

"I'd never cheat on you, Rosie. I haven't been to the club since we've been together, and if I do go again it'll be with you. And what's all this talk about me cheating on you? You of all people should know that I haven't been with anyone else. Either you, Andy, Scott or Kris have been with me every minute of the day."

"Lee-Anne told me all about your little threesome as part of her fiancé's initiation ritual. The two of you are going to fuck her at the same time in front of everyone, aren't you?"

His jaw locked together, Sam exhaled through his teeth. "Good investigative technique you've got there, sugar. Guilty until proven innocent. But thank you very much for believing that bimbo before askin' me. And no, I wasn't planning on being part of her plans. Ever."

Kicking the covers aside, he swung from the bed and paced. "Lee-Anne is a lying, scheming, social-climbing, cold-hearted, class-A b—". He stopped mid-stride and looked up, comprehension spreading over his face, blossoming into a wide grin. "That's what this is about, isn't it? It's not about the Rouge or me keeping secrets from you. It's not about your job or the stalker at all. You're jealous."

Rosie's jaw dropped. "Jealous? Of all the arrogant, self-serv—"

"Honey, whenever you think about that bitch, your eyes turn bright green."

"I am not jealous." Damn it, then why had she felt like pulling out her Glock and capping Lee-Anne right there in the middle of the party?

Sam's grin broadened. "Yeah, you are. That's why you're so pissed off." He leaned over the bed and touched his forefinger to her nose. "You, Rosalinda Maria Ramos, are jealous. It's driving you nuts thinking that I might sleep with someone else."

Damn it, he was right. When had she become such a possessive bitch? "It's not jealousy, Sam. It's disappointment. I trusted you. You gave me your word that while we were together it would just be us."

"Oh, baby. I don't know whether to turn you over my knee and spank you for not believing me or to get angry with you for not trusting me. But Lee-Anne Bennett lied to you. I am not going to the club on Saturday. I cancelled out weeks ago—you can check with Chad or Thalia, or even Cooper if you doubt me."

Intending to do just that, Rosie leaned back against the pillows. "Okay. Let's say Lee-Anne is lying. I'm not saying she is, but *if* she is, there's still the matter about your involvement with the club. Is it true that ménages are an accepted part of a member's initiation. Or was she lying about that too?"

He shook his head slowly as if trying to determine where she'd attack. "No-o, pretty much anything goes on initiation night as long as all the participants agree."

"So these women—the ones at the party tonight were members, right?—do they have sex with anyone they want? Anywhere they want? Or do you guys order them who to do claiming you're their masters?" *Do they parade around naked and shove their tits in your face? Do they wrap themselves around you like that Tawny woman who draped herself around Kris tonight?* How could she ever measure up to such surgical perfection? And yet the idea of the club wasn't as appalling as she'd first thought. As long as there were no other women in the club that looked like Tawny or Mandy.

"Ah." The mattress dipped when he resumed his place beside her. "You think I might be tempted by one of them?"

Hell yes. Even I found some of them attractive. "It's a reasonable concern."

He unclenched her fingers from the comforter and twined them with his. "I have not—" he lifted her hand to his mouth and kissed her knuckles, "—am not—" he kissed the inside of her wrist, "—and will not be with any other woman as long as you're in my life."

With a quick move, he tugged her until she lay on top of him. His hands cupping her behind, he leaned up and kissed the tip of her nose. "I will never cheat on you, Rosie. I promise."

She straddled him and sat up, feeling his cock twitch against her behind. "If I do find you've ever cheated on me, Samuel James Watson, I'll cut off your dick and...and..."

Sam snorted. "And what? Feed it to the lions at the zoo? Why not? Since Kris'll be tossing them my balls as a snack. That's what he threatened me with that first night you ran out of here and he and Scott were in the hall. Besides, Scott's already promised to shove my dick down my throat if I hurt you."

"Really? That's so sweet." She allowed herself a private grin. Looked like both Kris and Scott needed to get a big thank you. Maybe she could set one of them up on a date with Sandy.

"So are we good?" He arched his hips, his erection bumping into her ass. "'Cause I was thinking maybe it was time for some make-up sex."

She wiggled against him to add to his torment, and hers, but shook her head. "Not yet. I still have a few questions for you."

"Dang." He heaved a long suffering sigh. "All right, ask away."

"I guess my main question is why you hadn't told me about the club before? I mean, you had to know I would have heard something at the party tonight."

He shrugged "Never came up. I haven't been there in a while, and I wasn't planning on taking you there any time soon."

She let his evasion slide—maybe taking her there was one of those Freudian things that he'd avoided telling her but knew she'd find out...it was all too complicated. "If I do go to this place, would you expect me to have sex with you out in full view of everyone? Or with another guy at the same time as you?" Damn it, there had to be something wrong with her to be so intrigued by the idea. She thought back to the party, and all the leather pants and...Tawny's collar, and Sam's joke about not needing collars and leashes to get him hard. "You're not going to expect me to parade around on a leash like a dog, are you? Because I have to tell you, I'm not willing to debase myself like that."

"The Rouge isn't strictly for Dominants and subs," he explained patiently. "It can be whatever a member wants it to be. Yes, you'll see submissives being led around on a leash by their Dominant. Yes, you'll see public displays of sex, oral and otherwise. But some couples just use it as a way to get away from the kids, the in-laws, you know? They keep what goes on between them behind closed doors.

"And the singles, well, it gets all that will-she-or-won't-she out of the way. When a member walks in those big red front doors, it's a given they're looking for a partner for the night. They can hook up at the public areas just like any bar in D.C." He paused and she got the feeling he was censoring himself. So what wasn't he telling her this time? "There are a few rules but mainly as long as it follows the Safe, Sane and Consensual rule, anything goes."

"So there's all sorts of kinky stuff going on. Fetish stuff? Like guys who want to lick your feet? Or drip hot wax on you so they can get off?"

He nodded.

Images of Sam wearing the black leather chaps she'd seen him wearing when riding his motorcycle haunted her. What she'd give to see him wear them and nothing else. To feel the cool leather against the back of her thighs while he bent her over a table in front of Thalia or Cooper or... She exhaled slowly, pressing her thighs together to ease the throb in her pussy.

"How does someone even start a club like that? Do you put an ad in the paper or post something on the net saying 'Hey I like threesomes, let's meet, we'll do lunch then we can fuck each other senseless?' "

He snorted. "Not exactly."

Her curiosity got the better of her. "So how did you end up being a founding member?"

"Shit, you want the whole story?"

She nodded and rolled off him, snuggling under his arm.

"Okay." He scrubbed his hands across his face. "A little over eight years ago, while I was still with the FBI, the Bureau had been tracking a serial killer who targeted members of the scene. It started with two separate incidents in California. The killer shot his victims then ritually mutilated their bodies. When it made the news, police departments in Miami and Chicago realized they'd had similar cases over the previous couple of years. A couple months later, a group were killed in a dungeon scene in Houston that had the same markers. They had a general description of the suspect, and a credible tip that he'd headed here to D.C. The Porte didn't exist at that time, but there was a fairly active Dungeon scene. Back then there was no membership vetting as such. Anyone could show up at a couple of munches, talk the talk, get an invite to the scene and they'd be let in. No one knew your background or if you were there for the scene or to blackmail someone.

"I remember reading about it in the news. I was in college at the time so I didn't pay much attention, but I remember being surprised that someone hadn't been hurt before."

"These groups are usually pretty good at sniffing out anyone who might cause problems, and they let other groups know of any nutjobs to be wary of. Anyway, Chad was the Supervisory Special Agent in Charge; he decided to send a team in undercover in hopes that we'd find the killer before he struck again."

"How did they choose you? Or were you already part of the scene?"

"I wasn't into the scene at the time, but when you apply to the FBI they do a full background check and I guess they learned a few things from a couple old girlfriends. As you've already figured out, I was—am—more liberal about sex than most."

"I imagine going to a place where women are required to treat you like you're their lord and master was a huge sacrifice," she said drily.

Irritation radiated off him as he shoved himself off the bed and began pacing. "When you start off in the scene, even if you're a Dominant, especially if you're a Dominant, you undergo training to learn how to properly handle a sub. Not all clubs work that way, but this one did."

"Let me guess, Leash Handling 101? How about Flogging for Dummies?" He'd stopped pacing, his back turned to her, the muscles on his arms bulging as he tensed. She shook her head, "It was a joke. I'm sorry. I'll stop being such a smart ass. Go on."

"In order to be a good Master, you have to learn what you're asking of your slaves. So you start off as a sub."

She couldn't stop her laughter and quickly clamped her hand over her mouth at the mental picture of Sam wearing a leather dog collar while meekly being led around on a leash. More likely he'd rip the leash out of the person's hands and drag them behind him. "I'm sorry. I just can't picture you submitting to anyone."

After he'd shot her another look sideways, he continued, "I had to serve a mistress who acted as my mentor and taught me techniques that would help me be a good Dominant while—" he hesitated, swallowing hard, "—the other agent who volunteered pretended to be my girlfriend who wanted to learn how to be a good sub."

"And this was with the FBI's blessing?" What the hell type of report would have to be filed?

"We had to give reports to our supervisor regularly, yes."

"But no one in the club knew you were there as spies though?"

He scratched the long scar down the middle of his chest. "Cooper was in charge of the scene even back then, so he knew who we were, but he thought it best if no one else knew. Thalia is Chad's sister. At the time she knew he was sending someone in, but not exactly who. Since she was the most experienced Domme, we were assigned her as our trainer. I guess she suspected that we weren't who we said we were, but since there'd been a lot of emails flying around the scene about the murders, she wasn't sure if we were the killers or her brother's agents. So she questioned us."

Something about the way he said it told her the questioning was more than a standard interrogation. "What happened?"

There was a long silence but whether he was lost in his memories or trying to decide just how much information she could handle, she couldn't tell. He finally settled for "Unless you've been part of the scene, you couldn't understand, but there are techniques a Dom can use to scramble a sub's circuits so they'll not be able to dissemble. Neither of us broke cover but Thalia deduced enough to realize we're the good guys."

There was more to the story, but she didn't want him to lose momentum, so she decided to jump ahead. "Did you ever catch the killer?"

His hand drifted to the star-shaped bullet wound and his expression hardened. "Eventually."

Her breath drew in sharply. "Is that how you got shot?"

"Yeah." His pacing started again. "We'd met the guy before; he didn't set off any alarms with either of us. He was just a guy you'd wave to if you saw him washing his car in his driveway down the street. The other members said he'd been there quite a few times before we'd joined and taken part in a couple scenes. We figured that's when he was scoping out the place, picking his targets. Then when he felt secure that no one was suspicious of him, he came back."

"Makes sense. That's how I'd do it."

He continued as if he hadn't heard her. "Jill wasn't feeling good so we'd stopped in to beg out of a scene. We were leaving when he came in. I saw him raise his gun and went for my weapon but he shot me before I could get a round off." He took a deep breath, his eyes unfocusing as his memories took him back to that night. "Then he..." He cleared his throat. "He shot Jill."

Jill! The girl in the picture on his mantel.

His fingers curled into fists, the skin white over the knuckles before he stared at them and consciously flexed them. His voice hardened. "I got lucky. I walked out of the hospital with this." He gestured to his chest. "Jill died in my arms just as the paramedics arrived. And Thalia...well, I didn't shoot him fast enough to help her. She was already paralyzed by the time I killed the bastard."

Oh, Lord, so much pain he was carrying, so much guilt.

His eyes were bleak, his voice flat. "I failed them, Rosie. I was sent in to stop the killer, to protect them, and I failed."

She reached out then, stopping him mid-pace and dragged him toward her, then knelt on the bed and cupped his face in her hands. "It's not your fault, Sam."

"Yeah, it is." A dark look flickered behind his eyes. He rested his forehead against hers and swallowed hard. "Anyway, the other members kept me from going to pieces after Jill died. They visited me in the hospital, and when I got out, they phoned me if no one heard from me for a couple of days. Even though most of them were being harassed by the media and nutjobs that came out of the woodwork telling them they deserved to die. They looked after me, especially during the internal inquiry that ended up with Chad being fired. They were there when no one else was. Even Thalia kept in touch."

She patted the bed beside her. When he'd stretched out beside her, she lay her head on his chest, listening to the steady thump of his heart. Once his breathing slowed, she asked, "So how'd La Porte Rouge get started?"

"After the media finally got tired of their exposés of the group, and ruined more than one career, Cooper got together with some of the more influential club members. They decided to create an elite club. Somewhere they could feel safe from looky-loos and potential blackmailers, or whackjobs who wanted to cleanse the world of sinners like the guy who killed Jill. By that time I'd left the FBI, so Coop approached me about designing a proper security system for them. They made me a founding partner, which gave me enough money to start Hauberk. And it gave me access to influential clients who needed personal protection."

After a few minutes, Rosie shifted so she could look him in the eye. As much as she wanted to discuss the past, she knew she had to concentrate on protecting Sam in the here and now. "I know you trust the founding members, but isn't it possible that your stalker is one of the other members?"

"That was one of the first things I thought of. I went through the membership list, but frankly, there are days I trust most of the Rouge's members more than I do some of my own operatives."

Strange how he could find people into BDSM more trustworthy than her co-workers. But she supposed there had to be an incredible amount of trust to allow someone such power over your body and soul.

"How can you be sure?"

"The only way you can become a member of the Rouge is to be sponsored by a member who has been acquainted with you for at least two years. All initiates have to undergo a thorough psychological, medical and security screening before they're admitted. We don't allow anyone with a record, especially of drug use. We have to use a bit more leeway when it comes to abuse charges since sometimes society doesn't understand the games between scene players. Even once you're a member, we do regular background checks on everyone and all members have to pass semi-annual medical and psychological assessments to make sure no one's put at risk. And you have to sign a contract stating what your preferences are and agreeing to respect other members' choices."

"But surely there are personality clashes. People who object to something or other—either another member or perhaps a rule being enforced, or not being enforced?"

"The public areas are filmed so we can go back to the tapes to make an independent assessment. If the complaint occurs in a private area, then both the complainant and the accused must submit to another psychological assessment. And they'll have a hearing in front of the Board where they're required to answer any questions put to them. They fail any of the tests, they're out. No appeals."

"Sounds like it's tougher to be a member of the club than it is to be hired by Hauberk."

"It is."

She leaned back against him once more, and pondered the newly lit avenues of possibilities. "Has anyone been kicked out lately?"

"No. And there haven't been any complaints either."

She frowned. Damn it. Of course it wouldn't be that easy. "How many members are there?"

"Just over a hundred. But some of them don't live on the east coast, they keep a membership for when they're visiting."

Expensive if membership was a million bucks a pop. "How many founding members are there?"

"Ten now."

"Now?"

"There were twelve of us originally—but we've lost two in the last couple years."

She went still. "Lost? As in died?"

"You're thinking this may be related?" Sam shook his head. "It's not. Josh died in a plane crash about seven months ago, and Deidre died a couple years ago when some drunk ran a red light and T-boned her." He twined his fingers with hers, lifting them to his lips. "The stalker isn't a club member, Rosie. And even if they were, why stalk only me, why not Coop or one of the others?"

She huffed and untangled her fingers from his hold. "Even so, there could be a connection that you can't see because you're too close to the picture. I want to see the member files—I may be able to see something because I'm not familiar with them." Other than the ones she watched on the evening news or considered giving her vote. *Ay bendito!* No wonder they were so rabid about security.

He shook his head. "I don't want you at the club and Coop won't let the files leave. Send Andy to look at them. Please."

"I thought you said you trusted the members."

He sighed. "I do. But...I don't want you there."

She wanted to ask why, but considering the way she'd reacted about his membership, about the club's very existence, she could hardly fault him. He probably figured she'd freak out. But strangely, she found herself wanting an inside look— because that would allow her a peek into Sam Watson himself. A part she'd sensed he'd kept private, hidden, all along. And maybe she'd find out more about herself.

His cell phone chirruped and with a curse, he checked the caller ID and answered it. From his clipped speech and intense focus, it was important. Three minutes later he ended the call and cursed again.

"Colombia?"

"Yeah. Troy got word that the hostages have been moved again and we've lost track of them." He rubbed his hands over his face. "Look, don't tell Scott, all right? He's still blaming himself because he got out and they didn't."

They discussed the options for freeing the remaining hostages late into the night before she finally felt confident in returning to the original subject.

"I want to go to the club in the morning and see the files for myself, Sam."

He groaned. "No, Rosie. That's not gonna happen."

"It's a viable lead and as your team leader I have to check it out."

His hold on her tightened and his voice came out as a growl, "Then send Andy and Scott or Kris or someone. I don't want *you* there."

"Sam...either you trust these people or you don't. You can't have it both ways. And either way, I'm going to the club and take a look at those files."

"Has anyone ever told you, you're like a hound dog on a hare's trail?" He pinched the bridge of his nose. "All right, I'll take you over there in the morning myself and let you satisfy your curiosity about the place. But you're taking Andy as your own personal bodyguard and you do *not* leave the office area, you hear me?"

"All right, I'll take Andy with me, but will you please stop treating me like I'm breakable?"

How could she not realize that she wasn't immortal? He'd already lost one woman he loved, he couldn't bear to lose Rosie too.

He rested his forehead against the top of her head, pulling her against him. Somehow, when he wasn't looking, their relationship had become about more than just sex, more than just kink. She'd wrapped herself about his heart and he found himself enjoying being bound.

Ever since he'd lost Jill, he'd been careful in his choice of

169

dates. They had to be someone he couldn't imagine spending the rest of his life with, women who wanted him for his looks, his money, or simply for a good fuck. Women he could keep at a distance. Yet he'd totally ignored that rule with Rosie from the get-go.

Rosie was someone he could picture marrying, having kids with, taking home to his momma who would adore her almost as much as he...oh shit. As much as he loved her. He hadn't felt that way about anyone in years. Eight years.

She looked up at him, her eyes dark and promising in the dim light, her lips slightly parted in an open invitation to kiss her. Unable to pull away, he accepted her invitation. Her mouth was soft, her breath warm on his cheek, her body so tiny compared to his. His little rose, so beautiful, so fragrant, who opened only for him.

He was already hard when he tossed the sheet off her and rolled her onto her back. Her hair draped wildly over the pillow, a thundercloud around her creamy skin. Dipping his head, he took one puckered nipple into his mouth, reveling in the breathless gasp as she arched beneath him. He stole a look at her—her eyes were closed, her fingers clutching the pillow on either side of her head. If he were a painter, he'd paint her just like this and entitle it "Ecstasy Encaptured".

Releasing her breast, he laid a trail of kisses over her belly, then slid his hands beneath her hips and lifted her. She was already glistening as he dropped his head and tasted her again, reveled in her. Her hands clutched his head, holding him in place as she lifted higher, an attempt to control where and what his tongue touched. When she was swollen and gasping for breath, his cock harder than granite, his balls aching, he grabbed a condom he'd dropped on the night table and sheathed himself. Then he planted his arms on either side of her head, his cock nudging her entrance. Her lids slowly lifted she smiled at him, her eyes luminous, filled with such tenderness it sucked his breath from him.

She wrapped her legs about his waist as he entered her. He'd intended to make love to her slowly, gently, but as soon as her heat enveloped him he couldn't hold back and buried himself to the hilt. His hips pistoned, pounding into her until they were both gasping for air.

Her fingers wrapped around his biceps, her nails digging in as if she were holding onto him like a life preserver, half her body lifted off the mattress, clenching around him.

He dipped his head, caught her mouth with his, capturing her scream as she climaxed around him. The heat surrounding him, the pulses of her orgasm sent him over the edge.

Late in the night, as Rosie lay nestled against him, Sam smoothed her hair away from face, and wondered just how she'd managed to worm her way not only into his life, but into his heart.

Chapter Twenty-One

"Aside from the armed patrols with trained guard dogs patrolling the perimeter, there are security cameras installed on all access points and in all the public areas," Sam told Rosie as they walked up to the double front doors, Andy trailing behind. The brass door handle shone against the crimson wood panels. "There are alarms at various points in each wing as well as in each room. And you saw the manned security gates on the way in that require everyone to surrender any weapons and cell phones before they are allowed on the grounds."

She felt naked without her gun, but at least if they even took weapons from a founding member and Hauberk employees, everyone would be equally disarmed. Not that you needed a gun to kill. "Why take away people's cell phones?"

"Too many have cameras built in." Ah, possible blackmail. Right.

One of the front doors opened without a sound and a man about two inches shorter than Sam but with muscles to match blocked their way—she would have felt comfortable using him as a brick wall to stop a mortar attack.

"Good morning, Mr. Watson." He greeted Andy familiarly then turned to her and gave her a half-bow. "Miss Ramos, welcome to La Porte Rouge. Mrs. Harper is expecting you. Will you be showing Miss Ramos the way, Mr. Watson, or do you wish me to accompany her?"

"I'll take her myself, Igor."

She waited until the bouncer—she refused to think of him as a butler no matter what his tuxedo proclaimed—was out of earshot before murmuring, "Is Igor his real name?"

"Nah, his real name's Fred Fredriksson. Everyone just calls him Igor because he looks like a big Russian bear."

She followed him into the foyer. "You don't have to stay with me, Sam. Those hostages in Colombia need you more than I do."

Sam let out a soft exhalation before stroking the side of her neck. Though his face betrayed nothing, something flickered in his eyes but she couldn't tell if it was disappointment or downright frustration that she'd insisted on coming to the club instead of with him to the office.

"You go on to your meeting with Troy. I'll be fine. Besides, Andy will be here with me."

"I'm just going to make sure you're set up with Thalia, and then I'll leave you to your research. But remember, do not go out into the common areas, you're to stay in the office."

"Yes, Master."

"Rosie…"

She waved off his warning. "Yeah, yeah, I know. Just take me to the office. I won't wander where I'm not supposed to be."

Instead of taking her through the stained glass doors at the end of the vestibule where Igor had disappeared, Sam opened a plain white Colonial door to her left revealing a corridor done tastefully in muted tans with lots of polished wood trim.

The photographs mounted on the walls took Rosie's breath away. Black and white nudes—tasteful close ups of women's breasts, and a few other body parts that weren't as readily identifiable. She paused in front of one.

"That isn't a…is it?"

"A close-up of the head of a guy's dick?" Something rumbled deep in Sam's chest but when she looked at him she wasn't sure if it was a chuckle or a sound of embarrassment. "Yeah, Jocelyne's husband, Robert, is a professional photographer. Nobody'll own up to posing for him, so there's a bet that he used a macro lens on his own."

She continued walking down the hall then realized he

hadn't followed her.

"Come with me to the office, Rosie. Let Andy go through the files. Please."

She walked back to where he stood and put her hand on his chest, felt the strength in the muscles beneath her fingers. Remembered how they'd flexed over her the night before, how they'd glistened with sweat while he made love to her. Make-up sex with him was better than the best sex she'd ever had with anyone else. "It's safe here, Sam. You designed the security on this place yourself. You don't have to worry about me."

He fingered the thick gold choker he'd insisted she wear while she was at the club. A strange look—one of possessiveness, but also sadness—crossed his face before he dragged her against him, wrapping his arms about her.

She'd only had a momentary glance at the pendant dangling from the necklace before he'd clasped it around her neck. From what she had been able to see, one side held a circle divided into three swirling parts, but she hadn't had a chance to examine it close up. "Why's it so important I wear this anyway? Does it tell everyone else I'm your property or something?"

"It'll ensure no one else will bother you without my permission," he grunted. "Just make sure you don't take it off until you're off the grounds. In fact, don't take it off until you're back at the apartment, all right?"

"Let me guess, if I do, I'll find myself tied up in a dungeon?" She looked off to the side, thrown off by the heat that flooded her pussy at the image of being at Sam's mercy. "How about we go to your suite and you work off a little of your concern? I'll let you tie me up and blindfold me again."

Sam exhaled quietly and pinched the bridge of his nose for what had to be the fifth time that morning. "You're just trying to distract me again."

"Is it working?"

"Yeah." His gaze flicked to Andy before returning to set firmly on her. "But if I show you my suite, will you promise me you won't leave the office area once I leave?"

A sense of excitement, of expectation, set her heart racing.

"I promise."

He sighed again then relented and spoke to Andy, "Go tell Thalia we'll be there in a half hour or so."

Sam led her back into the atrium then through the double set of stained glass doors and down a wide hallway. More photographs hung on the cream colored walls—more nudes, most were men suckling women's breasts, but a few were of lips, male or female, licking or kissing engorged cocks. A number were of couples actually copulating. But on the whole she had to admit they were tastefully shot with soft focus and careful composition. Artistic, but not something she would feel comfortable hanging in her front room. However, she wouldn't object to displaying a few in her bedroom—as long as her mother never came to stay with her.

At the end of the hallway was another pair of stained glass doors. Sam swung them wide, revealing an ornate rotunda at least seventy feet in diameter with a dome rivaling the Capital Building. Three levels of balconies looked down upon a round dais ringed with vases of roses. More of the roses had been artfully woven through an archway over the dais, but they couldn't disguise a pair of leather cuffs dangling from the centre.

Sam dropped back, letting her explore the room on her own.

Numerous doors opened off each balcony, as well as three arched openings to more corridors. Craning her neck back, Rosie examined the erotic murals decorating the dome that soared high above.

On the far side was a smaller glass-enclosed grotto that jutted into a garden. From what she could see through the numerous plants, water trickled down a rough rock wall at the far side. Entranced, she wandered closer and discovered several benches and padded chairs, some with steel rings or hooks. She fingered one as she remembered Mandy saying she'd missed Sam's visits to the grotto. It disturbed her to think of Sam playing with other women here.

"Doms attach the subs' restraints to them depending upon what position they want them in," Sam said from the doorway. "Would you like to try them out?"

She could picture being tied up to the bench with Sam pounding into her from behind. As long as there was no one around. But yet...the idea of someone watching... Damn, her panties were wet at the idea. Would he think less of her if she said yes? But why should he, considering he founded this place?

Too confused to answer, she moved deeper into the room, following its curving path. At the end, she discovered a window that peered not to the outside, but to another room—from the looks of it, a communal shower.

"There are those who like to watch others bathing. Or being pleasured." Sam moved behind her and nodded to the far end of the shower room where there was an etched glass wall with holes at various heights. She didn't need an explanation for what would be done there. Especially with the leather kneeling pads in front of each hole.

Rubbing her arms, she eased past him and walked back to the rotunda. "Do you...do you use that room much?"

"The grotto?"

"No, the shower room." Why had she asked because she didn't want to know? She couldn't bear the thought of his cock being in another woman's mouth whether others watched or not.

"I prefer to see the woman pleasuring me, not hidden behind a wall. I prefer to use my own private suite."

She fingered the necklace, suddenly wanting to claim ownership of him the way he had of her. "Show me?"

Something flared in his eyes before he banked whatever emotion wanted out. He held out his hand, waiting for her to take it. When she did, he laced their fingers together. "Come with me."

He led her up the stairs to the top balcony, slowing so she could peer through the open doors. Some rooms were luxurious bedrooms not much different than Sam's penthouse. Some had X-shaped frames and strange benches, and one had a wrought iron cage like a jail. Almost all of them had mirrors or reflective metal on the walls or the ceilings. A whistling sound followed by a muffled cry came from behind one closed door.

Moving faster, as if he wanted to hurry her past that room, Sam turned right and headed down the last corridor. Bright sunlight streamed through the windows on the right hand side, overlooking a garden where many of the trees and shrubs had been planted to form private areas with more benches. In the centre of the garden was a Japanese style garden with an enclosed pavilion.

On the inner wall, the rooms were further apart than the ones ringing the rotunda. Gold Roman numerals had been mounted on the doors. X. IX. VIII. The founding members' personal suites. Beneath the numerals were stripes—but the colors varied for each member, some had only one or two colors, most had a half a dozen or more. "Is there a significance to the colors?"

"Yeah, it's a code that tells you what type of play the member is into."

She looked at the large V on the door where he'd stopped. So he was member number five of the dozen. The stripes on his door were a veritable rainbow. "What do they mean?"

"Black means I like to use a singletail or flogger," he growled. "Do you really want to know this about me?"

"I want to know everything about you." She ran a finger along the array. "Grey?"

His eyes hooded and he pressed her body until she was flat against the wall. He ground against her so she could feel his erection. "Grey means I'm into bondage—in my case that means tying other people up, not being tied up myself. The other colors mean I enjoy oral sex, I like to use clamps on my partner's nipples and various other body parts," his voice grew flatter with each recitation, "and I love fucking not only your pussy but your tight little rosebud ass." He captured her hand and flattened it over his fly. "And according to my partners, I've got a big cock."

He certainly did.

Her breasts heavy and aching, her nipples taut against his chest, it took an effort to raise her eyes to his. "How about we go inside?"

"You sure you wanna be alone in the private suite of a *loco pervertido*?"

"I'm sorry about calling you that but I was angry. You were right. I was jealous—I hated the thought that you might choose another woman over me."

His smug smile matched the sparkle in his eyes. "Shoot, you mean you don't think I'm a pervert anymore?"

"After what we've done already, if you're perverted then you're the pot and I'm the kettle."

Chuckling, Sam led her inside. The wider her eyes got, the lower her jaw dropped. "Holy crap."

She stopped in the middle of the room and did a complete circle standing in place, taking in the glass fronted cabinets on one wall, one displaying a variety of dildos and butt plugs, and another containing a variety of leather and latex hoods and ball gags.

He didn't say a word or move a muscle as she slowly wandered around the room.

Her palm skidded lightly over the padded leather bench that resembled a sawhorse. And again over the St. Andrew's cross that stood against the far wall. The purpose of the strange padded leather bench that resembled something from either her gynecologist's office or a sci fi medical bay wasn't as obvious.

If she'd seen this room before she'd agreed to his accord, she would have thought twice about knocking on his door that night. And here she'd thought she was so liberal, so open-minded. So daring for having gone down on Tony on the ferry. She was a rank amateur compared to Sam.

She leaned in to examine the erotic carvings on the end posts of the bed, her gaze lingering on the hooks and restraints mounted high and low. When she paused in front of the whips and floggers arranged in patterns worthy of a medieval castle, she touched the carved handle of one of the paddles mounted on the wall and flicked the ends of a leather flogger with one finger.

"When you did your training, did Thalia use a flogger or whip on you?" She still couldn't picture him allowing himself to be beaten.

"Yes. I'd never ask you—someone," he amended, "to do something I haven't done myself." He took a step closer. Then another until he was standing directly in front of her. "That's why I'm a stickler about safe words and slow words being used. And why our members have to fill out contracts with other members before they engage in any play so they'll know exactly what their partner will or won't allow."

"It sounds so...businesslike. So detached."

"Not between us, baby." He cupped her jaw with his palm. "I don't know what you do to me, but it's more than sex with you, Rosie. I've never wanted a woman as much as I want you. You don't want me to do anything just tell me no, and I'll stop."

She knew he would too. "Would you show me? Teach me?"

"Do you remember your safe word?"

"*Cochino.*"

Before she'd finished the word, he reached back to the door and flipped a switch to set the lock. When he spoke, his voice was a rough growl. "Take off your clothes, Princesa."

Thirty seconds later, she stood in the middle of the room completely naked, her clothes in a heap by her feet.

"See that bench?" He pointed to what looked like a wide padded sawhorse with leather restraints on each leg. "Lean over it. Face down."

"What is this thing?" Butterflies jumped in her stomach as she positioned herself against the cold surface. She'd never felt so exposed. Especially when he nudged her legs apart and fastened her wrists and ankles into the restraints. Considering the way her ass was high in the air, it didn't take much imagination. But was he going to fuck her pussy or her ass, the way he'd wanted to the night before?

He squatted down in front of her. "Why don't you tell me what you think it's for?"

"Um, so you can fuck me?"

A bright grin flashed across his face. "That's one side use, yes." His grin faded as he cupped her jaw in one hand. "But it's not fucking when I'm with you, Rosie. It never has been."

Did that mean he loved her?

He broke the connection by standing up and moving out of her line of sight. "As to your question, this is a spanking bench, Princesa. I use it when I have to punish my partner because they've disobeyed me." She jerked when he slapped first one ass cheek then the other.

"*¡Cabrón!*" Damn, her ass stung.

"That's for believing Lee-Anne instead of trusting me."

His hand struck twice more. He cooled the building heat by smoothing his palm over what had to be reddening flesh. It flared back up again when he trailed his fingers between thighs and tickled her clit. She squirmed at the building sensation. "That's for taking the butt plug out last night when you'd promised to leave it in."

The teasing stopped, and she cursed under her breath, but her pussy pulsed in anticipation of what might come next. It wasn't what she expected.

Instead of fucking her, Sam crouched down in front of her, holding up a paddle with holes in it. "I should be using this on you for what you put me through last night."

"But you're not?" *Please, don't use it, that sucker looked like it would hurt.*

He reached behind him and pulled out what looked like a whip. "I could also use a single tail—I'm a pretty good hand with them."

Closing her eyes, she shook her head. "No. No whips."

Multiple tails tickled the back of her thighs, were dragged across her back. She opened her eyes and discovered he'd moved behind her again.

"What about my flogger, Princesa? Would you like to meet one of them? I've got rabbit skin and deerskin and moose hide. Do you think you might like to try one of them today?"

"No. I don't think so." Her breath came in short gasps, partly because of her stomach being pressed into the bench, but partly from...damn, she wasn't afraid, she was excited.

His fingers played with her labia. "You're wet for me already. I think you like the idea of being punished. I think you find it exciting."

"You're crazy." Her hips arched against his touch, trying to force them over her pulsing bundle of nerves, needing him buried inside her.

"Yeah, you're ready for me, Princesa, and I've barely had to touch you."

She nearly screeched in frustration when he withdrew from her. A cupboard door opened. What was he doing? What was he planning?

"Last night you judged me guilty without a fair hearing. I think I deserve some recompense, don't you?"

"I take it I don't get a say in how you plan to extract your pound of flesh?"

He chuckled—but there was very little humor within it. "You gave up that right when you believed Lee-Anne instead of me."

Something cold and hard slid into her vagina. Damn it, a dildo? It started vibrating, teasing her deep inside, driving her crazy. She wanted him inside her, not some damned toy.

His breath was hot on her neck when he leaned over to whisper, "Don't forget, you can't come until I give you permission, Princesa."

Ah, fuck! Her breath came in short gasps as she tried to stop the building orgasm. "That's it, Princesa. Fight it until I get in there too."

Too?

Something ripped. Good! A condom, that meant she wouldn't have to wait long. But to her surprise, a cool liquid drizzled on the small of her back. She shivered. "That's cold."

"It won't be for long."

What was his game? His intentions became obvious seconds later when his fingers trailed the liquid around her anus. One finger breached her opening. Then another. Damn, it felt too good pressing the thin membrane against the vibrations.

Her hips thrust back as far as they could against the restraints, rotating into his impalement, her pussy throbbing. "Please, Sam, let me come."

"Not yet, baby." After he'd let her adjust, he removed his fingers. Moments later, the head of his cock butted against her rear entrance.

"*Necesito sentirte.* I need to feel you inside me when I come, Sam. Please."

She gasped, muttering both in English and Spanish as he

slowly entered her, letting her adjust to each thrust. By the time he was fully seated within her, every cell in both channels pulsed in a flame of need and desire.

Groaning, he grabbed her hips in his hands and withdrew partway. "Never doubt me again, Rosie." He surged back in, then set up a steady rhythm that had her pushing against him as much as she could, meeting him thrust for thrust.

She'd never thought being tied into place, totally captive to another's attention could be so erotic. He leaned over her and nibbled her neck, his chest resting lightly on her back. She shivered as his breath heated her neck. He nipped and sucked lightly, using his weight to emphasize his control over her, his protection of her.

"Do you feel me, Rosie? How much I desire you? How much I need you?" He rocked his hips, burying himself to the hilt then held still. "Do you feel my cock throbbing inside you?"

"Yes." She could feel his heart beating against her back and the synchronous beat in the bulbous head of his cock deep within.

"Do you have any idea of what you look like? How beautiful you are?"

No. But when he said it, she felt beautiful. "I've never given myself over to any other man like this before."

He laid his cheek against her shoulder, his body trembling, the vibrator inside her exciting both of them. "I never want you to give yourself over to any other man except me. Ever."

His whole body stiffened. With a roar he pulled back and plunged deep, then pulled back again and pistoned his hips in a frantic motion. His heavy testicles slapped against her clit, arousing her to a state of frenzy. The muscles in his forearms corded as he fought himself for control.

Her body trembling as she gasped for breath, she tightened her muscles around his cock, caressing him in the only way she could. He reached down with one hand and stroked her overly sensitive clit.

"Come for me, Rosie. Come with me."

At the touch, both her ass and her pussy clutched at him, pulling him deeper than he'd yet been. With a deep, almost primal groan, Sam shuddered as together they found their release.

He briefly sagged over her, his breath harsh in her ear. "Did you learn your lesson, Princesa?"

She heard the chuckle in his admonition.

"If the lesson...was being bad...results in a great orgasm," she panted, the aftershocks continuing to pulse both in him and in her, until she felt ready to orgasm again. "Then yeah, I guess I did."

"Smart ass."

To her regret, he slid from her. He pressed a kiss to each buttock as he retrieved the vibrator, leaving her totally bereft at the lack of sensation. "Pretty ass. Talented ass. I'll be back to release you in a minute."

It wasn't until he zipped his fly that she realized that while she'd been completely naked, he'd never undressed. He padded away, and she heard water running in what must have been an ensuite bathroom before he returned. To her surprise instead of undoing her restraints, he first cleaned the oil from her back.

Once he was satisfied she was clean, he released her and handed her her clothes. "I've got to go meet Troy." The look in his eyes was filled with both passion and concern. "Are you sure you won't come with me?"

"No, Sam. I'll be fine here."

He took her hand in his as they headed for the door, but paused with his hand on the doorknob. "Are you all right? I didn't take very long to prepare you..."

"I'm fine, Sam." She exhaled slowly and mentally picked up the spoon to eat the plateful of crow that hovered between them. "I'm sorry for not believing you right off last night. And I'm sorry if I came off like a prude about the club. I wasn't trying to judge you. Everything between us has moved so fast. I just got...scared. You know?"

Emotion flared in his eyes. "I'm not trying to pressure you, but I want to explore what we have together. I want more. I want..."

...*you forever*, she wanted him to say. The same way she wanted to say I trust you and would let you do anything you

want. The way she wanted to say I'm falling in love with you.
      But he didn't say it.
      And neither did she.

Chapter Twenty-Two

Without another word, Sam led her back through the halls and back to the front door. Where they'd turned right to the small waiting room before, this time he opened the door to a bright airy administrative office filled with greenery. Andy had commandeered a computer at one of the desks and was surfing the net from what she could see.

Crossing the room to a corner office overlooking the front yard, Sam rapped his knuckles on its half open door. "Thalia?"

"Samuel, come on in. And Rosie, welcome to La Porte Rouge." Thalia closed a file and smiled.

He kissed Thalia on the cheek and murmured, "Something's come up at the office so I can't stay. You'll make sure Rosie's given access to the files, but stays in the office, right?" At Thalia's soft assurance, Sam returned to Rosie's side and drew the back of his fingers along her jaw. "Give me a call when you're done—I'll come pick you up."

"You don't have to. Just have Kris or someone pick us up."

His hand dropped to his side. "I mean it, Rosie. Give me a call. I'll pick you up. And remember, stay here with Thalia." With a glance back at Thalia, and a nod, he closed the door behind him. She heard him talking with Andy, probably giving him strict instructions to stick to her side.

Thalia gestured toward a wing chair. "Come sit down, Rosie. Make yourself comfortable."

"Thank you for taking the time to help me with the files. I know you're busy."

"It's nothing that can't wait." Thalia tilted her head,

intelligent grey eyes assessing her as if they could hear her thoughts. "Now I understand you wish to look at the members' files, but is there anything you'd like to ask me first? About the club? About Sam?"

There were a million questions whizzing through her thoughts—since she liked being tied up did that make her submissive? Did being a submissive mean she'd have to be June Cleaver when she wasn't in the office? What else should she expect Sam to do to her? To expect of her? What type of a future would they have if she didn't want to join his club? Was this a phase that he might grow tired of? Was he still a member out of loyalty to those who had helped him all those years ago? Would Sam dump her if she wouldn't agree to a ménage? Or would he have one anyway, just not with her?

But none managed to make it past her mouth.

After a moment's silence, Thalia asked, "How long have you and Sam been dating, Rosie?"

"Just under a month." Though it felt longer. Yet in that time she'd revealed things to Sam, shown him parts of herself she hadn't even known existed. "I've known him for two years though."

Thalia leaned back and laced her fingers together, steepling her index fingers. "Forgive me if I'm getting too personal, but Sam's a dear friend of mine. I'm concerned that perhaps he hasn't been completely honest with you about his needs. Do you understand about his lifestyle and his association with the club?"

"He's told me about how he became a member. And I know that you were his mentor. He said that you taught him how to be a," she swallowed, "Dominant."

"My dear girl, Sam needed very little training from me. He is a natural Dom." She tilted her head. "Is there anything you'd like to ask me? Woman to woman?"

"I suppose I'm not comfortable with the idea that a woman—especially in this day and age—would allow herself to be subservient to a man. I mean, I get some of it—like being bound, even spanked, that's..." Spectacular? Mind-blowing? "...fun. But why would a woman allow someone to drag her around on a leash and find it arousing."

Why did she sometimes get the feeling Sam was holding back? That there were more secrets than just his membership at the club. But since she didn't know Thalia, or her relationship with Sam, she didn't ask that.

Thalia's fingers tapped together twice. "Good. He *has* introduced you to the lifestyle, at least parts of it. Tell me, were you were aroused by it? Is that what's scaring you—finding that you want to give up control to him."

Rosie stared at her hands and took a deep breath before meeting Thalia's gaze. "Why do I get so turned on by being spanked? I was raised to believe that people who were into such activities were mentally ill. Does liking a little pain make me a masochist? Or Sam a sadist? Does liking being bound mean I'm submissive?" Once the questions started, it was like someone had opened up a gate at a horse race. "Last night Sam said he was a Dominant. Does that mean he'll expect me to get on my hands and knees and crawl like a dog, or be his footstool? Because I can't see myself doing that."

A grimace flickered across Thalia's face. "That's been disproven you know—that being a follower of the BDSM lifestyle is a mental illness? Psychiatrists these days are much more open to the lifestyle than they were. And being a Dominant doesn't mean Sam is a sadist any more than you being a submissive, if you are a submissive, means you're a masochist.

"What you have to realize, Rosie," Thalia continued, "is that submission to Sam doesn't mean he wants a slave to use as furniture or a convenient cunt. To him it's much more personal. It's part of his nature that he needs you to rely on him in order to feel useful. He wants to protect you and provide for you. He will take as much pleasure from caring for you as he will give you."

"But I've worked so hard to prove myself independent. I don't want to be 'taken care of'."

Thalia waved her hand in annoyance. "Being a submissive doesn't mean you have to quit your job and be a nineteen fifties housewife. Many of our submissives are lawyers and doctors, male and female, professional people. They're people who are responsible for others all day long. But when they come through the doors of La Porte Rouge, they can shrug off their burdens and let someone else be in charge for a change.

"And Dominants like Sam...well, Sam's in a category all his own. He belongs in medieval times with a great big warhorse and battle-scarred armor. He's a warrior, Rosie. He needs to protect people. And he needs to know they'll let him protect them." Thalia patted the arms of her wheelchair. "Did Sam tell you how I ended up in this thing?"

"He said you were shot by a serial killer."

Thalia grimaced and nodded. "David Vandeburger. I wouldn't be here if it hadn't been for Sam that night. When David came in, he didn't say a word. He'd shot Sam before I realized he had a gun. I could have helped them, but I didn't. I panicked and ran. I was halfway down the hall when David shot me the first time. Then, even though he was shot, and had lost so much blood already, Sam dragged himself into the hallway and killed the bastard. If he hadn't, I would be dead too." Thalia's eyes were brimming when she looked away. "I was a coward, Rosie. I ran away when I might have been able to save Jill. Yet Sam saved me anyway. I'll never be able to repay him. Never."

Rosie leaned across the desk and laid her hand over Thalia's, squeezing it lightly. "You weren't a coward, Thalia. You did what you had to in order to survive. As FBI agents, Sam and Jill'd had training to deal with intense situations like that. You can't blame yourself for being human."

"That's what everyone tells me. But I still feel like I failed them both." Thalia closed her eyes, her hands absently smoothing the folds of her skirt over her knees. "Sam was devastated by Jill's death. He quit the FBI even before they released him from the hospital. We were all worried he might try to kill himself afterwards.

"As I said, he was devastated. He and Jill had fallen in love so quickly." Thalia took a deep breath. "They'd never dated or anything before they were teamed up for the assignment but I'd never seen a couple so perfect for each other. They'd only come in that night to tell me they were getting married on the weekend and so wouldn't be available for a scene I'd planned with a new trainee."

If someone had hit Rosie in the stomach with a breeze

block, the air couldn't have whooshed from her any quicker. She closed her eyes as her world whirled right along with her stomach. She'd seen the picture of him looking adoringly at Jill, but she'd never imagined he'd planned on marrying her.

Thalia took a few breaths to gather herself again. When she looked up and met Rosie's gaze, her eyes were clear and dry. "Sam was absolutely magnificent that day, Rosie. He saved my life; he saved a dozen other members who were there that night. People that David could have killed if he hadn't been stopped. But Sam still blames himself for Jill's death. And he blames himself for me being in this chair—even though I was the coward."

"You can't blame yourself because someone else was a sociopathic killer." And she'd have exactly the same talk with Sam. No wonder he had been so stubborn about her not taking a bullet for him.

"So you can see why it's important to me to see Sam finally happy. I'd hate to see you hurt him because you're too small minded to accept his sexual needs."

"I don't want to hurt him." *Besides, I'd be the one with the broken heart at the end, while Sam could come here to salve his wounds. I'd have to quit Hauberk and move far away.* "But this club, what it involves. I'm not sure if I can accept some parts of it."

"Sam's been using the club as a crutch, Rosie. You're exactly what he needs to help him move on. We're reminders of everything he's lost. But even without the club, he cannot deny his sexuality." Thalia narrowed her eyes. "What you don't realize, my dear, is that as Sam's partner, you are the one with the control, with the power. And if you're an *alpha* submissive, or even a possible switch as I suspect you are, there will be times when you can take charge and dominate him."

Rosie shook her head with a small laugh. "I don't think anyone could ever dominate Sam Watson. He's a force unto himself."

"I think you underestimate your power over him." Thalia leaned over and patted her hand, her sadness falling off her shoulders. "Sam needs to be challenged. He needs to learn to let his shields down again, to let someone get close to him. You're already halfway there, if not more. You'd keep him on his toes, especially if you tie him up and flog him one day—which, by the way, is something he quite enjoys even though he'll deny it if you ask."

"You're kidding?" The idea of having Sam tied up on the bed, or the bench he'd just tied her to, had her cream flowing. If she'd been wearing panties, they'd be clinging to her by now.

"No, I'm quite serious. Don't you think he gets tired of being responsible for everyone else on occasion?" Thalia sat back in her chair and waited while Rosie processed the image, tried to figure out how she could ever convince Sam to let her tie him up. "I'm hoping that in you, he's found a life partner. But you need to be open to learning about what Sam needs to be true to his nature. Because Sam needs someone who will not only let him take care of them but will take care of him. Heaven knows he deserves it."

After a moment, she held up a key. "And now I've done my little quack therapy for today and given you something to think about, how about I show you those files?"

Chapter Twenty-Three

The day at the club had opened Rosie's eyes to Sam's world. It was definitely not within the realm of anything she'd experienced before.

She'd spent the first part of the morning holed up in Thalia's office with Andy, searching through the members' files for a possible suspect. Then Thalia had suggested she visit the security office, telling her the guards might have more up-to-date scuttlebutt on any bad feelings between members. While the retired army major in charge of the detail talked, she'd found her eyes drifting to the security cameras monitoring the public areas. One screen displayed two men pleasuring each other, and a second showed a room that looked like a doctor's office with a man lying on an examination table. His cock stiffened as soon as the "nurse" snapped on a pair of latex gloves. A third monitor displayed a woman giving a man a blowjob while another man fucked her from behind.

It was like driving past a car accident—she didn't want to watch, but she couldn't stop herself.

She hadn't noticed that the chief of security left her alone in his office. She hadn't noticed Thalia join her. But she had noticed that she couldn't stop watching. Eventually she realized her hand was buried between her legs, pressing against her clit, her hips arching to increase the pressure.

And then the man from behind spanked the woman's behind, leaving a bright red handprint. Once. Twice. She didn't need the sound to be turned up to know the woman came when he spanked her a third time. Her hands frantically clutching at the hips of the man in front of her, the woman's whole body shuddered and jerked.

"Do you want to see more?" Thalia had asked. "I can teach you what excites Sam. Or perhaps you just wish to learn more about your own sexuality, understand your own triggers to arousal?"

At Rosie's flustered nod, they'd left the security office through a door on the opposite wall instead of going back through the office area. Thalia wheeled through the Rotunda, slowing so Rosie could observe a Master and his slave who knelt on the dais in front of him, pointing to the way the slave presented herself. She slowed again to watch a Domme training her sub in the grotto, each time murmuring quiet notes of instruction to Rosie before moving on.

By the time Sam had picked her up that afternoon, she'd been hornier than a mountain goat and they'd spent the evening exploring her boundaries. Once he was safely ensconced in his office the next day, she'd phoned Thalia and gone back for private lessons. As she had the day after that. And the next day too. She'd learned where a sub should look, and where they shouldn't, of how she should stand, how to kneel, tilting her pelvis to expose her pussy. But the main emphasis of Thalia's lessons was centered on letting go of her inhibitions. Of embracing her body and her sexuality. Of granting herself permission to embrace the pleasure instead of repressing her arousal.

On the fifth day, Thalia opened a cabinet, revealing a dozen different styles of floggers. "As Sam's partner, you must be trained in how to use one of these."

Unable to visualize Sam ever submitting himself to a flogger, Rosie nodded and listened as Thalia explained the different types of devices—rabbit skin to moose hide, riding crop to bullwhip. Thalia then positioned a velour pillow on a strangely shaped bench that vaguely reminded Rosie of the one in Sam's private suite. "Try imagining the place you want to hit before you strike. The tails will leave a track so you can see how accurate you are."

It was tougher than Rosie had thought it would be. After she'd finally mastered the placement of her blows, Thalia called Spencer into the suite and ordered him to strip. Without saying a word, he'd obeyed his mistress, revealing a well-toned body with an elaborate ivy tattoo that trailed from his shoulder, down his chest and around his hip, its end embedded in the deep cleft between his buttocks. He knelt in the middle of the room, his thighs wide apart, his eyes discreetly lowered, his hands clasped behind his back.

"Spencer," Thalia had said. "I understand you watched Mistress Grace and her sub at play earlier this morning."

"Yes, My Lady."

Thalia proceeded to question Spencer, determining that although he hadn't specifically disobeyed her, he had allowed the sub to fondle him at Grace's instructions.

"You'd only said I mustn't pleasure myself, my lady. And as you instructed, I didn't come," Spencer had said proudly.

"But you found pleasure in it. And thus went against my instructions. For that, you will receive twenty stripes of the flogger. And I think I shall enforce your chastity." Thalia handed him a strange looking device of acrylic and metal and ordered him to attach it.

Rosie watched, half fascinated half horrified as Spencer wrapped the acrylic ring around his scrotum, cinching it so his balls drew away from his body, then enclosed his cock within the metal chamber that would prevent him from having an erection.

Once Thalia gave her approval to his effort, Spencer bent over the angled bench that left him with his ass high in the air, and his head nearly to the floor, waiting passively as Thalia locked him in place. She then turned to Rosie and gestured to the flogger she'd been using. "Mistress Rosalinda will be administering your punishment today, Spencer."

Rosie started to protest but Thalia shook her head.

"You must practice, Rosie. In a controlled environment."

If it was possible for Spencer to look even prouder in that position, he did. "I would be honored to receive your punishment, Mistress Rosalinda."

Gripping the braided handle, she'd brought it down across his buttocks and cringed at the sharp sound and the red trails that bloomed on his skin.

"Thank you, Mistress," Spencer whispered. The bench had been designed with an opening for his cock, and she could see through the hole that his cock had inflated and was straining against its metal bonds. The device must be causing him even more pain than she was with her flogger.

By the tenth strike, Spencer's ass was bright red and drops of liquid quivered on the end of his cock. And Rosie was so turned on, she was having trouble breathing. She looked at Thalia in confusion. "I have to go..."

"Don't be embarrassed, Rosie," Thalia said quietly. She took the flogger from Rosie's hand, allowing Rosie to flee the room and seek the solitude of the office once more.

While she wasn't prepared to be publicly paraded through the halls as Sam's submissive, maybe it was time for her to experience more of what Sam might require of her.

Pity she couldn't go back to Sam's private suite and sneak out a flogger. Maybe Thalia might give her one. Except Sam would not recognize it and ask where she'd got it. And then she'd have to admit she'd left the office area that first day, and her subsequent visits.

But Sam had a secret store of things at home, didn't he? That night he'd blindfolded her, he'd come up with leather restraints and what she realized now was probably the tails of a flogger. And before the party, he'd produced that butt plug and harness. So there had to be some sort of hidden cabinet somewhere in the apartment.

Ideas flitting through her mind, she called the office and left a message with Sandy that she was heading out to do some shopping.

After hitting a mall, and a few other specialty stores, she dropped her bags in Sam's condo, then checked in with Scott, snagging the blueprints to Sam's apartment.

It took her fifteen minutes studying the blueprints to notice how Sam's apartment didn't quite align with the walls in 1202. It took her another forty-five minutes to find the hidden panel concealing the keypad in the closet, and thirty more to crack the code to open the door.

The heavy bulletproof door swung open soundlessly revealing not just a cabinet, but an entire room.

"Holy crap."

About the size of his bathroom, the safe room was equipped with everything needed to last out an attack including a bed that folded into the wall, a toilet and phone which was probably hooked up to a second line separate from the main one. But Sam had added a few extra touches, like a bench exactly the same as the one Spencer had been restrained on in Thalia's suite. Hooks gleamed from various heights on the opposite wall and even on the ceiling. Several cabinets had been built in, but there were no floggers or whips in artful arrangements the way they had been in Sam's private suite. Damn it, surely he had something here he could use.

The first cabinet held clothing. Leather pants with laces and zippers that extended all the way around the crotch, a variety of vests, some leather, some black satin. There were laced jock straps, harnesses and belts. She opened the first drawer of the second cabinet, revealing various sized dildos and butt plugs. The two drawers below contained numerous ball gags and bits, cock rings, leashes, and hoods both full masks and half masks, and all types of restraints. The fourth drawer contained the motherlode—a collection of floggers, some furry—rabbit skin, others of soft leather.

Perfect.

Chapter Twenty-Four

Sam worried when it was Scott who met them by the garage elevator instead of Rosie. Where was she? She'd put in a cursory appearance at the office in the morning before disappearing for nearly five hours. Which was lucky for him because it had given him a chance to duck out of the office to arrange his surprise. Hopefully Kris would keep his mouth shut about that trip.

"Rosie isn't upset about something, is she?" he asked Scott as they rode the elevator to the top floor.

Scott shrugged. "No, she seemed fine when she got back this afternoon."

"Do you know what she'd been doing?"

"Shopping from the looks of the bags she was carrying." He grinned. "One of the bags was from Victoria's Secret. Looks like she's got plans for the night. Oh, and she grabbed the floor plans to your place, but she didn't seem to be worried about anything. Why?"

He unlocked the door to Sam's penthouse, a sure sign that Rosie was inside since Scott hadn't felt it necessary to check it out first.

Sam closed the door and locked it, listening as Scott's footsteps retreated down the hall. "Rosebud? You here?"

"I'm right here. Master."

"Holy fuck," he breathed as Rosie sashayed toward him wearing only a fire-engine red leather bustier and a matching pair of stilettos. And here he'd been expecting trouble. This type of trouble he'd take on any day.

"I take it I meet with your approval. Master?" She stopped in front of him and lowered her eyes, her hands demurely clasped behind her back.

Just like a properly taught submissive. Goddamn, if Rosie had managed to sneak past Andy and watch some scenes at the club that day, he was going to strangle them both. Unless Thalia had given Rosie private lessons in her office. His blood pressure lowered slightly.

"Rosie? You want to tell me what's goin' on?"

Rosie kept her eyes trained on her toes as she answered, "I would like to learn to be a good submissive, Master. Will you train me?"

From the immediate hard-on he got, his cock definitely approved of the plan. Did she have any idea what she was asking of him? What he might ask of her?

"Do you mean for the night? Or for the long haul?"

She looked down, frowning, before answering slowly, "Which would you prefer? Master?"

He didn't want her just as a playmate for the night. He wanted this—her—for a lot longer. Except that would put her in danger from whatever psycho was stalking him. She was probably already in danger.

Maybe there was a way... He was getting ahead of himself anyway. She might not like what he planned for her. For tonight, it would be a game he'd play, then they could discuss the scene and decide if she wanted to take further or not.

"I don't expect you to commit to the lifestyle based on one night. It takes a lot of discussion to make that commitment, Rosie. And we've barely scratched the surface. Let's see if you feel the same way at the end of the night."

"Yes, Master." A question flickered across her brow. "Except if we did it long term, would I have to call you Master at work?"

He slid an arm behind her, flattened his hand over the small of her back as he pulled her hard against him. "I'd never do anything to embarrass you at work. I'll only ask that you call me Master during our scene play. And we'll save the scenes for special times—you don't always need to be the sub. The rest of the time we can just be Rosie and Sam."

Her body relaxed against him and the playful look returned to her eyes.

"But," he continued, "should we decide to continue your training, I reserve the right to start a scene whenever and wherever I choose. And that's not always going to be here in the privacy of the apartment. I won't call upon you at work, but one day when we're out with friends who may not know about our agreement, or when we're at a party, or walkin' down the Mall, I will call you Princesa and you will obey me, no questions asked."

She tilted her head, tossing her hair over her shoulder. "So we could be sitting at a restaurant, and if you told me to slide under the table and go down on you, I'd have to or you'd punish me. Have I got that right?"

"Exactly."

"I think I can handle that. I've always been a bit of an exhibitionist." When she unzipped his pants and slid her hand inside to stroke his cock, he leaned his head against the wall, struggling to maintain control. "It's nice to know you—Christ, that feels good, baby—won't have any problems with that little scenario."

She flicked her thumb over the head of his cock, smearing a dab of pre-come over it, before removing her hand. "What do you wish for your slave to do for you first, *Master?*"

Pity she didn't still have her hand wrapped around his cock when she'd called him that. She would have felt it throbbing even more than it already was.

He held her by the shoulders, letting her feel his strength. Then once she got his message to stay in place, he strolled around her, slowing for a prolonged appreciation of her backside.

"You're not my slave, Rosie." Though Jill had preferred complete domination and referred to herself as his slave, he'd never believed in the Total Power Exchange of the Master/slave relationship.

He forced himself to concentrate. "With me as your Dom, you'll always have a choice. And by choosing to follow my instructions, you'll prove your obedience and loyalty."

"Just so you know—while I'm up for almost anything, I do have limits."

"So do I. That's why you have your safe word. And before we begin I'll give you a list of things that you'll agree or disagree to do or allow to be done. We'll write up a contract so there are no misunderstandings."

"I've already filled one out—it's on your desk."

Thalia had to be behind tonight's adventure. Tomorrow, he was definitely going to pay a visit to his former mentor and find out just what had happened after he'd left Rosie at the club that day.

He wrapped his arms around her, drew her against him, and rubbed her back. Her heart was racing but whether from fear or excitement he couldn't tell. "Trust me, Rosebud, I'll never do anything you don't want to do. Everything will be safe, sane and consensual. And we'll take it slow. I'm not going to expect you to understand and do everything that I will ask of you, but I hope you'll trust me enough to at least try."

"I know." She rested her head on his chest. "So how do we start?"

"You still wanna use *cochino* as your safe word?"

She nodded. "It's as good as any."

"What's the proper way to respond?" he gently reminded her.

"Oh. Yes, *Master.*"

"Once we start tonight's scene, you will do what I tell you to do with no argument. If I tell you to crawl across the floor, you'll crawl. Willingly. If I ordered you to answer the door naked, you would do it with a smile." When she frowned, he amended. "We've already established I won't demand anything of you around your co-workers, right? So I wouldn't ask you to do anything like that around Andy or Scott, anyone. The point is, if I give you an order, you will obey me without question. And when it is time for your punishments, you will offer your pretty ass up to me with a smile and then you'll thank me afterwards."

"Yes, Master." A hint of a smile crossed her lips before she bowed her head again.

What was she so pleased about? That he'd agreed to her

terms? Or...oh, who knew? Whatever man could figure out the inner workings of a woman's head deserved a Nobel Peace Prize. Time to regain control, because he had a feeling he'd just lost it.

"Just so you're warned, if you disrespect me or ignore an instruction tonight, I will spank you."

Did her eyes just widen? Yeah, her pupils were dilating and her breath was shallowing. Son of a gun. So punishments may actually be a reward to her.

He let his smile broaden. "And if you're very disobedient, I will flog you. Maybe you'll even beg me to punish you."

"Yes, Master."

Minx. "By the way, I should warn you. By agreeing to my terms tonight, you're giving me permission to fuck that beautiful rosebud ass of yours again."

She stuck one hand on her hip and struck a pose, her head tilted to one side. "Do you know what I think? I think you're deliberately trying to scare me. But I'm still here, aren't I?"

"Yeah," he said softly, the predatory animal hidden deep inside leaping to the surface. Miss Rosalinda Maria Ramos's reaction couldn't have pleased him, or challenged him, more. "Yeah, you are. Now go into the kitchen, Princesa, and fetch me a beer."

To his surprise, she readily agreed. "Yes, Master."

She returned less than thirty seconds later, Heineken opened and poured into a glass. He sat down on the couch. "Whenever we're in a room together, you will always stay lower than me." Considering her height compared to his, that wouldn't be difficult.

She surprised him again when, instead of sitting on the couch beside him, she knelt at his feet in a supplicant position as if she'd practiced for days. Maybe she had. A niggling feeling started in his chest, wormed through his intestines. Where had she seen someone in this position if she'd stayed in the office? Unless Thalia brought someone into the office to demonstrate. Just what other demonstrations had Thalia provided?

"Take off the bustier."

"Yes, Master." He was rather disappointed that she didn't fight him, didn't yell about how he was from the dark ages.

Push her, see what she might tell you. Because she's obviously trying to push you...somewhere. But where?

With a smile suggestive of more, she undid the laces of the bustier and let it drop on the floor. Her hair draped over her shoulders, the curls pointing toward the dark brown buds of her nipples. Beautiful. Luscious. His.

How far should he test her limits? Start with something simple.

"Go stand in front of the window, facing out."

Her glance darted toward the picture window and the first sign of hesitation appeared. "But the people in the condo on the other side of the street might be able to see that I'm bare-assed naked."

"That's the point."

He wouldn't tell her that he knew exactly who would be watching, or how they reciprocated for him.

He waited until she was in position before saying, "And questioning me has earned you your first punishment."

"Cr—" She started to protest then stopped. She straightened and gave him a regal nod. "Yes, Master. Sorry, Master."

Like hell she was sorry. She looked like the proverbial cat with canary feathers stickin' out of her mouth. But what was her game?

"I'm sorry for speaking out of turn, Master," Rosie said. "And I'm sorry I forgot to call you Master, Master."

"Apology accepted but I will still have to discipline you. Later." Once he figured out what she was after. "Pull that chair over and put one foot up on it." Once she'd obeyed him, he said, "Now play with yourself. Pinch your nipples and get them good and hard, and make your sweet little pussy real wet. And don't leave your position or stop pleasuring yourself until I return."

"Yes, Master."

He flicked off the light beside him, and turned on a halogen above her, spotlighting her. Turning his back on her, he snagged the contract and list she'd left on his desk, then walked into the bedroom. He ditched his suit, exchanging it for a black silk shirt and set of leather pants with a laced fly that would let him completely free both his cock and his balls. "You playin' with yourself like I told you?"

"Yes, Master. I'm SO hot."

He snorted quietly at her exaggerated tone. A check of the list revealed little he hadn't already guessed about her preferences. Hmm, that was interesting. Where he'd have bet big money she'd check "definitely not" under ménage, she'd checked "might consider". And she'd checked "definitely" in the flogging and spanking column. A scan of the rest of the items showed, with few exceptions, Miss Rosalinda Ramos was game for just about anything he would want to do with her.

"Does the idea that someone might be watching me masturbate make you jealous, Master? Or does it make you horny?"

Oh, yeah, she was deliberately racking up the points. Getting her to submit, to obey him, was going to be such a challenge.

"Just keep touching yourself, Princesa. And you're up to punishment number three." He opened his safe room, and ran a finger along the shelf containing his collection of dildos and butt plugs, choosing a remote control vibrator that would pay particular attention to her G-spot. He tucked the remote in his pocket so she wouldn't realize it would vibrate. Yet.

If she'd done what he'd told her, he probably wouldn't need any lube, but he grabbed a tube just in case, then added a harness.

She was where he'd left her, following his instructions to the letter. A light sheen of sweat dewed her skin. Lord, what a picture she made, her skin and fingers glistening under the halogen, her nipples dark, hard berries waiting to be suckled. And...oh, yeah, those little hitches in her breath she made when she was close to orgasm were starting.

He palmed his groin, resetting his burgeoning cock. "That's another rule. You are not allowed to come unless I give you permission."

He allowed her a huff of exasperation. It was his fault he hadn't reminded her of that rule beforehand.

Standing behind her, he cupped her mons, letting his

fingers trail through the slick cream coating her labia. "Very nice." He withdrew his fingers and drew them across her lips. "Lick your lips, baby. Taste how sweet you are."

Her tongue slowly slid over her top lip then she turned her head and looked up at him. "Don't you want a taste, Master?"

"Baby, you're going to have to remember you're not supposed to speak. That makes punishment number four." Before she could protest, he captured her mouth with his. While she was distracted, he slid the dildo into her, rotating it so its curve would press against her most sensitive spot every time she moved. She'd tell him later that was mean, and maybe it was, but she had to learn to control her orgasm to his command.

He draped the leather harness over her shoulder and stepped away. "Put that on."

"Yes, Master."

He grabbed the chair she'd braced herself on and turned it around to face the window, then tossed a throw pillow on the floor. No need in her hurting her knees. He sat down, splaying his legs wide and pointed to the floor between them. "Kneel."

After unlacing his fly and freeing his cock, he stroked himself. "You know what I want, Princesa."

"Yes, Master.

She bent over him, her hair brushing his thighs in a silken caress. When she put her lips around his cock, he buried his fingers in her hair. "Remember, I can come, but you can't."

His cock filling her mouth, she muttered something indecipherable. The vibrations drove him insane so he decided to share the experience by using the remote to her vibrator. When she realized what he'd done, he held her head in place and pumped his cock deep into her mouth. From the way she squirmed, he could tell the vibrator was doing its job, driving her as insane as she was driving him.

Her tongue flattened against his length, her cheeks hollowing as she sucked him deep. The little moans she made drove him over the edge, his climax rocketing through him.

As she licked the lingering drops of come from his head, she smiled up at him. Damn she looked so perfect there. She'd look even better lying beneath him on the couch, her eyes unfocussed as he drove into her. But tonight, she was playing a game, thinking she knew about the lifestyle. So he'd show her exactly what happened when you played with fire.

"Go make me dinner, Princesa. Your master's hungry."

"Aren't you—" A look of disappointment flickered across her face, mutating into frustration. "Yes, Master."

Smiling to himself, he removed a cigar from his humidor and listened to her muttering to herself as she banged pots and pans in the kitchen. She'd expected him to reciprocate, to let her climax in return. Soon, she'd realize his denial of her pleasure was part of her training. Would she be so enthusiastic about her training when she realized she'd have to hand over such control to him?

Realizing Rosie was being extremely quiet, he wandered into the kitchen, and found her grabbing the counter with both hands, hunched over as she panted.

He hurried to her side. "What's the matter, Rosebud?"

She could barely breath as she glared at him. "I'm trying really hard here not to come, goddamn it." She closed her eyes and forced her breath out through her teeth. "Oh, God, Sam, I need to come so bad."

"Poor little Rosebud, I left the vibrator going, didn't I?" He wrapped one arm around her waist, and pulled her back against him. He dipped his fingers into the cleft between her legs. "Come for me, Rosie."

It took only a single swipe of his finger over her swollen clit before she shook in release. They stood entwined, Rosie trembling as the aftershocks died down. He could have stood there forever, holding her, comforting her. Loving her.

After turning off the vibrator, he bent down and kissed her. "You go take out the vibrator and I'll help you with dinner."

The meal was almost complete when his Berry buzzed, Andy texting him that he was about to have visitors. Ah, now this might be an interesting test for her resolve. Sam composed a reply instructing Andy to allow his guests through but to go back into the apartment and leave the hallway clear. When the doorbell chimed, she looked to him, frowning when he didn't get it.

"Someone's at the door, Princesa. Wouldn't do to keep them waiting."

She turned slowly, carefully placing a paring knife down on the table. Ooops, good thing it wasn't stickin' in the cabinet an inch from his head. Or in the middle of his forehead. He had a feelin' she had a damned good aim.

"You expect me to answer the door naked?"

"Yup. Andy's back in his apartment, so no one will see you."

"Did you forget about the cameras monitoring your door? Master."

Crap. He had.

He pulled a face and shrugged out of his shirt. "Here, put this on."

The doorbell chimed a second time just as he reached the front door. "Hey, Thalia, what brings you to the neighborhood?"

Spencer pushed Thalia into Sam's foyer before Thalia replied, "Jocelyne invited us to dinner. After seeing Rosie's little show in the window, I thought I'd drop in. Since I'm in the neighborhood."

"Wasn't that convenient for you? I'm surprised you didn't convince Jocelyne and Robert to come here with you."

Thalia chuckled. "Next time perhaps. Robert thanks you for the show, by the way."

Sam shut the door behind Spencer and called, "Rosie, come out here and greet our guests." He lowered his voice. "I want to know exactly what you said and showed Rosie at the club the other day. Everything, Thalia."

Rosie peered around the corner. His shirt enveloped her like a dress, reaching nearly to her knees. And damned if that didn't look just as sexy as when she was naked.

"Hello, Thalia. Spencer. I'm, uh, just in the middle of making dinner."

"Come here, Princesa."

Muttering under her breath, she took a deep breath and stepped to the middle of the doorway, her hands clasped in front.

"Rosalinda," Sam growled when she didn't come any closer. "Come. Here."

Chapter Twenty-Five

Thank God, Sam had given her his shirt. Although considering Spencer had stripped down in front of her, maybe Thalia would insist she do the same. A sort of quid pro quo. Damned if the idea of stripping down wasn't making her horny.

A quick glance showed the only eyes on her were Thalia's and Sam's which were shuttered, his emotion unreadable. Spencer stood in proper submissive form, two paces behind Thalia's chair, eyes on his toes.

"Rosie, your master has given you an order," Thalia said quietly. "By hesitating, you defy him which not only insults him, but embarrasses him in front of his guests."

Order? Oh, right, Sam asked her to go over there. Her legs carried her to the middle of the foyer, just in front of Sam, and assumed a position mirroring Spencer's. "I'm sorry for insulting you, Master."

Shit, this submission stuff was tough when there were witnesses.

"How is dinner progressing?" Sam asked, just a little too casually.

She narrowed her eyes at him, then glanced at Thalia who smiled right back at her. "It'll be a while yet. *Master.*"

"Will you be joining me, Thalia?"

"Thank you, but no, I've already eaten."

He nodded. "Princesa, you may continue cooking. When dinner's ready, you will wait for me beside the table."

Thalia waved a hand toward the kitchen. "Spencer, help Master Samuel's slave."

Did he think that just because she wasn't in the room she couldn't guess they were going to talk about her? It was like being back in high school where the rich kids huddled together in their group and snickered at the kids from the barrio. Gritting her teeth, Rosie tromped into the kitchen and pulled two dishes from the cupboard.

"You'll only need one place setting," Spencer whispered. "Slaves eat what their master or mistress serve from their own plates."

With a huff, she shoved a plate back into the cabinet, wincing slightly at the crash it made. At least it hadn't broken.

"Tell me you didn't, that she didn't." Sam's voice rose, echoing through both the foyer and living room. "What the *hell* were you thinking?"

The rest faded back down to a harsh whisper, low enough that she couldn't hear what they were talking about. But she had a pretty good idea, especially when he practically shouted, "She what?" followed by "Rosalinda. Get your ass out here. Now."

Drawing herself up to her full five foot one, she sauntered to the foyer as if she were a queen. "You called, Master?"

"I understand you disobeyed my orders and left the office area of the club the other day. And that you've since returned several times."

Oops.

Narrowing her eyes, Rosie shot a glance at Thalia. So much for women sticking together.

"I also understand," Sam continued through clenched teeth, "that you helped punish Spencer this afternoon."

"I— Yes, Master. Mistress Thalia—" was that how she was supposed to address another slave's mistress? "—Mistress Thalia was instructing me in the use of a flogger. She wanted me to demonstrate my ability with it."

"Were you aware that by administering the punishment to her slave, you bestowed her the right to administer punishment to you if she caught you misbehaving?" Every Hauberk employee had heard the legend that when Sam's voice got quieter, when he lost his drawl completely, he was beyond anger and it was every man for himself.

She took a half-step back and ran smack dab into Spencer. Oh, crap. Did that mean she was Thalia's slave? "As my master, isn't it your duty to administer punishments? Your right?"

"It should have been my privilege, but the club rules are that in accepting the flogger from her, you granted her the right." If his teeth clenched any tighter, they'd shatter. "Let's get this over with."

He stalked down the hall and into the bedroom.

"Why didn't you tell me you would get to do this, not him?" Rosie snapped.

"You have to trust me on this, Rosie. It's for Sam's own good."

"*Sam*'s good? I'm the one whose ass is about to get flogged."

"All part of your training, my dear. Now you'd better follow him before he completely loses his patience and doubles your punishment." Thalia signaled to Spencer to take his position behind her chair.

Her heart beating so fast and so loud she could hear the whooshing of blood in her ears, Rosie followed them to the bedroom. If she'd been facing just Sam, she knew she'd be running to follow him, as horny as hell. But knowing it would be Thalia wielding the whip, her confidence fled so quickly she was surprised they hadn't heard a sonic boom.

Sam stood in the walk-in closet, the panel hiding his secret room wide open.

"Come here."

Hoping her legs wouldn't give out and betray her nervousness, Rosie strode into the room. When he snorted, she realized she'd made a mistake by not acting surprised at the room's existence.

He pointed to the bench. "Kneel down on the lower part of the bench then grab the handles on the other end."

"Yes, Master." Wiping her palms on her thighs, she followed his instructions so she ended up in the same position Spencer had been earlier.

Leaning over her, Sam adjusted her so her ass was even higher in the air, then firmly fastened the leather restraints around her legs and wrists, along with a strap over her waist. There was no way she could move if she'd wanted to. Which probably was a good thing because she was beginning to shake.

Satisfied she couldn't move, he opened the cabinet containing the floggers and stepped aside so Thalia could choose from the selection.

"She's never been flogged before so I have no idea what level of pain she can take." His voice was flat. Cold.

The shaking in her legs increased.

"She'll take what is administered," Thalia replied calmly. "Spencer, we'll use the deerskin."

Rosie jerked against her bindings. Would Thalia be administering her flogging? Or Spencer? Crap. Once she'd seen his reaction, she hadn't held back that afternoon. Would he try to return the favor? Would Thalia be any less forgiving? Between the two of them she knew she didn't stand a chance.

Sam returned, crouching down so she could see his face. "You are so in over your head, baby, and I can't help you. Just remember, if it gets too much, don't be afraid to use your safe word. But once you use it, the scene is ended. Completely. And you'll be sleeping alone tonight."

She had a feeling that, with or without the safe word, he'd never allow her to try another scene again. Why hadn't Thalia told her what administering Spencer's punishment meant? She wanted Sam to be the one punishing her. Wanted him holding the whip, not Spencer. Not even Thalia.

"How many stripes did you give Spencer, Princesa?" he asked quietly.

"Ten. I was supposed to give him twenty but I chickened out." Because it had made her too horny, but suddenly she didn't want to admit that to him.

He winced. "Damn it, Rosie, that means Thalia can give you ten tonight, and you only deserve a third of that. Why in hell did you leave the office area when I specifically told you not to?"

Because she'd trusted Thalia. Something she wasn't going to do again any time soon. And gave her somewhere else to look in her hunt for the stalker. Maybe despite Thalia's insistence that she didn't hold Sam to blame, there was a lingering resentment.

"I'm sorry. I wish it was you giving me the punishment."

Oh boy, did she wish it was him. With him she knew she'd come with no problem. With him, she'd be begging him for more.

"Do you wish your slave to be ball gagged, Samuel?" Thalia called.

"No. If she wants to use her safe word, I want to be able to hear it. And she's not my slave."

"Has she any device inside her that will stimulate her?"

"No."

There was a pause. Then the sound of a drawer sliding open. "Use this one." Was she choosing a different flogger? One that would hurt more, or less?

Two seconds later, she jumped when someone touched her labia. Her face flamed that Spencer might have touched her so intimately.

"Sam?"

"It's all right, baby, it's me." Something cool pressed against her labia, and slid deep inside her vagina. Shoot. Another dildo. A big one. Hopefully this one wouldn't vibrate, her inner tissues were still sensitive from the orgasm she'd just had. But who had inserted it.

Sam smoothed a hand over her behind before stepping back into her sight.

"Now that she's ready," Thalia said, "we shall begin."

Rosie jerked against the restraints at the sound of a flogger striking something. She waited for the burn on her ass, but none came.

As if sensing Rosie's rising panic, Sam placed a hand on her shoulder to comfort her. "Stop trying to psyche her out, Thalia. Just get it over with. You've got ten lashes. No more."

He knelt down so she could see his face, putting his hand over hers. "Look at me, baby. I'm right here."

As soon as he'd finished speaking, the flogger snapped across her ass. She let fly a curse. Damn, it stung more than when Sam had spanked her. She scrunched her eyes closed as the flogger cracked through the air again.

Sam's fingers tightened slightly on hers. "Open your eyes, Rosebud. It'll help you concentrate on something other than the pain in your ass."

The flogger struck again. Strangely enough the pain changed to heat that radiated from her ass to her pussy. It got worse when Sam let go of her hands and slipped his hand beneath her, teasing her nipples. When he tugged on them sharply, the sensation shot straight down to her core and had her moaning. Her hips writhed beneath the third punishing strike. Her thigh muscles trembled, clenching together, the dildo exciting her already inflamed sheath. Wow, now she understood Spencer's reaction.

She bit the inside of her cheek to try and distract herself from the impending orgasm.

No, she wouldn't come. She wouldn't come when the attention didn't come from Sam. That was for Sam. Only Sam.

The flogger hit for a fourth time. Then a fifth.

Oh, God, she couldn't hold back. She needed to come. But she didn't want to get off knowing it was someone else administering her punishment. "Sam?"

"It's all right, baby. Just let yourself feel it." He was further away now. Standing beside Spencer?

Another punishing strike that had her barely able to hold back her orgasm.

"Sam? I have to come, please, Sam. I don't want to do it for anyone but you."

She cried out when the leather harness holding the dildo in place was removed and again when the dildo itself slid from her body. Oh, God, was this part of her punishment to feel so empty?

The flat of a hand cracked against her already heated cheek, then quickly hit the other. And then she felt warmth against her thighs, and a blunt object, a cock, slid into her pussy in one smooth stroke. Tears ran down her face as she struggled against the straps, struggled against her body's internal need to clench around the cock no matter whose it was, to milk it dry.

"No. Oh, please, no. I want Sam. Only Sam."

"It is me, baby," Sam said from behind her. "Thalia and Spencer left."

Before he'd finished speaking, conscious thought took flight and her body responded, her head arching back and her body tightening around him, milking him as he pumped into her.

Sam bent over Rosie, holding himself up on shaking arms. He'd been so angry that Thalia had insisted on the game. But he was also grateful. If Rosie had changed her mind, if she'd used her safe word, she'd remember Thalia as the giver of pain, not him.

Beneath him, around him, her muscles continued to spasm and quiver, stroking every inch of his cock. A lightning sensation speared from the base of his spine and through his balls. He reared back and shouted as a second climax rocketed through him.

He tried to hold his weight off her as his legs gave out. Nope, no good. Fumbling, he released her ankles from their restraints, then padded around to the front and similarly freed her wrists. "Come here, baby."

Slinging one of her arms around his shoulder, he carried her into the bedroom and collapsed onto the bed. He cradled her on his chest, smoothing his hands over her warm behind.

Bath. That's what she needed. He should get up and run one for her. In a minute.

The minute turned into an hour before he was ready to take his arms from around her. He rolled off the bed and plodded to the bathroom. While the tub filled with water, he tossed in a cup of Epsom salts. Once the water was to the right height and temperature, he went back to the bedroom and lifted Rosie, who slumped in his arms, utterly content.

Leaving her to soak, he wandered out on the terrace and lit up a cigar. He lifted a hand to Jocelyne's husband on the balcony across the way. Robert waved back then ducked his head to look through the telescope pointed at Sam's building, but several floors below. Ah, the couple in 906 were giving Robert a show tonight also.

What the hell was he doing? He'd gotten carried away back

there. He'd forgotten to use a condom when he'd replaced the dildo with his cock. He'd forgotten what it felt like to take a woman bare. He'd felt every tremor of her pussy, like a thousand tongues lapping his cock, how the heat increased as she'd come, the tiny rippling aftershocks. She'd wormed her way so deep into his heart that he'd never be able to let her go now. Not after tonight.

The cigar was almost a stub by the time the door to his bedroom opened. Rosie padded out, wrapped up in one of his bathrobes. The danged thing trailed behind her like a queen's mantle.

"When did Thalia and Spencer leave?"

"After the fifth strike." Spencer had simply tapped him on the arm with the flogger and presented it to him, then turned around and left. Thalia had smiled at him then silently wheeled out behind Spencer. Quid pro quo for Rosie walking out on him earlier perhaps?

Whatever, he was grateful to have had the chance to be alone with her. And furious that he'd been a spectator rather than a participant.

"Was that planned? For you to switch over like that?" She flipped a strand of hair out of her eyes, tucking it behind her ear.

"No. But I'm glad he di—"

Without warning, she'd hooked her leg behind his and pushed him to the ground, splaying her body over him.

Sam chuckled and wrapped his arms about her waist, cinching her up higher so he could nuzzle her neck. "Honey, if you wanted to do it out here, all you had to do was ask. You didn't have to ambush me like that. Not to mention I've got some perfectly fine furniture over there with pillows that'll make it a helluva lot more comfortable on my ass. Or your knees."

"Stay down," she whispered. "There's someone across the road with a rifle." She patted her waist. "Damn it, I left my Berry in the bedroom. We have to get you inside."

Sam jerked as if he'd been tasered. He flipped her over, shielding her body with his. "You're tryin' to shield me from a *sniper*? Are you fuckin' insane?"

"Of course I'm trying to protect you. It's my job, remember?"

The thought of Rosie willingly taking a bullet had him seeing scarlet. "Where is this fucker?"

"Penthouse. Middle balcony. I saw a flash off his scope."

His muscles relaxed when he realized what she'd seen. He rolled off her, leaning against the concrete planter while he fought the adrenaline rush. "That wasn't a rifle scope you saw. It was a telescope."

"What? How can you be sure?"

He leaned his head back, forcing oxygen into his lungs. "That's Jocelyne's apartment. Robert's a voyeur—he spies on his neighbors with a telescope. That's who you did your little show for earlier. I saw him out there while you were in the tub. He was watching the couple in 906 getting it on—they always leave the drapes open for him."

"Eeew. You mean there really was someone watching me? That's sorta creepy." Rubbing her arms, she scooched over to peer through the slit in the balcony then scooted back out of the way. "Are you sure it's just a telescope and not a gun?"

He couldn't do this.

Things were right back to the way things were eight years ago. How had he forgotten someone was out to kill him? He couldn't make Rosie a target. Couldn't let her be hurt. Couldn't lose her the way he'd lost Jill.

But damn it, he couldn't set her aside either. He needed her more than he needed the air around him. He loved her. And would do anything to keep her safe. Whether she wanted him to protect her or not, dammit. Even if that meant making her as mad as hell to keep her away from him, to keep her safe. And safe meant away from him.

His jaw clenched, Sam pushed himself to a stand and stalked to the bedroom.

"Ay!" Rosie scrambled after him, catching the door before he could slam it shut. "I'm sorry. All right? I didn't mean to ruin your game. I'll be good and obey you. Master."

Sam glared at her. "I will not have someone else die because of me. I'll not have one hair on your head hurt. Not now. Not ever. Do you understand?"

Damn. He was thinking of Jill. How had she forgotten what he'd lost already? In an effort to distract him, she sank on her knees in front of him and once again assumed a subservient position. She caught the laces of his fly in her teeth and tugged.

"Stop it, Rosie."

"Princesa, remember?"

"Stop it! It's not a fucking game, Rosie. This is important, why don't you see that?" His shout echoed off the walls.

"Sam..."

He retied the laces and folded his arms across his chest. "We need to slow things down between us, Rosie. It's best if you sleep at the other apartment from here on in."

He was sending her away? After what they'd just shared? After he'd held her for the past hour as if she were fragile porcelain, even drawn her a bath?

When she moved toward him, he took a step back, the distance between them forming an uncrossable abyss. An overwhelming agony compressed her chest. She was losing him. "You mean break things off, don't you?"

He shook his head. "No. I don't know. I can't... I just know I need... I can't do this again."

A chill rippled beneath her skin at the fierce look on his face. Until she remembered that she wasn't just his girlfriend or his lover. She stood up and rounded on him, jamming her finger into his chest. "I'm your bodyguard, remember? I'm supposed to protect you. So if I have to jump in front of a speeding car to push you out of the way, I will. If I have to cover a grenade with my body to protect you, I will. If I have to push you down on the pavement and cover you with my body, I will. I will not let someone kill you." She poked him again. "Got that?"

Sam shook his head but wouldn't look at her. Instead he stared over the terrace, a bleak look on his face. "Don't sacrifice yourself for me, Rosie. *Ever.* Promise me."

"I won't. I mean, I won't promise you that I wouldn't do that again." She flattened her hand on his chest, felt the muscles bunched beneath her fingers, the thick scar down the center. "Even if I wasn't your lead op, I couldn't stand by and watch you get killed."

He whirled away and slammed his fist into the wall, punching a hole in the drywall. "Damn it, promise me! You will not get yourself hurt because of me. Please." He lowered his voice. "Please, Rosie. Don't you ever put yourself in the path of a bullet for me. I'll transfer you to Australia if that is the only way to keep you safe. I'll fire you if I have to. I'll destroy your credibility so you'll never be hired by another protection agency, you'll never be able to get a job that'll put you in the line of fire again."

"You wouldn't do that."

"Damned straight I would."

She searched his eyes, saw his determination. He wasn't exaggerating. "All right. I promise I won't put myself in the path of a bullet for you." For the first time in her life, she made a promise she knew would willingly and knowingly break.

God forgive her.

Sam forgive her.

His back to the wall, he sipped his Guinness, only half paying attention to the flatscreen over the bar. Chad allowed himself a small smile of satisfaction as the Saints' quarterback heaved a pass to the end zone. According to the phone call he'd received, Sam was completing his own pass. Thalia's harebrained scheme had worked.

As a cheer went up when Washington intercepted the pass, the door to the bar opened. A frown on his face, the bar's newest patron scanned the crowd and found his target. He pushed his way through the throng and slumped into the booth.

"What are you doing here, Andy? Why aren't you at Sam's place?"

Andy signaled to the waitress and ordered a cola. "Because he just fired me."

"What? Why?" Had Sam found out about their plan? Would he be next?

"He said I put Rosie at risk by letting her go with Thalia into the public part of the club." Andy worried his goatee. "I didn't know she'd left the security office until they returned. But he's right. I should have been in the office with her and at least gone with her."

"Crap. All right, first off, you're not fired. Take a week's vacation while I talk to Sam and calm him down. It's my damned sister's fault, not yours. When Thalia gets something into her head, there's no stopping her." He waved toward the television. "Those football players have nothing on her when it comes to offensive strategy."

Look at him. He'd let her talk him into assigning Sam and Jill to her club in the first place. And ended up in front of a media firing squad, his career in flames.

Andy chugged half his drink before the waitress had managed to get two steps away from the table. "You guys may have to come up with a new plan 'cause there's trouble in paradise."

Acid from his stomach slicing at the back of his throat, Chad stilled. "They were fighting?"

"Rosie thought she saw a sniper in the building opposite and threw herself over him. Livid doesn't even begin to describe Sam right now."

Crap. Crap. Crap. When Thalia had proposed the scheme of having Rosie as Sam's bodyguard, he'd argued against it for this very reason. All they needed to make Sam withdraw from Rosie was to remind him of how he'd lost Jill. He rubbed his temple against the headache that stabbed behind his eyes.

"All right. We'll wait and see how things shake out. Rosie won't let Sam pull away without a battle."

"And if she does?"

"Then I guess I have to call in the big guns."

Chapter Twenty-Six

When Chad walked into his office, Sam held up his hand motioning for Chad to wait. "Isn't there any way we can get someone in there without raisin' their suspicions?"

"Sorry, Watson," squawked a voice from the speakerphone. "Your guy Phillips' escape made the terrorists frickin' paranoid about the rest of the hostages. They've doubled the guard on the camp and have booby trapped all the buildings. They're suspecting their own shadows right now. There's no way you're going to be able to put a new face in their midst without having them suspect something."

"I'm not about to let my guys rot in that hellhole they've taken them to. I want them out of there by whatever means necessary. I've got manpower and I've got money. Just tell me what you need and you've got it."

"I appreciate the offer, but at the moment, you have to put your faith in the American and Colombian governments' negotiations. I'll call you when I hear anything else. Sorry I couldn't be more help."

Sam stabbed the button, cutting the connection. Another curse befouled the air. He rubbed his temples against the headache forming at the back of his eyes. "What do you want, Chad?"

"Got a question for you."

"What?"

"What the fuck is going on with you? Why are you being such an ass to Rosie?"

Good question. Things had spiraled out of control ever

since that night he'd tried to slow things down between them. "None of your fuckin' business."

"You made it my business when you tried to fire Andy."

"Yeah, okay." Sam's shoulders slumped and he stared at the ceiling. Shit, he missed Rosie, but he couldn't take the chance while there was still a stalker possibly gunning for him. But Chad was right; it wasn't Andy's fault that Thalia—or Rosie—had deliberately kept Andy out of the loop. "Yeah, I was pretty pissed off that night and took it out on the wrong person. I'm glad you told Andy he's not fired. I need to apologize to him for that."

He stalked to the bathroom and grabbed a bottle of Tylenol from the cabinet and downed two caplets dry. When he returned, he stayed in the doorway to the bathroom and met Chad's gaze. "As for what's going on between me and Rosie, that's between me and her. It's none of your business."

"It is my business because it's possible you've given her a reason to sue the company for sexual harassment. I'm in charge of the D.C. office, remember? It's my job to look out for the company even if the owner doesn't like my advice."

"Rosie won't sue."

He rubbed his eyes. Shit he was tired. Between worrying about Rosie and the Colombia situation, he'd been putting in twenty-hour days. Hell, he'd fallen asleep at his desk the night before. Make that early this morning.

Chad waved an arm toward the door to the outer office. "Then let's talk about how you've got Sandy on edge, how Troy's about to throttle anyone who walks into his office, and the whole accounting staff is having fits over your last memo. Not to mention that you look like shit, Sam."

When Sam flipped him off, Chad sighed. "You're exhausted because you've been staying here late every night for the past week. Go home, Sam. Go talk to Rosie. Straighten this mess out before you lose her completely. Before she comes and asks me for a transfer because damn it, Sam, that's going to happen too fucking soon."

"This from the man who let his wife slip through his fingers because he was too fuckin' busy feeling sorry for himself to pay any attention to her."

Chad stiffened. When he spoke his voice was quiet, but he couldn't disguise the bitterness filling it. "Who better to give advice? Yes, I fucked up a good thing with Lauren. I was too blinded by everything that happened to see that I was driving her away. That's why I hate to see you make the same stupid mistake."

"It's not a mistake, goddamn it. It's for her own damned good. I won't see Rosie hurt."

Chad slammed his hand flat on the desk. "Goddamn it, Sam. What the hell's wrong with you? *You're* hurting her!"

Because then she'll continue to be in harms' way. "You may be my manager in the office, which gives you the right to make suggestions about my business decisions but you sure as hell have no right making judgments on my love life."

"Someone's got to get through that thick skull of yours and make you see what you've got right in front of you before you crash and burn. You're Hauberk, Sam. You go down, we all go down with you. Rosie loves you. Or is that what's scaring you?"

"I'd rather lose her and know she's alive than have her in the stalker's cross hairs. Or have you forgotten I'm a target right now?"

"You stupid, pigheaded, shit-for-brains asshole, haven't you figured it out yet? There is no—"

"Uh, Sam? Chad?" Sandy stuck her head in the door. "You guys want to keep it down—you're starting to attract a crowd out here."

Sam shook his head and stared Chad down. "It's okay, Sandy. We're done here. Chad's leaving right now."

Chad cursed once then stalked to the door. "Fine. You want to play it that way, asshole? You've got it." Chad pushed past Sandy, who stared after him open-mouthed.

"Idiot," she muttered and shut the door behind her. But Sam couldn't figure out who she meant. Chad. Or him.

Her eyes fuzzy from reading the files for so many hours, Rosie stretched and realized Scott was standing at the door. He looked as tired as she felt. Not surprising considering the nightmares he was still suffering. She doubted he slept more than two hours straight in a night. Not that she'd been sleeping much better. The bed seemed so empty, so cold, without Sam beside her. But she didn't buy this crap about having her move back into 1202 to keep her safe. He was pissed off that she'd gone to the Rouge behind his back.

"Hey, Rosie. There's a guy here to see you. Said his name's Spencer Harper."

If Spencer was there, surely Thalia was close by. Just what she needed, the Dominatrix herself reaming her out. "Is there anyone else with him?"

Scott shook his head. "Nope, just Harper. You want me to tell him to beat it?"

She glanced at the files stacked in piles on the bed. They'd cleared all the usual suspects weeks before, but the latest spate of threats had them combing the files once again. "No, it's all right. I needed a break anyway."

Spencer stood in the hallway, Kris hovering between him and the monitors. Dressed in a pair of tan Dockers with a white shirt covered by a plaid sweater vest, he looked like he'd just gotten off a golf course. The memory of him tied to a bench while she flogged his ass, and how little she'd been wearing when he'd flogged her sent heat flying up her neck and into her face.

"Hi, Spencer, what's up?"

He tucked a pair of sunglasses into his pocket. "I hope I'm not interrupting you, Miss Ramos, but Thalia would like to see you in her office right away."

"I'm tied up right now." The heat that had been dying in her face rebounded. Not the best way to phrase that considering their history. "Besides it doesn't look like I'm going to be needing any more of Thalia's training. But thank her—"

"No, it's not that," Spencer hurried to say. "I believe she has something about Mr. Watson's stalker that she wishes to discuss. She was quite emphatic that you come with me."

She didn't want to face Thalia for what she was sure would end in a lecture about Sam's needs, but she couldn't ignore what might turn out to be the only lead they had. Might as well get it over with. Because she had a feeling that if she didn't go with Spencer, Thalia would come to her. Besides, she had a thing or two to say to Thalia herself.

"Hey, Scott? I'm going out for a while, okay?" She snagged her purse and walked down the hallway, aware of how Spencer stayed precisely two paces behind her. Remembered the night he'd come to Sam's apartment, and how wonderful it had been for part of that night. Right before everything went to shit.

Chapter Twenty-Seven

A check of his watch showed him Troy wouldn't be landing in Bogota for another seven hours. Seeking something to keep him busy while he waited, he meandered into the inner sanctum. Chad had stormed out right after their fight, and Sandy had disappeared. With Troy's departure, the place was as quiet as a mausoleum.

Other than Scott, who had shown up a couple hours ago and was yakking on the phone at one of the spare desks, and Kris who was working out in the gym, the central office area was deserted. He wound his way through the IT area, eyeing the computer geek's cubicles with their collections of action figures—*Star Wars, Star Trek, Lord of the Rings* and a few *SpongeBob SquarePants* figures. Beyond them was a double set of revolving doors leading to the raised floor computer room. Which reminded him of tomorrow's meeting with John Lake, the IT manager, to discuss enlarging the raised floor computer area yet again.

In the glass-enclosed area monitoring Hauberk's client security systems, some of his employees yawned as they finished up the last hour of their night shift. The operators manning the main computer console had shut off the lights to the data centre, preferring to work in the eerie glow of their monitors.

What was he doing here? He had no excuse to keep him in the office. But he had no one waiting for him at home. Not now that Rosie had moved back to the other apartment.

It was better that way. Better that he not get more involved with her than he already was. But she hadn't understood that.

Hell. He didn't understand it. He missed Rosie. He missed her smart mouth. He missed watching that blue butterfly flutter when she walked naked to the bathroom. Or when it heaved in tumult while he drove into her from behind. He missed watching her sleep as she lay curled up beside him in bed. He even missed the straightening irons and diffusers and bottles of hair lotion cluttering up his bathroom counter.

But she was safe when she wasn't around him. And that's what counted.

"Hey, Sam?" Scott called moments before Sam entered the mantrap to the firing range. "Got a minute?"

"Yeah, what's up?" So much for working off his mood with his Glock. Damn he missed being out in the field. Being useful. But fate had proven he was better behind a desk than he was at protecting someone's life.

"I found something I think you should see."

Something in Scott's tone got Sam's attention. "What?"

Scott hitched a thumb over his shoulder. "I think I might have found your stalker."

While he should feel relief that he wouldn't require babysitting anymore, finding the stalker also meant Rosie would request a transfer and he'd lose her completely. As if he hadn't already set her on that path. "All right. I'm comin'."

As they walked toward the desk Scott had been using, Scott explained, "We've been suspecting someone inside, right?"

Sam nodded.

"So earlier today, I noticed my computer updating a program all by itself. I thought maybe I'd been hacked so I called the IT guys. They told me all Hauberk computers have a bot program installed so the geeks can do updates without having to go to every computer. So it got me wondering..."

Sam stopped. "Are you tellin' me someone's hacked into our system?"

"No." Scott shook his head. "The system's secure. But I convinced the manager to give me access to run a search on everyone's hard drives. Search for photos they'd uploaded. IM conversations they may have stored that might mention you. That type of thing."

By this time they'd reached the desk. Scott turned the monitor so Sam could see the undoctored photo of him helping Cynthia Stewart from his Jag.

"Who's computer was this on?" he breathed.

"Chad Miller's."

Sam stared at the screen. *Revenge is a dish best served cold.* Was Chad seeking revenge against Sam for leaving his sister in a wheelchair for the rest of her life?

But if Chad was seeking revenge, why wouldn't he have just shot him years ago instead of going through this circuitous route? They'd been alone so many times when Chad could have killed him without witnesses. Like any one of the numerous times they'd been out on Chad's boat, Chad could have dumped Sam overboard and no one would have been the wiser.

Or was killing Sam not Chad's game? If he wanted revenge on someone, how would he best get it? By going after something they cared about, the nasty part of his psyche whispered.

He whipped out his Berry and speed dialed Rosie's number. Damn it, no answer. "Rosie's at the apartment, right?"

"Ah, no. Some guy named Spencer Harper came over earlier and picked her up. Told her Thalia wanted to talk to her at the Rouge. She went over there a couple hours ago."

Dear God. No.

"We've got to get to the club. Fast."

"I'll drive."

As they raced to the front door, Sam whipped out his Berry and punched in Rosie's number again.

It rang the standard four times before dumping him once more into voicemail. Shit, all electronic devices had to be left at the gate.

Scott unlocked the doors to the limo, holding the back one open until Sam threw himself in. He braced himself as Scott peeled the limo out of the parking lot and headed for the beltway, then dialed Thalia's number and started praying that she'd pick up.

She did, on the second ring.

"Why, Thalia? If it's revenge, don't take it out on Rosie. Please."

Even over the noise of the car engine, he could hear her sigh. "Oh, Samuel. It's not revenge we're after."

We're? Plural. So she and Chad were in on it together, Spencer too. "Then what is it you want?"

"Come to the club, Sam. We'll talk about it when you arrive."

He clutched the Berry so hard its case cracked. "Don't hurt her, Thalia. Don't let anyone else near her. Promise me."

"We'll talk when you get here. But Sam? Don't take too long." She broke the connection, leaving Sam staring at his phone.

"Scott?"

"Yes, sir?"

"Floor it."

Chapter Twenty-Eight

Spencer held open the door to Thalia's office, motioning for Rosie to go in. She walked in and found herself facing not only Thalia, but Chad, Andy and a dark-haired Hispanic man she recognized as Sam's junior partner from Dallas, Mark Rodriguez.

"Hello, Miss Ramos. It's a pleasure to meet you again." Mark stood and greeted her, though she couldn't miss the thorough assessment he made of her.

"I didn't realize you were in D.C., Mr. Rodriguez." Rosie put her hand on Andy's shoulder, worried that he might blame her for Sam trying to fire him. "Hey, Andy, how you doing?"

"I'm okay, Rosie." But he didn't meet her gaze.

Chad however did meet her gaze, nodding his head only slightly, his expression unreadable.

"Sit down, Rosie," Thalia said. While her voice was quiet, it contained an unmistakable order.

What the hell was going on? It was like facing a firing line, or...oh, my God, while she'd been obsessing about combing through the files, something must have happened to Sam. Her breath tight in her throat, she stared at Chad. "Is it Sam? Is he hurt? Did the stalker get him?"

Mark firmly grasped her shoulders and led her to the chair, pressing her into it. He knelt beside her and laid his hand over hers as it clamped onto the arm of the chair. "Sam is fine. He's safe in his office. You don't need to worry."

"Then what—"

"Rosie, we need you to listen and not say anything until

we've finished," Chad interrupted. Since she'd taken his chair, Mark walked to the door, closed it and then leaned against it. Was he standing there to stop her from leaving? What the heck was going on?

"We ask that you keep an open mind about what we tell you," Thalia said.

Not knowing who to look at or what to expect, Rosie grasped the arms of the chair and nodded.

"All right. I'll keep an open mind." But that's all she'd promise. "Now what's going on?"

After exchanging a glance with the other three, Chad took a deep breath. "There is no stalker, Rosie. There never has been."

She glanced at Andy, who stared at his feet, then at Thalia, who met her gaze evenly and nodded slowly. Mark smiled as if he were in on some huge joke. Except there was nothing funny that she could see.

"I don't understand. What about the photos? The phone calls?"

"All of us took the photos." Chad circled his finger at the group. "Thalia took the one at the club, Andy and I took the rest. And I made the phone calls using a spoof card, just like you originally surmised."

No wonder they'd not found any fingerprints at the phone booths. Considering Chad had made the calls, he'd probably never had them checked in the first place.

"But someone broke into his apartment and trashed it."

Chad held up his hand. "That would also be me."

Andy shifted uncomfortably in his chair. "And I diverted the guard."

"Why? Why did you do this?" *Damn it, what the hell was going on here?*

The four of them exchanged a glance. Chad nodded and began explaining, "You know about Sam's part in the club right? You understand why he's involved?"

"Yeah, the FBI sent him and his partner—" his fiancée, she couldn't say, "—in to catch a serial killer. Except she got killed in the process. What's going on, Chad? Why did you need to stalk him?" She glanced toward the door assessing how she could take Mark down and get past him. How far she might get before they caught up to her? Would she have time to reach a panic button?

"It's not what you think, Miss Ramos," Mark said quietly. "You're in no danger from us."

Chad leaned forward in his chair. "You know that Sam holds himself responsible for Jill's death, right?"

"And for me being in a wheelchair," Thalia added.

Rosie nodded. "Is that what this has been about, Thalia? Vengeance."

"Not vengeance. Compensation." Thalia folded her hands in her lap and frowned. "Sam's not allowed himself to become emotionally involved with anyone since Jill died."

"I still don't understand—"

"Don't you remember what I said to you that first night Sam approached you?" Chad picked up the conversation. "About how Sam was attracted to you? That's why Jodi asked that you bid on Sam at the auction. We'd hoped he'd make a move on that date he took you on afterwards. But then you came back and said he'd behaved like a *perfect gentleman* and nothing happened between you after that.

"So we decided to force his hand. To put him in daily contact with you. The only way we could think of doing that was by setting you up as his bodyguard. We figured that at some point one of you would act upon your attraction for each other."

"So it's all been some gigantic matchmaking scheme?" She sank back into the chair when they nodded as one. "Well, I hate to tell you this but your plan failed." Miserably. "Sam broke it off with me."

Chad ran his hand through his hair. "I know. But Sam's just as miserable as you are. That's why we figured we needed to come clean with you."

Thalia leaned forward. "We have a plan, Rosie. But we need your help."

Chapter Twenty-Nine

Sam threw the car door open before the limo had stopped. Scott hot on his heels, he raced to the front door, which opened seconds before he could open it himself.

Fredriksson stepped into the doorway; Sam tried to cannonade past him. The floor rushed up to meet him, his forehead hitting the tile with a resounding thud. When he tried to roll to his feet, more than one body held him down and the cold steel of handcuffs bit his wrists.

Fighting them, he shouted for Scott to call the police. Restraints were fastened around his ankles. An unseen force tugged on one leg, the other moving with it. Shackled, goddamn it.

"That should hold him," Scott said from behind him. "And there's no need for the police, Mr. Watson."

"What the hell... Are you in on this too, Phillips? How much they paying you? Because I'll double it." *And then I'll rip off your fuckin' nuts with my bare hands.*

A pair of legs came into view, then hands slipped beneath his arms and he was hauled to his feet.

Chad, arms folded across his chest, nodded his approval and murmured to Cooper Davis who stood beside him.

Coop eyed Sam's restraints dubiously. "Are you sure they'll hold him?"

"Should do. I tested 'em myself," Andy replied from one side of Sam, Scott bracketing his other side.

"You sons of bitches," Sam spat out. "Where's Rosie? If you have harmed one hair of her head..."

"Calm down. Rosie's fine," Chad said. "You'll see her in a little while—you got here faster than we expected. But first we want to talk with you."

Sam struggled against his restraints to no avail. "I want to see her for myself. Make sure she's okay."

Cooper made a noise in the back of his throat. "I hate to point this out, Sam, but you're not in a position to make demands." He glanced at Andy and Scott. "Bring him up to my suite. No point in giving the members any more to gossip about."

It took three of them to wrestle him into the elevator and down the hall to Cooper's private suite. He managed to elbow Andy in the chin once, and Scott took a blow to his chest, but they still managed to clip a chain to his handcuffs. That chain was then fastened to a block and tackle attached to a hook in the ceiling and his hands were hauled over his head until his feet barely touched the ground.

Goddamn. He forced himself to relax. As Andy and Scott flanked the door, Chad and Cooper had positioned themselves on the opposite side of the room.

Hmm. That was interesting. The curtains were open on either side of the mirrored window leading to Cooper's private room. Was Rosie in there? Watching? But was she there voluntarily? Was she in on whatever scheme they had planned? Or were they holding her hostage too?

His fingers curled around the chain as he wondered if the entire affair with her had been orchestrated. If she'd been playing some sort of game with him.

For what purpose? Blackmail?

Sam let his entire weight transfer to the block and tackle unit overhead. When it creaked, all eyes trained on the hook in the ceiling. Good, there was a slight possibility of freedom there. Maybe a couple good tugs and he could get free.

"Relax, Sam. We just want to talk," Cooper said.

"So talk." And while they talked, he'd plan his escape. Because sure as shootin' there was no way he was gonna be found in another guy's suite trussed up like a Thanksgiving turkey.

✧

In the adjoining room, watching Sam through the one-way mirror between them, Rosie spoke over her shoulder to Mark Rodriguez.

"Why do they have to tie him up like that? Why can't they just tie him to a chair? Let him have some dignity?"

"A chair wouldn't hold him," Mark said. "And from what I've heard, Sam broke through several restraints during his training. Thalia says this is the only thing strong enough. Plus she says she trained him this way. So she's hoping his training will kick in and he'll listen to her." He chuckled. "Besides, it's fitting considering what he did to me last summer."

Rosie pulled herself away from the unfolding drama and focused on Mark. "Last summer? What exactly did he do to you?"

He cleared his throat, his smile dimming as he shot her a sideways glance. "He tied me up. Amongst other things. Said it was the only way he could make his point. But he had way too much fun doing it."

"Are you sure your part in this is completely altruistic? Or are you exacting a little revenge?"

"As satisfying as the payback is, Rosie, Sam needs to let go of his guilt. He loves you but the stubborn ass is fighting it. If this is the only way to get him to realize that, he deserves whatever Thalia does to him."

She couldn't deny Sam had been an ass lately. But did the means justify the end? She paced the room twice before facing Mark again. "How do you know he loves me? Did he tell you?" Because he hadn't said anything to her.

"He's not said it in so many words, no. Sam's the type who thinks actions speak louder than words," Mark allowed. "But we talk every week. Last night in fact. When he says your name, I can hear it in his voice. It changes somehow." He tilted his head toward the mirror where Sam was straining against his bonds again. "Plus you'd have to be blind not to see it."

Then someone had put a leather hood over her eyes.

"You don't see it, do you?" Mark said quietly. "Sam's not worried about what they'll do to him, or why. He's only worried about you. You're all he's asked about since he arrived. You're the reason he's here."

Maybe. But he'd also gone out of his way to put distance between them over the past week. Even though she'd moved out, he was staying late at the office, even falling asleep at his desk from what Kris had told her.

It had taken Thalia, and Chad, to open her eyes about why he'd been pushing her away. It wasn't that he was ticked off that he was being stalked and that she'd put herself in harms' way the way he'd claimed. It wasn't a fear of commitment like she'd thought it might be. He felt guilty about falling in love with someone other than Jill.

And now they were trying to convince him—while he was bound and forced to listen—to let go of that love? Could you force someone to do that?

Tying Sam up couldn't be the way to convince him. If someone did that to her, she'd dig in her heels and stop listening, convinced she was right and they were wrong. Unable to think in any more depth, she shook her head. "So how come you waited eight years before trying so unselfishly to help him."

A frown flickered over his face. "I didn't realize he was still mourning Jill. I thought he'd let go of it years ago. But then Thalia realized what was going on, especially when Sam asked you to move out. That's when we knew we had to take action."

"Action." Rosie snorted. "Why couldn't you have just phoned him and told him to get therapy?"

He snorted in response. "Come on, Rosie, you know Sam as well as I do. Or at least you should if what Chad says about you is true. Can you see Sam voluntarily going to a therapist?"

No, she couldn't. He'd have to be bound and gagged and... Oh, right. Except for the gag, that's exactly what they'd done. "Then why couldn't you have just... I don't know, told me right from the start that it was a scheme?"

There was a moment's hesitation, as if he was considering whether to tell her the truth. "We had to make sure that you wanted Sam as much as he wanted you. And that you were with him for the right reasons."

Her lips firmed. "You mean that I wasn't after his money."

Mark nodded. "There is that."

Uncomfortable with the direction of the conversation, Rosie returned to her position of spectator.

"Just bring Rosie out here. I don't have time for whatever game you're playing."

"Don't you understand, Sam?" Thalia asked. "It's not a game."

Sam's voice was flat when he replied, "Why don't you tell me, Thalia? Get this damned charade over with but let me make sure that Rosie's okay."

Wait a minute. If Chad and Thalia were his stalkers...what the hell was this about if not revenge? Why were Cooper and Scott and Andy just standing around helping them?

"You want to tell me what the hell's going on here, Chad? Scott found the undoctored photos on your computer."

"Jesus, Sam, you got some of the highest scores in Quantico, and you haven't figured it out yet?" Chad rolled his eyes. "It's all been a set up, Sam. All of it. There's never been a stalker. There's been no threat. And Scott found the photos there because I told him where to look so you'd come running to us."

What the fuck? "Is it money you're after? Or do you think I owe you part of Hauberk? What is it, Chad, because frankly I haven't got a clue what this is about if not revenge?"

"Oh, Sam." Thalia wheeled over to him and put her hand on his thigh. "It's never been about revenge. It's been about you getting on with your life."

Thalia sighed. "Sam, you need to move on. You need to put the past behind you and not hide out here. You need someone permanent in your life. Any woman with half a brain would consider you a good catch."

"That's about sums up the type he dates," Cooper rumbled. "Half a brain."

Sam sneered. "Maybe you should take a look in a mirror, Coop. Or is this not your suite we're in? And you could at least let me down from here? I'm starting to lose circulation to my hands."

"I don't think so, Sam, not until you've listened to us." Thalia wheeled herself back in front of Sam, her head tilted back to look up at him. "Everyone knows you loved Jill. And no one would ever try to take her memory away from you or deny your feelings for her. But she's gone—through no fault of your own, she's gone. It's time for you to accept that and move on."

Why don't you stick a hot poker in my gut? That would hurt less.

He tested the tackle again. A smattering of dust floated over his shoulders. One more good jerk, maybe two should do it.

"You think you should have been able to save Jill. Well, guess what. You couldn't. It wasn't your fault. People get killed, Sam. You can't save them all. People have car accidents, they get cancer, they get shot. You can't save everyone, and you can't shut everyone out for fear of losing them. Let yourself love Rosie. Accept her love too. Don't destroy this chance at love, Sam. You may not get another one."

Damn, she wasn't just stickin' the poker in his gut, she was slicing his whole damned intestines out with it. "In case you haven't heard, Thal, that boat's sailed. Rosie moved out."

"Rosie moved out because you ordered her to."

"Because she threw herself over me to protect me. If Robert had been an assassin she'd be dead. We both thought I was being stalked, remember? I figured she'd be safer if she wasn't in the line of fire. I was trying to protect her, not lose her."

Like I lost Jill.

"Just like Jill." Chad walked up behind Thalia, put his hand on her shoulder. "Thalia's right, Sam. I understand that you want to protect Rosie, I do. And maybe we've gone about this the wrong way..."

"Ya think?"

"We couldn't think of another way to get you two together after the date we'd arranged went nowhere."

He'd wondered why it had been Rosie who had bid on him,

but Jodi had said Mark didn't think it would be proper for Thalia to bid. "How many times do I have to tell you, Chad, Rosie's my employee. You know I was trying to protect Hauberk from a lawsuit."

"It doesn't matter now. If you didn't know you weren't being stalked, if Rosie worked for a different security firm who was protecting you, you'd have still found a way to push her away."

"Bullshit."

"Is it?" With a nod from Thalia, Chad walked behind him. The rope holding Sam's hands above his head slackened and he lowered his arms with a groan of relief.

Thalia caught his hands with hers, chaffing them as the blood flooded back. But instead of undoing his handcuffs, she turned his wrists until his right hand was face up and rubbed his ring with her thumb.

"Then tell us why you still wear this, Sam. The wedding ring Jill bought for you? The one you've put on and never taken off since you got out of the hospital."

Jeezuz, what more did she want? His entrails spread over the floor like a goddamned rug so she could roll over them? "You know it is, Thalia. Leave it alone."

"I can't. You deserve to find happiness, Sam. You lost more than I did that day, and it left you as crippled as me. But you have the ability to get up and dust yourself off and move on."

"In other words," Cooper said, "it's time to get off your ass and stop feeling sorry for yourself."

Damn it, why couldn't they see what was going on? "I'm not keeping Rosie away because I feel sorry for myself. I'm doing it because she'll be safe that way. I won't see her hurt because of me."

"Don't you see? You are using the stalking as a way to keep Rosie at arm's length. The same way you use the club. It's a crutch, Sam. You don't want to get hurt the way you were when Jill died, and you know that the women you meet here aren't looking for long term involvement. So instead of taking a chance and meeting someone special, you spend your time here and avoid commitment." Thalia paused, shaking her head. "Marriage, children, commitment of that type anyway. And the women you date..." she waved her hand toward the door, "...out there. They're no better. I swear half the ones you date couldn't find their way out of a hall with one door."

"What in the hell makes you think I was looking for commitment? I've been coming to the club because I enjoy it. I love havin' sex without my partner complaining that I'm too kinky. That's the whole point of the place, isn't it?"

"But Rosie's different, isn't she? You can see a life with her. And that makes you feel like you're disloyal to Jill, doesn't it?" When he didn't answer, Thalia lowered her pitch assuming her Domme persona, the one that made him respond without thinking. "Do you love Rosie, Sam?"

"Yes," he shouted. "Yes. I love her, all right? But that doesn't mean she should stick around me. That doesn't mean she should throw herself in front of a goddamned bullet for me. I don't want to lose her like that. I won't lose her like that. I'd rather she stayed safe. That she stayed alive."

The door to the back room opened and Rosie appeared, her arms jammed on her hips. He relaxed to see her unharmed, unbound.

"Rosie, thank God you're safe." Desperation mixed with relief filled his voice. "I'm sorry if I got angry the other night."

This morning she would have accepted his apology at face value. But she couldn't now she knew the significance of his ring. That awareness created an ache in her heart, in her soul. Chad moved Thalia back to where Cooper stood so they no longer blocked her from Sam, but Rosie stayed where she was.

"Now that we know there's no real stalker, you can move back in and we—"

"No. Sam." The ache in her heart became a knife sharp pain. She blinked away the tears and held her head high. "I'm not moving back in with you. At least, not yet."

Not while you wear that ring. Not until I come first.

He shook his head and tugged at the restraints then gave up with a sigh. "Look, I know I've been an ass lately. I know I reacted badly the other night but—"

"I'm not prepared to spend my life with someone who doesn't love me as much as I love them." She wrapped her arms about her stomach. Andy put his hand on her shoulder, steadying her. "It hurts too much, Sam. Even if it's only us in the room, I feel like there's still going to be another person between us."

"I don't think of Jill when I'm with you, Rosie. You have to believe me, I love you."

Why couldn't you have said "I love you" last night. When you weren't handcuffed and shackled and under duress?

"When we were making love," her voice wavered so she took a couple of breaths before she felt steady enough to continue. "Sam, when you touch me and you're wearing that ring, are you thinking of her?"

"No."

"Then why do you still wear it?"

He looked away from her. "I couldn't get rid of it. It's all I had left of her."

"Oh, Sam. Thalia is right. I hoped she wasn't, but she is, isn't she? Jill's been between us every minute of every day. She's been in every conversation we've had and every decision you've made."

"What do you want of me? I can't just stop loving someone like you'd flip off a light switch. What would that say of how I feel about you?"

What did he feel? she wanted to scream. *Where am I in your life compared to Jill? Will I always be second? How much longer before you let go of her and see me standing right in front of you?*

"I've never lost anyone I care about like that, Sam, so I can't begin to understand how much losing Jill must have hurt. I'm not expecting you to forget her. But she died eight years ago. If we're to have a chance, if that's where we're headed, you've got to put the past in the past. And if you can't, well, I'm not prepared to come second to a ghost in any relationship."

"What are you saying, Rosie?"

"I'm saying I love you, but I'm not convinced you're ready to love me the way I deserve to be loved, the way I need to be loved." She drew another deep breath, shuddering as she did, conscious of how quiet the room had become, of everyone's eyes on her. "I'm saying good-bye, Sam."

Before he could say another word, before she could change her mind, she walked out of the room. Out of his life.

Chapter Thirty

It was as if someone had taken a vacuum and sucked all the light out of the apartment, all the air. Everywhere he looked he saw Rosie. If he sat in the living room, he remembered making love to her in front of the fireplace, of her standing naked in front of the window calling him Master. Of watching the football games, Rosie catcalling the umpires if they made a call she disagreed with, doing little dances when her beloved Jets scored a touchdown. How she'd stood in his arms in the kitchen, trembling with aftershocks after he'd made her come. Or even just the times they'd worked in a companionable silence making dinner.

And his own bedroom? He'd not find another night's sleep in that bed.

Even the spare bedroom reminded him of when she'd lain beneath him that night he'd acted on impulse and admitted his attraction. He could still feel her writhing beneath his touch, still taste her sweet honey on his tongue, still hear her moans echoing in his chest.

He stared at the ring he'd placed on the coffee table. By keeping it, by wearing it, had he used it to keep Jill alive? Had he created his own personal albatross?

Yet taking it off had been like losing Jill all over again. As if he were to say he hadn't loved her, that she didn't matter. And that seemed wrong too.

The doorbell rang. Must be one of his neighbors since the front desk hadn't called to announce any visitors.

He stayed where he was, letting the bell ring twice more.

Whoever it was gave up on the bell and knocked on the door.

"Sam, I know you're in there. Let me in, buddy."

Mark. The traitor who had refused to release him until Rosie had disappeared from his life.

A key rattled in the lock and the door opened. "Sam?"

Shit, the bastard must have gotten the master key from the guard. So much for his own security people protecting him.

He rubbed his palm across his knuckles, the absence of the ring strange after all these years. "What do you want, Mark? Fixin' to rub more salt in my wounds?"

"We were worried about you."

"Kinda hard to tell considering what you did to me earlier. How you wrecked my life."

"Can I turn on a light here, Sam? I can't see worth shit in this dark."

Before he could answer, Mark flicked on the overhead fixture, its light bouncing off the ring.

"Turn it off, goddamn it."

The light flicked off, and a dark shadow appeared beside him. "You okay?"

"Rosie's gone. I've lost her." Thanks to Mark's fucking interference. If Mark had let him down right away, he might have had a chance to catch Rosie before she left. And then he'd discovered Mark had agreed to the plan months before. The bastard had probably been sitting back there in Dallas laughing his fuckin' ass off during all the conversations they'd had about Rosie. Now Mark would go home to his pregnant wife, while Sam had just lost the woman he loved. Again!

He surged from the couch, tackling Mark, pinning him face-down to the floor. "You made me lose her. If you hadn't interfered, she'd be here now."

Mark grunted, but didn't struggle. "I'm sorry. We didn't think she'd walk out like that. We thought you'd listen to reason and—"

"She left me! Because of you and Chad and Thalia, and your fucking quack psychology, I've lost Rosie." *Fight back, damn it. Fight so I can hit you. Hit me, hurt me so I can concentrate on something other than this god-awful pain in my chest.*

"You'd already pushed her away, Sam. She was talking with Chad about transferring. We had to do something to get you to realize what you were doing."

Sam tightened his grip, fighting the urge to pound Mark's head into the floor. "I was trying to keep her safe. You would have done the same thing with Jodi if you thought she was in danger."

"Yeah, I would have, you're right." Mark sucked in a breath. "We fucked up, all right? I admit it, everyone admits it. But when Thalia suggested her plan to get you two together, she just thought it was time you settled down. And after what you'd said to me about Jodi, I thought..." He exhaled in a long slow stream. "None of us realized that you were still mourning Jill. I didn't mean for you to end up hurting again. I was trying to find a way to, I don't know, thank you for forcing me to see how much I loved Jodi. And it was sort of funny too, to see the tables turned on you for once. I figured you'd end up hitched. None of us intended for it to turn out this way. We're sorry. I'm sorry."

"It's too late for apologies, you fucking bastard. Rosie's gone." His voice caught in his throat.

"No, she's not."

"I went straight to her apartment once you let me go. Her neighbor said she'd come home but left ten minutes later with a suitcase. I've tried phoning her Berry, but she's not answering, I've texted her. I've checked with her friends and either they don't know or they're not telling me. I even phoned her parents and they don't know where she is."

"I know where she is, Sam."

Sam pushed his knee harder into Mark's back, tightened his hold on his arms. "Where? Where is she? You tell me now, damn it!"

"Let me up first."

After a moment's hesitation, Sam rolled off of him and leaned against the couch. He scrubbed his face with his hands. "Where is she? And how do you know?"

"Andy drove her to the airport. She's gone to visit her

brother in Puerto Rico."

"I have to go." Now he had direction again, he jumped to his feet. "I've gotta arrange a flight. I've gotta find her, tell her I love her."

"Sam."

He picked up the phone. Shit, he didn't know the number of the travel agent. Damn, it was after midnight, they'd be closed anyway. He'd have to phone the airline directly, book a seat himself. Ignoring Mark, he hurried into his study and grabbed the phone book.

"Sam," Mark had followed him and now leaned against the doorframe, his thumbs hooked in his belt loops, "Rosie was pretty upset. She may not listen to you. She may not even want to see you. Not for a while yet. Maybe you should let her calm down for a couple days."

He put the book down, willing the threatening panic away. "Don't you see? I have to go after her, I have to try. I have to tell her I love her and I want to marry her and... I have to make her listen. If I have to get on my knees and beg, I will."

Rosie pulled on her collar as the chilly December wind blew down Zerega Avenue, taking her breath away. When she reached the familiar white wrought-iron fence at the corner, she turned right.

She should have stayed in D.C., or at least used her ticket to Puerto Rico as she'd originally planned instead of running home to New York.

Her parents had sensed something was wrong when she'd arrived out of the blue. Her mother immediately started questioning her, but she wasn't ready to talk about Sam. Not yet. So she'd come up with an excuse that she had a meeting at the Hauberk offices and booked it out of there first thing that morning.

Instead of going to the office, having to face Rick's inquisition, of possibly having him phone Sam to find out why she was back in the city, she'd spent the day examining the

Christmas displays in the shops. When the cold grew too much, she took refuge in the Guggenheim. But no matter where she went, no matter how hard she tried to pretend Sam didn't exist, she couldn't convince herself that the constant ache in her chest was jet lag.

As she reached the warm vestibule of her parents' building, she heard voices at the top of the stairs.

"You broke my daughter's heart. You think I don't know why she came home to her mama?"

"I know I did, Mrs. Ramos. That's why I'm here."

Sam. He'd followed her.

She hurried up to her family's apartment and found Sam standing in the doorway, her mother blocking the door, her arms folded across her chest. Her gaze dipped down to check his right hand to see if he still wore the ring, but he'd stuck his hands in his coat pockets. Surely he wouldn't be still wearing it if he were here.

"You made my Rosie cry."

"Mama!"

Sam turned at her call. "Rosie! God, I've missed—"

"No, no, no." Her mother insinuated herself between Sam and the top of the stairs, forcing Rosie to stay on the second step. "You don't try to sweet talk my Rosie, you big *oso*."

"Mama," Rosie whispered. "It's all right, you don't need to protect me. And for heaven's sake, I wasn't crying."

When her mother switched to Spanish, Rosie didn't bother to tell her that Sam would understand every word. "You think you can fool your mama? You think I couldn't tell from your eyes this morning that you weren't crying half the night? Or that I wouldn't hear it in your voice, or see it as you drag yourself around like a puppy that had been kicked?"

Sheesh, did her mother have some hidden camera in her room? And what was wrong with her eyes—she'd looked in the mirror this morning just in case and they'd looked fine. Maybe Rick should think about hiring her mom to do interrogations. Heck, Homeland Security should hire her.

She chanced a glance at Sam and instead of the amused grin she'd expected him to be wearing, he looked mortified.

"Senora Ramos," not taking his eyes from Rosie, Sam addressed her mother in their own language though he used a European Spanish rather than their Puerto Rican, "I never meant to hurt Rosie, and I certainly never—"

"Sa-a-m." Rosie clenched her teeth together. He was going about this all wrong if he wanted to win over her mother. He needed to smooth talk her, compliment her, not admit he was wrong. Once he'd shown a weakness, her mother would never let him forget it. But depending on what he was here to say, maybe she didn't want him to charm her mother.

"Let the man speak, *cariño*." Her mother lowered her voice and spoke out one side of her mouth, still not getting that Sam could understand every word. Or maybe she did, but just didn't care. "It doesn't hurt for a man to grovel once in a while. Especially when he's hurt someone he loves."

"Mama, Mr. Watson's my boss." God help her if her mother discovered she'd been sleeping with him without benefit of a wedding ring.

"Pssht." Her mother batted her hand in Rosie's direction. "You're in love with him, Rosie, don't argue with your mama. If Mr. Watson's here looking for you—at your home—that means he loves you too."

Rosie stifled the urge to roll her eyes. Sam however hadn't taken his eyes off her, the heat from them as intense as a laser beam.

"You come in, Mr. Watson, you talk with my daughter. Tell her how sorry you are that you made her need to run home to her mama and papa."

"Mama!"

Her mother grabbed her arm and hauled her into their apartment only half-whispering, but loud enough that Sam, who was following, could hear. "He's not married, is he? If he is, I'll get rid of him, don't you worry."

"No, Mrs. Ramos, I'm not married. And Rosie came home because she knew it was the only way I'd listen to her."

"Ay, my Rosie tries to teach you a lesson, no? And what did you not want to listen to that was so important?"

"That the past is the past, and she's my future." His voice

grew soft, soothing.

Rosie forced her legs to keep walking away from him instead of turning around. She knew if she looked at him, she'd melt and accept everything he said.

"Ah." Her mother stopped in the middle of the room and pushed Rosie toward the couch. "Sit. Both of you. I'll get coffee and some nice cake I baked this morning."

When she started to shrug off her jacket, Sam's hands brushed hers. The electricity between them still crackling, she dropped her hands. He folded her jacket and laid it neatly over the arm of her father's chair, and stroked it once before turning back to her.

Feeling dwarfed by him, feeling the walls closing in about her, she took a step away from his towering presence but couldn't go any farther because of the Christmas tree jammed into the corner of the tiny room.

Once, twice, she opened her mouth to speak but couldn't find the words.

"I would have gotten here sooner, but I'd been told you'd gone to Puerto Rico so I flew there first." He stayed where he was, as if he sensed her reluctance to be near him.

Her gaze darted up to his then fluttered away again. He'd flown first to Puerto Rico and then all the way to New York? Surely that meant he wanted her back. Didn't it?

"I had my ticket in my hand and was ready to go through security and then..." She didn't think she could have survived making small talk while watching Jose and Elba coo over their new son, painfully aware that she wouldn't be a mother any time soon. Besides her eldest brother would have asked why she'd decided to visit them on such a whim, and asked questions she didn't want to answer. Not that her mother had been any better. "I just changed my mind, that's all."

"It's a woman's prerogative."

She toyed with an angel her mother had hung on the tree, still not willing to look at him. "I wasn't sure whether you'd want to see me again."

He chuckled, but it held no humor in it. "I was thinking the same thing in the taxi coming over here. About whether you'd want to see me."

"I wasn't in on their plan, you know. Not until that day." *When I realized you were in love with a ghost.*

"I know. I don't blame you for anything that happened, if you're worried about that."

"I'm not." She was.

Her mother bustled back in, carrying a tray loaded with two coffee cups from her grandmother's special collection, and her grandmother's sugar and cream set. "There, I'll leave you two alone for a while. Call me if you need anything."

Rosie perched on the couch and added two teaspoons of sugar to one cup. "You should be honored, Mama only uses this china for special occasions."

"Rosie..."

She hurried to speak before he could say anything more. "My grandfather worked for a week building shelves for a jeweler when they'd first come to New York. He'd wanted to buy my grandmother a birthday present, but they didn't have any money, so he negotiated with the jeweler that if he built the shelves, he could..." *Why was she babbling?* "...he could choose something of equal value in trade. It's pretty, isn't it?"

Sam knelt in front of her, placed one hand on her knee. His right hand. He wasn't wearing the ring anymore. "If you don't want me here, if I make you uncomfortable, or unhappy. I'll leave. Just say the word."

"Would you really leave if I asked you to?"

The expression on his face changed so she couldn't read what he felt. "Do you want me to leave, Rosebud?"

His nickname sliced through her objections. "No. I don't want you to leave." She carefully placed the coffee cup back on the tray, grateful her hand didn't shake betraying how everything inside her quaked and roiled. "But why are you here, Sam?"

"To tell you I love you." He lifted his hand and stroked her cheek with the back of his knuckles. "To tell you you'd never come second to anyone in our relationship."

"I love you too. But I also know you were right that day. About love not being like a light switch you flip on or off. You can't tell me that in the two days since I last saw you, you've been able to forget about Jill."

"Jill will always be a part of me, Rosie." He touched a finger to her grandmother's coffee service, ringing the top of the empty cup. "Same as your grandparents will always be part of you. Same as your mother and father, and your brothers and sister, will always be in your heart."

"It's not the same."

"No, it's not. But it doesn't mean I don't have room for you too. I promise Jill's memory won't ever come between us. When I'm with you, I don't think of her. But I don't know how to convince you of that. I can't hand you something concrete to prove it, I wish I could."

So did she. Still he'd removed the ring, that was a start. But had he hung onto it? Was it still tucked away somewhere safe for him to look at now and then? Or had he gotten rid of it?

"If you're wondering what I did with the ring, I asked Mark to send it to Jill's parents."

Feeling guilty over the relief flooding through her, Rosie turned her hand over and twined her fingers with his. "Jill was only part of why I left, Sam."

"Oh?" His voice was a study in casualness but from the way his fingers dug into hers for a moment before gentling his grip, she knew he was forcing himself not to react.

"There's the question of how you didn't respect me as an operative. How you wouldn't let me do my job."

A moment passed before he said, "I told you at the start not to try to get between me and a bullet."

Especially you, she heard him not say.

"I thought Robert was a sniper. You were my principal. That's what Hauberk hired me to do. To protect our clients."

"So you threw yourself on top of me prepared to take the bullet in my place. That wasn't a tactically sound move, Rosebud. You should have just taken me down out of the line of fire, and sought backup. If you'd been shot, I'd have been just as vulnerable as if you hadn't been there at all."

"A tactically sound move?" She narrowed her eyes. "What about you racing into the club when you thought I was being held hostage, huh? You charged in, expecting to have to fight for me even though they'd taken your weapons at the gate."

He opened his mouth to speak but she barreled over him. "Yet still you came. Unarmed. Unprepared. Alone. Did you even think of calling the police? The SWAT team or hostage negotiation? Nope. Big old Sam Watson walked straight into a trap. You deliberately put yourself in harms' way. Now tell me that was a tactically sound move."

"That was different."

"No, it wasn't. In fact it was worse than what I did on the terrace." She poked her finger into his sternum, pushing until he lost his balance and fell onto the couch with an oomph. "What you're saying is that you're allowed to sacrifice yourself, but I'm not allowed to. So what does that mean, Sam? That I'm not allowed to love you as much as you love me?"

He clambered to his feet. "It's not a matter of allowed or not allowed, or who loves who more. It's about how I don't want to lose you, and I hope you don't want to lose me either." He held up his hand stopping her from speaking. "It's got nothing to do with Jill or anything Thalia or Chad said at the club. I love you, Rosie. I want to spend the rest of my life with you. I want to get you pregnant and have children that I can teach to ride a bike and throw a football."

"You want children?" she spluttered, unable to form a coherent thought. The course of this conversation had taken a turn she hadn't expected. The hope she'd squelched when she thought about Jose and Elba cooing over their new baby boy flared up, sensing a fresh source of oxygen.

Great, if he was this protective of her when she wasn't pregnant, think what Sam would be like when she was. She'd barely be able to make a move without him coddling her.

Is that so bad? Yes! She might as well be living at home, dependent upon Mama and Papa. She'd spent too long gaining her independence to give it up now. But somehow she also knew Sam's type of coddling would be different than Mama's. It probably meant spending long hours in bed with him.

Sam sat on the couch and pulled her onto his lap, resting his forehead against hers. "Come back to D.C. with me, Rosie. Give me a fresh start. Let me take you out on a date, go with me to a restaurant, maybe a movie. Just Sam and Rosie, not Samuel Watson and his bodyguard for once."

"We skipped that part, didn't we? Dating, I mean."

"Yeah, we did. So what do you say?"

"All right. But I have some conditions."

"Ah, a negotiation." His grin returned. "Name your terms, sugar."

When she slid off his lap and began pacing, he spread his arms out along the back of the couch, and straightened his legs, forcing her to divert her path around him.

"First off, you've got to stop treating me like I'm some china doll. I'm a Close Protective Officer with Hauberk Protection. And we're the best on the whole eastern seaboard. Got that?"

"Yeah, but—"

"Shut up and listen, you big jerk." She stopped in front of him. "I can drop a two-hundred-and-twenty-pound man and have him crying for his mommy in two seconds. I carry two Glocks and I know how to use them."

"Right. You're tough. Keep going." His grin widened.

"Damned right I'm tough. And like it or not, if someone threatens you, I'm going after them." She climbed back on his lap, straddling him. "They want to get to you—" she jabbed his sternum with her thumb, then pointed at herself, "—they have to go through me. You got that?"

She narrowed her eyes, growling, "I said—*got. that?*"

"Yes, ma'am."

Her gaze dropped from his face to his bulging erection. "Are you getting off on this, Watson? Because I know that's not where you keep your Glock."

A grin flashed on his face before he wrestled control back and replaced it with a bland expression. "No, ma'am. I mean, no, that's not my Glock. And yes, ma'am, you sure make me hot when you get all riled up."

A choked sound echoed down the hallway. Damn, how had she forgotten her mother would have been eavesdropping?

"Do you agree to my terms? That you don't try to wrap me in cotton wool and protect me like some china doll?"

"Agreed. Reluctantly. But agreed. Now you mention it, I

have a couple conditions too."

"Which are?"

His grin faded. "You don't run out on me again, Rosebud. You stick around and hear me out if we ever get into an argument."

"Right back at you."

"I'm not the one who flew to New York."

She rested her head on his chest. "I'm sorry about that. I just needed to get away to think."

"You could have stuck around a bit longer before hopping on a plane. It's not like I could have chased after you, if that's what you were expecting." His hands kneaded her behind before pulling her on top of his erection. "You left me handcuffed and shackled, remember?"

"How long did they leave you there?" She wondered who'd had the guts to release him, and if they could still see out of both eyes.

"Hard to tell, they were so busy yakkin' at me I zoned out." More likely he was shouting and cursing them. "Then they started arguin' with each other and walked out and left me hanging there until Fredriksson came to check on me." A sensible precaution, once freed he probably would have taken them all on. "By the time I got to your place you were gone. Anyway, that's in the past, right?"

She nodded and shifted closer. "You said you had a couple of conditions. What's the second one?"

"That you remember I love you, and that I know you're my here and now. That you're my future."

"I think I can agree to that. Provided that you accept that while we're together, I'm going to be your personal bodyguard."

Sam chuckled then kissed her until she was lightheaded. "Then that means you'll be guardin' me for life. Because, Rosebud, when you're around I'm gonna need a lot of personal protection."

About the Author

The only woman in a houseful of men, Leah often takes refuge in her office in an effort to avoid the dishes and dust bunnies. Writing about hunky heroes and hot sex is so much more rewarding than housework.

To learn more about Leah, please visit www.leahbraemel.com. Send an email to Leah at leah@leahbraemel.com or join her Yahoo! group to join in the fun with other readers as well as Leah at http://groups.yahoo.com/group/Leah_Braemel.

When love is threatened by truth, every moment counts…

Steve's Story
© *2009 Jess Dee*
Circle of Friends, Book 2.

Steve Sommers is having a gut-wrenching week. His fiancée has left him, the woman who broke his heart is back in town—and they're all gathered at the bedside of his best friend, who's in a coma. The emotional ties between them are strained to the breaking point. Like it or not, it's up to Steve to find the strength and compassion to support the four of them through the toughest ordeal of their lives.

In the midst of the turmoil and trauma, passion unexpectedly flares anew between Steve and the woman he loves. Suddenly the future he'd believed lost lies within his reach. But she still carries the secret that once tore them apart, and determined to protect Steve from the truth, she fights their rekindled relationship every step of the way.

Now the fragile bond they've developed hangs in the balance, threatened by a reality that love may not be strong enough to overcome…

Warning: This book might just make you cry, but it'll make you smile as well. The story will probably get you all hot and bothered too. It contains naughty activities in the car, sex on the kitchen counter (and up against the wall), a quickie in the garden, a little experimenting with scarves—oh, and some hot loving in the bedroom.

Available now in ebook and print from Samhain Publishing.

LaVergne, TN USA
30 December 2010
210631LV00001B/152/P